"Who

Kristin's voice was a muffled choke.

It took Alex a full heartbeat to understand what had happened, that there had been another explosion—but he didn't need any time to realize that he was on top of Kristin. He pushed himself up quickly and pulled her to her feet.

Dirt streaked one cheek, and tendrils of hair had been loosened from her ponytail. "I'm sorry," he murmured, meaning to pull back and be free of her. But his best intentions died when his hand swept along her jaw, brushing at the strand of hair that clung there.

He heard the other men getting to their feet, muttering curses, but he didn't look away from the lavender-blue eyes in front of him. He lowered his hand to Kristin's shoulder, and it unnerved him to feel her trembling.

"This is all I'm going to take," he muttered. Before he could stop himself, he was lowering his lips to hers. . . .

Dear Reader,

Merry Christmas! This is the season for good wishes and gift giving, and I hope that one of your gifts to yourself this holiday season will be the time to read this month's Silhouette Intimate Moments. As always, we've put together what we think is a pretty special package for you.

For starters, try Marilyn Pappano's *Room at the Inn*, a very special—and especially romantic—book set around a country inn, the holiday season and, of course, a man and a woman who are destined to be together forever. Snow is falling in tiny Angel's Peak, North Carolina, when Leah meets Bryce for the first time. How can she know that he's the man who will change her life and bring joy to her heart, becoming not only her husband but a father to the four children she loves so much? There's "room at the inn" for you, too, so why not join her for a very special Christmas?

Then, if you're tired of winter, escape into summer with ever popular author Heather Graham Pozzessere. *Lucia in Love* reignites Lucia Lorenzo's once torrid relationship with Ryan Dandridge. With her entire lovable, wacky family on hand, Lucia expects their reunion to be eventful, but never downright dangerous! And Ryan isn't the only threat; someone else is stalking her. Surrendering to Ryan might very well be the *best* thing she could do.

Complete this month's reading with new books from Mary Anne Wilson and Doreen Roberts, then look forward to next year and more compelling romances from your favorite authors, including Maura Seger, Linda Howard and Barbara Faith, to name only a few.

Happy Holidays!

Leslie J. Wainger
Senior Editor

Mary Anne Wilson
Home Fires

Silhouette Intimate Moments
Published by Silhouette Books New York
America's Publisher of Contemporary Romance

SILHOUETTE BOOKS
300 East 42nd St., New York, N.Y. 10017

Copyright © 1988 by Mary Anne Wilson

ISBN: 0-373-07267-8

First Silhouette Books printing December 1988

Printed in the U.S.A.

Books by Mary Anne Wilson

Silhouette Intimate Moments

Hot-Blooded #230
Home Fires #267

MARY ANNE WILSON

fell in love with reading at ten years of age when she discovered *Pride and Prejudice*. A year later she knew she had to be a writer when she found herself writing a new ending for *A Tale of Two Cities*. A true romantic, she had Sydney Carton rescued, and he lived happily ever after.

Though she's a native of Canada, she now lives in California with her husband, children, a six-toed black cat who believes he's Hungarian and five timid Dobermans, who welcome any and all strangers. And she's writing happy endings for her own books.

For my parents, Herb and Mary Bignell, with love.
They've made it work for forty-seven years.

Prologue

I called to tell you that I'm going to kill him.'' Alexander Jordan made the pronouncement into the cordless telephone, then sank down into a lounge chair on the terrace of his sprawling adobe home. He stretched out his six-foot-five-inch frame, propped his bare feet on the low brick wall that divided the clay tile flooring from a sea of ankle-deep grass and waited.

When there was no response over the line, he frowned into the darkness of the night that surrounded him. ''Jessie, are you still there?'' he asked.

He heard Jessie Moss sigh, and he could almost see the tiny, gray-haired woman rolling her eyes heavenward. ''It's fifteen minutes to midnight, Alex. What's going on?''

''I told you. I'm going to kill Jake Warner.''

''Oh, really?''

The sarcastic edge to her tone grated across his nerves. Then he relaxed, feeling the pleasant sensation of the warmth of a gentle night breeze brush across his bare skin, exposed except for the pair of well worn cutoff Levi's. He knew what he was going to do. Settling back, he ran his fingers through his dark curls. He just wondered why he expected her to understand. Jessie never had understood why he'd come back to Vespar Bay.

"Yes, really," he said evenly.

"It's that place—the isolation. It's getting to you. It's not as if your family still lived there."

"I'm not isolated. I've got friends, and this is home." His eyes scanned the pines and redwoods rimming either side of the thirty-foot expanse of lawn that ran to the cliffs. The Pacific, a dark smudge at the horizon, had been Alex's pool, the place his father had taught him to swim the summer of his third year.

He felt a stab of nostalgia for what had been before life had shuffled and his parents were gone. Then he steeled himself for the sermon he knew was coming. He didn't have to wait long.

"I know your breakup with Kaye was hard on you, but you shouldn't have gone back up to that place to hibernate and lick your wounds at the old family home. You're on that boat so much I can't reach you half the time, then the first time I hear from you in weeks, it's almost midnight on the Fourth of July, and you're calling to tell me that you want to kill Jake."

"You're my agent, not my psychiatrist," he said quickly. He took a deep breath and found himself countering her opinion with, "This has nothing to do with Kaye. The marriage was over. I knew it. She knew it. It just took me a while to realize it. And I'm not licking any wounds." He said it and he meant it. "But I've been having problems, and it finally hit me that I can't get going on anything because I'm sick and tired of Jake Warner." He paused for emphasis. "I want rid of him—once and for all."

"You can't get rid of him, Alex. He's been with you for ten years, since you left the army."

He inhaled the sweet night air and closed his eyes. "I think I hate him."

"You don't have to like him."

Alex couldn't stop a rough chuckle and the upward tug of a smile he could feel at the corners of his mouth. "True."

Jessie waited for a moment, then asked, "Why aren't you at a party tonight with some gorgeous woman?"

"I was at a party earlier. They have a big blowout at the town hall every Fourth." He sat forward with a sigh and ran a hand over his face, feeling the bristling of the beginning of a beard. He ignored the "gorgeous woman" comment. "I came home to think." He reached for a drink he'd left on a wooden table to his right. "I'm on the terrace, alone, and in two minutes I'm going to go down, get on the boat and watch the midnight display of fireworks from there."

"Alex?"

He held the damp glass in his hand, then abruptly swirled it. "What?" he asked as he watched the melting ice cubes catch the light from a partial moon, sending the shimmer around and around in the amber liquid.

"Write another Jake Warner book. You can do it."

"There isn't another Jake Warner book in me."

"Sure there is. A big one. Number seven. *Jake Warner, Bounty Hunter—His Greatest Adventure.* That's got a nice ring to it, doesn't it? Your fans will eat it up. Going two years without a new A. V. Jordan novel has really whet their appetites." Jessie was on a roll, her nervous energy channeled into making Alex change his mind. "Lucky number seven, and you can do anything with it that you want. Let Jake go wild, all blood and guts and action. Then send him off into the sunset heading for his next adventure. Leave everyone satisfied."

Alex grimaced and sipped at his drink before saying anything. "Jess, please..."

"Alex, I know that Jake Warner is your alter ego, the part of you that you stopped using when you left the special forces. And I don't believe you can go cold turkey. You have to taper off. Make him a sheriff. Make him an outlaw. Make him a sensitive hero. We'll get a big promotion campaign started. Lots of PR. Banners in all the book stores reading Jake Warner Is Back. It could be big, *really* big. Just do it."

Just do it. Alex wished it was that easy and that Jess would understand how hard it had become to put words on paper lately. "I'll think about it." He downed the last of his drink. "Happy Fourth of July, Jess," he murmured, and laid the phone facedown on the table. He waited a moment, then turned it over and clicked off the Receive button. He didn't want a callback right now.

Settling in his chair, he rested the cool dampness of his empty glass on his bare stomach. How did Jessie do it? She pushed the right buttons and as good as had him agreeing to keep writing the Jake Warner books.

He fingered a quarter-sized tattoo on the back of his right wrist, the emblem of his platoon in Nam, still faintly irregular after all these years. Jake Warner...his alter ego? Maybe Jess was right.

Actually that didn't make a difference. Jake Warner had run out of life. Writing the books had become work—hard work. At one time they had come so easily that Alex had barely had time to type them into the computer. But the creative flow had slowed. He frowned. Slowed—hell, it had become little more than a trickle.

He stood abruptly and set his glass by the phone before stepping over the low wall and onto the lawn. The cool grass felt delicious on his bare feet and around his ankles. Slowly he headed toward the cliff, away from the empty house.

He reached the wooden stairs set into the granite cliff and climbed down to the narrow strip of rocky beach. His thirty-foot cabin cruiser rose and fell on the gentle swells of the ocean where it was secured at the end of the pontoon pier.

Alex stepped onto the unsteady wooden plank path to the boat and walked along it to the *Dream's End*. Getting on board, he didn't go near the controls but walked to the bow, flopped down on the brass-trimmed deck and looked out at the moonlight rippling on the ocean's surface.

Maybe he should have stayed at the party in town. He could have talked more to the houseguest Gwen and Dailey had invited up from San Francisco for the barbecue and fireworks display. The girl had seemed pretty enough in a tiny, dark-haired way. Maybe something would have come of it, would have clicked after he got to know her a bit. He could have asked her back to the boat to watch the fireworks display.

The idea died before it had fully formed.

He realized that, in a way, his personal needs were changing as surely as his professional needs were. He was past the stage of simply smiling at someone and feeling that basic response—the physical awareness that had nothing to do with what the person had inside. He'd actually come to a point in his life where he wanted to make an investment in another person, to work on a relationship that would last. "God, you've finally grown up, Alex," he muttered aloud.

The girl at the barbecue had been cute but nothing special. At thirty-eight, if he was going to get involved, he wanted *very* special. He didn't want a woman just to have a woman. Not anymore. He wanted a friend, a lover, a companion. But he wasn't going to worry about that now. He didn't have the time.

What he needed to worry about now was getting his writing back on track, getting the passion back into it. He inhaled sharply at the realization that he *did* feel passionately about his writing. He passionately wanted an end to the Jake Warner series.

Suddenly everything fell into place. If Jess wanted a book, he'd give her one. She'd get a Jake Warner book to end all Jake Warner books. Jake *was* going to die whether she liked it or not. Alex didn't know the how or the where, but Jake Warner—bounty hunter, cowboy, loner, hero, male chauvinist—was going to end up on Boot Hill.

Alex smiled. He liked that idea. He liked it a lot. And suddenly the dam burst, ideas coming one over the other. He stood, ready to head back up to the house and into his study to turn on the computer, when a long, low whistle drew his attention south. A white ball catapulted into the night sky, then at its apex it burst into a blue shower of vibrant sparks, the beauty echoing on the dark waters. Immediately, red and yellow explosions followed.

Alex stood for a better view, absorbing the beauty of the display that blotted out the moonlight. After ten years he owed it to Jake Warner to send him out in a blaze of heroic glory.

Three miles farther north

The Hunter felt pain. He'd never realized that anger and betrayal could cause this physical ache that permeated his whole body. He was on the verge of losing everything he'd worked for these past six months, and he hadn't seen it coming. He'd been too involved in trying to make the last job perfect.

From his hiding spot behind the rusting chute that had long since stopped guiding cut timber to the beach below the rugged cliffs, the Hunter stared at the deserted logging camp. Fletcher had been told midnight, and it was ten minutes to the hour now. Nothing moved in the sharp shadows cast by the rising moon.

Then he heard a different sound above the clamor of crickets and night birds—a creak of metal on metal, then silence. Wind? No, the ocean far below the cliffs was calm, the air warm, and the only breeze was gentle. A rustling of dead leaves and brush drew his attention across the camp to the shadowed, decaying buildings huddled around a dusty clearing that had once been used for deliveries.

A fleeting flash in the shadows by a sagging-roofed cabin made the Hunter catch his breath. Ever so slowly the shape moved toward him, gradually taking the form of a medium-built man dressed in dark clothes. The Hunter's pain began to subside as Ronald Fletcher walked forward, totally unaware that he'd been set up.

Hatred was rapidly replacing the anger. Everything had been figured down to the last detail. The Stuart robbery was the last, the culmination of six months' work. The thief who didn't get caught was the one who knew when to walk away and not look back. The Hunter knew that was why he'd get away with the robberies: he knew when to walk away.

He'd been the one to put the five jobs together, to give them a time limit of under six months. He'd found Fletcher, set him up here at the cottage and laid out the jobs. The first four had been trial runs for the big one.

For a moment the Hunter wished he'd been there to see the blaze at the Stuart home, to watch the smoke rise into the night air over San Francisco. It had been his idea to use fire as the cover for the robberies. A brilliant idea, he'd thought, since Fletcher was a pro at making things burn. But the television news coverage hadn't done it justice.

"The Nob Hill estate of Parker Warren Stuart was leveled tonight by fire that raced through the wooden

Victorian structure. Before the fire units arrived on the scene, the house and a separate guest house were totally involved. Parker Warren Stuart, seventy-three, was found dead of smoke inhalation in his bed on the ground floor. Lost in the blaze was an art collection whose value is still unknown and personal property.''

Personal property. Nearly a million in diamonds seemed personal enough, the Hunter thought, as he watched Fletcher coming closer, moving cautiously across the open space. Ronald Fletcher—a visually forgettable man. Medium height, medium build, medium intelligence.

The sound of heavy breathing echoed in the crisp air as Fletcher passed the chute heading for the cliffs. Once he got to the top of the stairs set in the cliff, out in the open with no place to run, the Hunter could make his move. Fletcher reached the side rails, two dark silhouettes against the night sky, stopped, faced the ocean and lit a cigarette.

The Hunter broke from cover then, silently coming up behind the unsuspecting man.

Ronald Fletcher let the smoke trickle out of his mouth and nose as he stared out at the Pacific.

"Fletcher?"

For a split second he was certain he was hallucinating, that he was imagining the worst thing that could happen. But as he turned, his partner was very real in front of him.

"Hunt, I . . ." His words faltered to a stop. A gun leveled at his middle made talking hard, yet the fear he should have known didn't come. He felt strangely resigned to the fact that he'd messed up again. He waited.

"You're such a fool, Fletcher. It was all over. We were going to get away clean, then you had to get greedy."

After so many years of being around death, Fletcher didn't feel any dread. In some way, it seemed a natural end to the life he had chosen. "Jack..."

"Jack Blair and I talked for a long time today, right after you contacted him to fence the jewels."

"I thought a fence could keep his mouth shut," he muttered around the cigarette as he drew more acrid smoke into his lungs. "So much for honor among thieves."

"He might be the best fence around, but Jack and I go back a long way. He owes me. Let's go somewhere and get this straightened out."

Fletcher shrugged and took another long drag on the cigarette. He glanced at the gun. No, he wasn't about to walk meekly to what he knew would be his death. He took a step backward. "We can talk here."

Hunt matched the step, keeping the distance between them undiminished. "Where are the jewels?"

"They're safe."

"But they aren't at the cottage. I checked before coming here. Where's the box?"

Fletcher needed another drag on the cigarette, but he could feel his hand beginning to shake. "Being stuck here between jobs for six months forced me to get to know this place like the back of my hand."

His partner inhaled sharply. "And gave you time to think about stealing everything we've worked for?"

"Can you steal something that's already stolen?" he asked on an unsteady laugh.

"Knock it off!"

Fletcher blinked but stood his ground. He had nothing to lose. "If you want the goods, you're going to have to make a deal with me—whether you like it or not," he ground out. He felt suddenly bold. "It's that or nothing. Take it or leave it. I stashed the goods where you'll never find them. Somewhere between the cottage and this spot." Fear did come when Fletcher saw the pure rage in Hunt's eyes and felt the gun barrel dig into his middle. "If...if you use that, you'd better be ready to spend a long time looking for the stuff," he stammered.

"Shut up!"

"You'll never find the box without me."

"Damn you!" Hunt muttered, and lunged toward Fletcher, his free hand reaching for the front of Fletcher's shirt.

Fletcher spun away and started to run forward into the darkness. But suddenly there was no solid ground, just the night. His hands grabbed at nothingness. For a single moment in time, Ronald Fletcher felt as if he could fly.

The Hunter stumbled and fell sideways onto the rough ground as a scream ripped through the night. It had died out long before he scrambled to the edge of the cliff to look over to the beach below. The roof of one of three old wooden storage sheds at the base of the cliffs was completely gone. Inky blackness inside hid any signs of Fletcher. Then a flame of light flickered in the shed and a hissing glow began to grow.

For a fleeting instant Fletcher was visible, splayed on top of rotted timber down in the building. Then, fire blazed in the night. The cigarette had ignited the tinder-dry wood.

The Hunter pushed the gun into his pocket, got to his feet and ran for the stairs. Before he stepped down onto the beach the fire had engulfed the sheds completely. He sank slowly to his knees on the warm sand, and his violent curse echoed off the granite cliffs.

As a blue shower of fireworks flared to life and canopied in the skies overhead, he realized the two tickets he had for

Canada were useless to him. He couldn't leave Vespar Bay now. He struck his leg with his fist.

Thanks to a stupid, greedy man named Ronald Fletcher, he might be in this godforsaken town a lot longer than he'd intended. And he hated this town—almost as much as he hated Fletcher for sending him on some damned treasure hunt.

Chapter 1

Late afternoon sunshine glared off the windshield as Kristin Delaney drove her blue rental car toward Vespar Bay, feeling more tired than she had in her life. During the past six hours she'd flown into San Francisco International Airport from Spain and sat in her silent apartment near the Marina for over an hour, waiting for her boss to come by. But when David Allcott, the head of Allcott Investigations had contacted her, it had been by telephone.

His briefing had been just that—brief. Go to Vespar Bay. Find out who's trying to destroy the new resort being built by Restcorp, the large Los Angeles-based development company. Use the prearranged cover of being a house sitter for an elderly couple who live north of town, on the boundary of the Restcorp development. The couple were on a month-long cruise to Mexico. Watch the house, take care of a pet called Boy and blend into the community.

Hammon Insurance, the company that had underwritten the construction phase of the development, hadn't been able to find out anything. They wanted to replace their investigator with a fresh face, someone who could fit into a small town without drawing undue attention.

"Let's face it," David had told her over the telephone. "Who's going to think you're a threat? Blond, blue-eyed— and even though you're fairly tall, you look delicate." He laughed softly. "You don't look threatening, Kristin. People will feel differently about your presence than they do about the man on the Hammon payroll."

Kristin listened intently, jotting down notes. But all the while she'd been thinking about arson. She hated the idea of arson, of violence of any kind. That was one of the reasons she'd joined a company that seldom dealt in cases of that nature. White-collar work, embezzlement, fraud... those were her preferences.

"David," she interrupted finally. "You know I don't like this sort of case."

"And I wouldn't ask unless I needed you there," he countered softly.

He hadn't said, "I'm your boss. You work for me." He hadn't said, "You owe me, Kristin." And he never would. But all three things were true, and she gave in without any more argument. Reluctantly she agreed to go to Vespar Bay.

After getting the last of the information from David, she'd repacked her luggage with casual clothes, replenished her toiletries, then dressed in Levi's, tennis shoes and a T-shirt. Leaving her silvery blond hair loose around her shoulders, she'd applied minimal makeup and glanced at herself in the mirror in the bathroom.

Her usually wide lavender-blue eyes framed by dark lashes had looked heavy-lidded with weariness. The idea of sleeping for twenty-four hours had been terribly seductive, but she hadn't had the luxury of time. David had wanted her on the job as soon as possible.

Kristin inhaled the fresh, tangy scent of the nearby ocean through the open car window and felt the warmth of an Indian-summer day lingering as the sun set in the west.

"A lot of small fires were set at the construction site," David had explained. "Then the first phase of construction on vacation condos went up in smoke."

As she got closer, Kristin could make out the old houses and small businesses huddled into the land at the top of the horseshoe-shaped bay cut into the cliffs. Maybe an enemy of the company was doing it, and it wasn't because of this particular development. There were other possibilities beyond the few David had told her about.

"The mayor, Charles Overton, started a Save Vespar Bay Society. Then there's a lumberman, Bob Lipton. He's really outspoken against development. He's actually made threats against Restcorp." David had sounded as if he'd been reading from a list. "The high school math teacher, Dailey Cook, seems to be a lifelong protestor for liberal causes. Then there's Alexander Jordan, Vespar Bay's local celebrity. He's been very vocal about getting Restcorp out of there."

"What sort of celebrity is this Alexander Jordan?" she'd asked David.

"Haven't you heard of A. V. Jordan?"

"The author of the Western novels?"

"Yes. His property is right beside the Donaldsons', where you'll be house-sitting."

"My brother, Danny, reads those books, and he's read excerpts to me about shoot-outs, ambushes and bloody fighting—they're definitely not my type of reading."

David had laughed, but Kristin had felt vaguely sick. Talk about violence, she thought now, looking through the windshield at the panoramic view. The setting sun was creating a surrealistic look, bathing everything in a strange pink glow. Almost like the light cast by the flames of a fire.

Kristin cringed. Arson. She hated the sound of the word. Maybe she should have tried to talk her way out of the assignment. She didn't want anything to start her thinking about what had happened in the past—about past mistakes and pain. Not now. She would get the information, and then she'd hand it all over to Hammon Insurance. That sounded simple, neat enough.

She drove slowly onto the main street of the town, an all but deserted road with wooden sidewalks and false-fronted businesses. She spotted one of the few places still lit, a low-roofed, old-fashioned store with a porch area at the front that held soda machines and wooden benches. She swung onto a graveled parking lot, passed a single gas pump set on a high concrete island and parked near the door.

One of the things Kristin had learned in her five years as a private investigator was to start at the most basic level and build. A small store where she could talk a bit and get a copy of the local paper was as good a start as any.

She studied the flat roof and dull gray wooden siding, the windows along the front, wide, deep and blacked out with paint. Two clear windows on either side of the screened entry door ran from the floor to the low-pitched overhang.

There were no other cars in the parking lot, and she could see only one person in the store. A bulky man sat with his back to the window at a counter to the left of the door. He was hunched over as if reading something spread out in front of him.

Kristin grabbed her wallet and climbed into the gathering dusk. While she slipped the wallet into the pocket of her Levi's, she glanced up and down the street. The only thing she saw was a black-and-white police car slowly cruising out of sight in the opposite direction.

"They haven't gone more than a week without a fire or vandalism at the Restcorp site," David had told her. It figured that the tourist business must be as good as dead. She turned and walked up the single shallow step onto the porch and pulled the screen door open.

A bell jingled as Kristin stepped inside, and she paused while the door swung shut. Shelves that ran from the front to the back of the store seemed to offer a sampling of anything anyone could ever need. A bank of freezers and coolers lined the rear wall, and the slight staleness of age hung in the warm air being stirred by three slow-moving ceiling fans.

Kristin sensed the clerk watching her, and as she turned, she found she was right. The middle-aged man stared at her, ignoring a newspaper spread on the counter in front of him. He didn't look away while she walked across the green-tiled floor toward him.

"Help ya?" he finally asked, sitting back on the high stool and folding his arms across his middle, where buttons strained to keep the front of a blue work shirt closed.

"I'm looking for a newspaper," Kristin said, not letting herself become discouraged when her friendly smile was met head-on with a sober head-to-toe assessment.

After his pale blue eyes had flicked over her five-foot-eight frame and come back to her face, the man motioned to a long magazine rack on the front wall beyond the door. "Over there," he muttered, and pointedly went back to his reading.

Kristin had a feeling it wasn't just the fires that had driven off tourists. If everyone who showed up here got that sort of greeting, this place would be a ghost town in no time at all. So much for a country welcome, she thought as she walked over to the racks that displayed an assortment of San

Francisco papers and glossy magazines. An empty slot right at the front read *Vespar Bay Guardian*.

She moved farther along to see if there was another local paper and bumped into a revolving paperback rack in the corner by the candy display. As she steadied it, she read the sign on top: *Jake Warner, Bounty Hunter* by Local Author, A. V. Jordan.

The softcover books all had red bands at the top of their covers with their titles and the author's name, A. V. Jordan, splashed across them in gold. The cover art all seemed nearly the same—a lone cowboy on a well-muscled horse, his face shaded by a wide-brimmed hat, a heavy gun in his hand and a blurred vista of the old west in the background. The covers looked innocuous, almost pastoral, quite unlike the stories between them.

She chose one of the books at random. *The Day of Reckoning*. Flipping the book to its back cover, she quickly read the blurb that teased the reader with a promise of "the roughest, toughest Jake Warner book yet."

The bell on the door sounded, and a deep male voice asked, "Have you seen him, Len?"

Kristin looked up at the man who strode into the store. She had the immediate impression of size and strength. Tall, well over six feet, he came close to brushing the low ceiling with loosely-curling black hair that was long enough to lie on the nape of his neck. A white T-shirt and worn Levi's defined obvious strength, and the way he walked as he crossed to the counter made Kristin think of the old adage about a bull in a china shop. But not because of any awkwardness. Far from it. He seemed in control but gave the impression that if he strode too quickly the motion would rattle the foundations of the old building and things would tumble off the shelves.

Len looked up from the newspaper and shook his head. "No, nothing yet. Ain't been by here."

Kristin looked away, flipping through the book without reading it.

"Damn, he's hard to find," the stranger said, in a voice deep enough to more than match his size.

"He's always out and around talking to folks. He's pushing for a meeting. That guy from the insurance company made people real mad. Dailey thinks we need a meeting to get things out in the open."

"He may be right." The stranger paused. "This whole thing is getting ugly."

"Damn right," Len muttered. "Makes you wonder..."

Their voices dropped to an indistinguishable whisper, and Kristin chanced a glance at the two men. The stranger was leaning over the counter toward Len, supporting himself with both hands pressed flat on top of the open newspaper.

Knowing she couldn't move closer without being obvious, she stayed where she was, but she continued to watch the two men.

The tall man didn't seem terribly handsome in the traditional sense—not with a slightly crooked nose and a heavy jaw. Yet there was something about him that was raw and strong and almost uncomfortably male. And it was making Kristin so totally aware of him that she forgot about the open book in her hands.

A man is a man. So why did she notice the way this man's hair curled at his ears and at the nape of his neck and the way his arm muscles flexed? What was it about him that sparked that glimmer of the dreamer in her, that part of her that could almost imagine being touched by him?

She brought herself up short. It had been almost three years since her divorce, and she'd stopped thinking about any man that way long before that. Stop it, she ordered herself as she tried to pull her thoughts back to business.

But she was too late. The stranger turned abruptly, and fathomless dark eyes under a straight slash of brows caught Kristin staring. The clean-shaven face held little expression, but the eyes made a contact that stunned her, changing merely intriguing to startling.

The book slipped from her hands and hit the top of her shoe with a soft thud. But she didn't move. Heat rose in her face—mingled with another heat, dormant for so long she'd wondered if it had died altogether. It had only been hibernating, she managed to think. And if this incident was any example, it had gained in intensity.

It let her remember the full meaning of "sexual chemistry," that potent reaction to a man on the most basic level possible—a man she didn't even know.

"Len, call Gwen and see what's going on," he said, his voice breaking the spell. Then he strode toward Kristin.

Her gaze dropped self-consciously to the book at her feet. But before she could stoop to pick it up, the stranger was in front of her. In one lithe motion he'd retrieved the book and straightened to his full height.

An easy smile crinkled fine lines at either side of his rich, sable-colored eyes. He held the book out to her. "Yours?" he asked.

She shook her head. "Yes . . . er . . . no. I mean, I was just looking at it."

He glanced at the book then back to her, his gaze holding hers completely. This close, he overwhelmed her senses, and she killed the urge to take a big step backward. Instead she focused on his face and realized that he looked expectant, as if waiting for her to do something. She reached for the book. "Thanks," she managed to say in a tight voice.

He shrugged, his broad shoulders testing the soft cotton of his T-shirt. "Is Jake Warner your hero?"

She held the book tightly to her middle with both hands. "No. I was just curious. I . . . don't read books like that."

"Books like what?" he asked with the lift of one dark eyebrow.

She almost said "Garbage," but held her peace. She didn't want to say anything to damn her with a local resident. "They're not to my taste," she hedged.

"You're not a reader of macho-men books?"

She couldn't tell from his expression, but she wondered if he was teasing her. "Excuse me?"

"That's what most women say about them: books for men who want to feel macho. I've heard that more than once."

She shrugged, a vaguely unsteady motion of her shoulders. "Well, aren't they?"

"Maybe . . . maybe not," he answered cryptically as he crossed his arms over his chest. That was when she saw the tattoo on the back of his right wrist. Less than an inch across, it seemed light and faded, and without looking directly at it, she couldn't make out what it was. She wasn't about to stare at the man one more time. Worse yet, he'd said something and she hadn't the vaguest idea what.

"Pardon me?"

"I'll concede that they probably aren't great literature."

"And they're violent."

"The world is violent."

"So why read about it?"

He studied her for a moment, then took her completely off balance by saying, "Maybe they should kill Jake Warner off."

"Kill him off?" This didn't make sense at all.

"Isn't that what you think should be done with that sort of hero?"

Kristin held tightly to the book below her breastbone, as flustered by his conversation as by his catching her staring. It didn't help matters that he seemed surrounded by an appealing scent of fresh air and maleness.

"If someone said you could do away with the man, how would you do it?" he asked when she didn't respond.

If he was being foolish, so could she. "I'd put him in therapy and make sure he got help."

A flash of white teeth accompanied a soft, very pleasant laugh. "Therapy? I thought you'd want him shot at high noon, hung in the town square or set out over an anthill with honey all over his body."

She crinkled her nose with distaste. "That's quite a vivid word picture. But, no, I think *he's* done enough violent things. He should be committed and treated with some of the compassion he's never shown."

He flashed a smile again, and this time she could barely get air into her lungs. "I thought you said you never read any of these books?"

"I haven't," she said quickly. "My brother told me about them."

The phone rang, and Len answered it then called, "Hey, Gwen said Dailey left half an hour ago. He didn't tell her where he was going, but he headed down for the beach. He might have jogged to your place."

"Thanks, Len," the man said over his shoulder without looking away from Kristin. "Something you should remember is that these books—" with one finger, he flicked the book she held "—are only fiction." With that he turned, waved to Len and strode out the door.

Kristin watched through the window as he got into a large black pickup truck parked by her car and drove off to the north.

"Find what you're looking for?" Len called to Kristin.

She brought herself up sharply. Only if she'd been looking for a verbal tug-of-war with a stranger, she thought as she crossed to the counter. "I . . . I was looking for a local paper, but you seem to be out of them." Was that tight voice really hers? She took a deep breath. "I was hoping to find one."

The man closed the paper he was reading, folded it and pushed it across the scarred counter to her. "Here. *Vespar Bay Guardian*. On the house."

"Oh, no, I can't let you do that."

He shook his head, his expression almost pleasant now. "Don't want you to think Vespar Bay ain't a friendly place to pass through." He looked at the book still clutched in her hand. "I suppose you'll be wanting that book now?"

She laid it on the counter and smoothed the cover where she had twisted it slightly. "No, I don't."

"I thought you got it autographed."

"Excuse me?"

"Alex." He tapped the cover. "A. V. Jordan. You was talking to him just now."

Kristin barely kept a groan from passing her lips.

Chapter 2

He's the man who writes these books?"

"Damn right. Alex Jordan. I thought you knew when you was staring at him like that."

He'd seen it, too. She shook her head and nibbled nervously on her bottom lip. Why had she reacted like that to him at all? She could remember passages of the books that Danny had read out loud—gore and blood and violence. She felt vaguely sick at the memory. Yet that hadn't stopped the awareness and heat that Jordan's presence had produced in her. "No, I didn't know who he was."

"Most people do." He tapped the book again. "Reckon he can be anonymous around some folks."

"He's anonymous all right," she muttered, and wished David had given her pictures of any possible suspects instead of a verbal list.

"Around here he don't make no airs. He's real obliging. At least he was..." The thought trailed off, and the man's expression took on an edge. "Are you passin' through?"

"I'm enjoying driving around here," she evaded.

His eyes narrowed. "You here for the company?"

"Pardon me?"

He shook his head sharply. "Nah, a pretty thing like you ain't their type. They got real hard cases doin' their dirty work."

"Their dirty work?"

He shrugged. "Don't matter none."

Kristin looked at the man and instinctively knew he wanted to talk. All she had to do was ask the right questions. "Oh, I've heard a bit on the news about some big company—er, Restway, isn't it?"

"Restcorp," he corrected, and sat back on the stool.

"Yes, that's it. They own a lot of land around here, don't they?"

He frowned at her, his heavy eyebrows narrowing his pale blue eyes. "Own?"

"They're building an exclusive community, aren't they?"

"Yeah, that's what they're callin' it."

Here goes, Kristin thought, and plunged right in. "That has to be wonderful for your town. All the money and taxes. What a boon to Vespar Bay."

The frown deepened, and Kristin knew she'd hit the right nerve. When Len began to talk, the words spilled out, one over the other. "Sure, a real boon. That's what most think. But Restcorp bought up some of our land north of here, right from under the dead owner's family. Took advantage of the poor grievin' souls. Got it real cheap from the Harris family, then started in to tear it up. They're callin' it development. Progress." He said the words as if they were the worst form of blasphemy and raked his fingers through his thinning hair. "Just runnin' roughshod over the town as if it don't count for nothin'. Just the way they did to the Harris family. Two days Joe's dead—not even buried yet—and Restcorp lawyers started badgerin' poor Rose and the boys.''

Kristin felt a degree of sympathy for the man and for his town intimidated by Restcorp. "She...the man's widow, she sold it to them?"

"Yeah, the whole bundle."

"Why did she sell if they were so terrible?"

"They was real smart, settin' up trust funds for the boys and giving Rose enough money to be fixed for life."

And most people would take the money and run, she thought, but said to Len, "That's a shame. Too bad you can't get the company to leave."

He exhaled loudly. "We tried protestin' to block zonin' and such, but they're real set on doing it, and they got high-powered lawyers doin' their dirty work. Someone did get on their case, though. That's what's been in the news off and on."

Kristin could truthfully say, "I haven't paid much attention. I've been moving around a bit, and I just arrived in the area this afternoon."

"They were havin' fires up at the construction site, little ones, and some nuisance things, but then there was the biggest damned blaze I ever seen in my life. Last week a whole bunch of them condominiums went up. Five miles from here. It lit up the sky like it was day, and it was after midnight."

Kristin wondered if Hammon's investigators had been able to get this man to talk. "Do you mean someone deliberately started the fires?"

He lowered his voice a bit and leaned toward her. "That's the word that's goin' around."

"Who?"

"Ain't no one sayin'...if they know."

"Any guesses?"

The man's mouth opened, but before any words came out the bell on the door rang out. "Hey, Len!"

Kristin looked up at a tall, very slender man in red nylon running shorts, a loose tank top and jogging shoes. His narrow face, with high color at the cheekbones, looked sharp and angular. His long brown hair was pulled back in a low ponytail. He looked dressed for running, but he was neither out of breath nor sweating.

He came directly to the counter and smiled coolly at Kristin. "Hello. I don't think I've ever seen you around here."

"I just got here. This gentleman was telling me about what's going on in the town."

The man cast Len a sharp glance. "You shouldn't be talking to this pretty lady about our problems, Len. Bad manners, very bad." His voice was as educated as Len's had been unschooled. "We don't want to give a bad impression to someone just passing through."

Kristin knew that she was witnessing a lesson on how to get rid of strangers without offending them. "Len was just giving me some background on the town."

"That's all town business."

He wouldn't be nearly as easy to get through to as Len, but a challenge was a challenge. Kristin worked on a knowing smile. "I understand completely. I've lived in small towns, and it's only right to keep town business with the town. What I really need to know is how to find the Charles Donaldson place."

The man cocked his head to one side, and his green eyes under short lashes seemed less remote. "If you're a friend of Charlie and June's, you're out of luck. They just left this morning for a vacation. They won a trip—a cruise."

"Yes, I know."

His eyes grew sharp again, and he came a step closer. He pressed one hand flat on the counter beside the paperback and studied Kristin. "Who are you?"

Kristin shook her head and stuck to her cover story. "I wanted to get here before they left, but I couldn't manage it. I'm going to house-sit for them while they're away. I'm part of their prize."

"Damned if I ever got a prize like that," Len chortled.

"I heard they had a house sitter coming," the man said without a trace of a smile.

"That's me. I stay there and make sure nothing happens to their house and property, which—" she pushed a bit because the thin man was beginning to annoy her "—seems like a good thing considering what's been going on around here."

"You'll be here until they come back?" he asked abruptly.

"Until they come back," she echoed, "Mr.... er..."

"Cook." His green eyes had the most unnerving way of never blinking. "Dailey Cook."

Damn David! The next time she'd ask for pictures of everyone and their pets or she wouldn't come. She hated being taken off guard two times in a row. And she hated knowing instinctively that her smile wasn't fooling this man, not any more than he was fooling her by keeping his voice level. He was defensive and she was probing.

She knew she should be acting a bit more deferential, so she made herself flutter her eyelashes at him in her best imitation of a "helpless female," as much as she disliked doing it. "Could you please give me directions I can understand? I'm not very good at finding things from written directions. I even have trouble with maps."

She could almost see him thinking, wondering what she was up to. "North for two miles out of town, then left. It's

Tideway Lane. Go until it ends and butts into the coast road. Make a right. Charlie's got his name on the mailbox.'' Cook never looked away from Kristin. "I didn't catch your name?''

"Kristin Delaney.''

"You work for the company that gave Charlie the trip?''

"Yes, I do.'' She cut off any more questions by adding, "I just met your resident celebrity.''

Cook frowned down at her. "What's that?''

"A. V. Jordan. He writes Jake—''

"I know what Alex writes, but I hardly think of him in terms of being a celebrity.'' He saw the book lying on the counter. "Were you bothering him for an autograph?''

"No. I don't read this sort of book. There's enough violence in this world without reading about it, too. You should know that, living up here with everything that's going on.''

She saw the instant flare of emotion in his eyes, but any response was cut off when Len spoke up. "Change your mind about the book?''

She glanced down at it and almost shook her head. But for no reason she could think of, she found herself agreeing to buy it. "Yes. I'll take it.'' She paid Len and waved aside a bag for the book. "That's fine,'' she said, and picking it up along with the paper, she walked around Cook and headed for the door.

When she touched the screen, Cook called after her, "Go slowly, Miss Delaney. Our roads aren't in very good repair. Big equipment's been tearing them up.''

She turned to nod to him. "Thanks for the warning.''

He motioned north. "It won't take you more than ten minutes to get to Charlie's.''

"Miss?'' Len said from behind the counter. "Keep a good eye on Charlie's place, won't you? You're awful close to Restcorp up there.''

I know, she thought, but said out loud, "That's what I'm getting paid for." She looked at Cook. "I'll be seeing you again, I suppose."

The eyes never faltered. "Yes, you will."

Kristin didn't look back as she strode out into the softness of the approaching evening. But she stopped in her tracks with her hand on the door handle when she saw a man getting out of a Jeep with Restcorp printed on the side. He was slender, around sixty years old, and he tugged at the sleeves of an immaculate green uniform, then slipped a hat on over thick gray hair and strode toward the store.

Kristin watched him coming closer. As his blue eyes lifted and met Kristin's shocked gaze they widened ever so slightly. Ben Lewis never broke stride, but quickly, before Kristin could do or say anything, he lifted one hand to smooth his gray mustache and turned it palm out to stop anything she'd say or do. He deliberately broke eye contact to look at the store.

Kristin knew she'd been warned off, and the greeting for a man she hadn't seen for over a year died immediately. Dailey Cook and Len were probably watching, and Ben didn't want them to see him talking to her. Ben Lewis had crossed her path in New York when she'd been investigating an embezzlement case and he'd been working for the government on the same case.

He came within two feet of her, nodded as one would when he passed anyone in a small town. He took the step in one stride, crossed the porch, and the door closed behind him. Kristin ran an unsteady hand over her face. The federal government was interested in Vespar Bay?

Quickly she got into her car. She tossed the paper onto the front seat by her, started the motor and snapped on the headlights. Slowly she pulled out onto the main street without looking back. The federal government. Alexander Jordan. Dailey Cook. Kristin's thoughts went in circles where nothing made sense.

She found the turnoff easily and swung left onto a wide dirt road. After a few hundred yards it angled to the right and paralleled the shore. But this road was narrower and lined by redwoods and pines whose branches canopied overhead, almost making a tunnel.

When the road suddenly widened and the trees thinned, Kristin saw Alexander Jordan's house to the left.

David had given her the information during her briefing. "Little more than a mile's drive separates the Donaldsons' house from Jordan's. Jordan is shut off, protected by brick and chain-link fencing on three sides, steep bluffs on the water side. Access by stairs in the bluff is blocked by a security chain. You can identify Jordan's home by oleander bushes lining an adobe-brick wall."

The wall was over six feet high, the bushes dark shadows against the uneven bricks. Farther along Kristin saw double wooden gates the height of the wall, then more fence and bushes until they disappeared into the heavy forest. She drove about half a mile, the trees fell away and she spotted the Donaldson house.

In a broad clearing the softly blurred shape of an old bungalow set back beyond a sea of deep grass stood against the early night sky. Kristin turned onto an uneven brick driveway, the headlights of her car sweeping over the house showing faded green shutters on double-hung windows that were shielded by a wraparound porch. A worn, shingled roof steepened to a central ridge and beyond, and a detached single-car garage stood to the right. Side steps led up to the porch and a wide entry door.

She stopped the car near the steps, got out into the lingering warmth and paused. A gentle whispering of the leaves from a cluster of old elms that shaded the house to the south carried on the soft breeze. She tilted her head back to look up at the velvety sky dotted with stars and a rising moon to the east. She'd been brought up in the city—not the small towns she'd mentioned to Cook—an army brat who'd never lived more than a year in one place. In the city the stars were blotted out by the artificial lights below. Here, each and every star sparkled brilliantly. The peace and beauty could almost mask what was going on here. Almost.

Abruptly Kristin went up the two steps, got the key out of her pocket and inserted it into the brass door lock. With a click, the knob turned, and Kristin pushed back the heavy door. She stepped into shadows touched by the confined heat of the day and air that carried the scent of lemon wax and age.

She groped to find a light switch to the right and flipped it up. A three-bulb, tulip-shaded fixture overhead cast a yellow glow that exposed polished wainscoting, hardwood flooring partially hidden by a braided rug and cabbage-rose wallpaper—all old but immaculately cared for.

Tossing the key onto an oak chest that sat against the wall facing the door, she glanced at a mirrored hat rack that towered to the ceiling on her right. Then, anxious to get some windows open to let in fresh air, she looked left to a doorway with darkness beyond. Surely that was the living room.

Leaving the front door open for ventilation, Kristin walked to the darkened entry of the next room and stepped into the thick shadows. She reached to the left in search of a light switch, but her hand closed over something warm and alive. It flew at her, its unholy screech vibrating through the empty house, and a staggering weight struck her arm and chest.

Reeling backward, Kristin heard her own scream as her head and elbow struck the door frame. Pain shot red shards through her, and the next thing she knew, she was falling into the foyer with her attacker at her throat. Strangled by fear, she ended up sprawled on her back on the soft throw rug.

Any scream beyond that first shriek of terror caught in her throat. Her hands shot out for protection, closing over a tangle of hair and heat. A gray blur blocked her vision and the crushing weight on her chest moved lower to settle on her diaphragm.

She gasped and blinked, finally able to focus on amber eyes that belonged to the largest cat she had ever seen. The long-furred animal regarded her intently, its surprisingly dainty feet pressing sharply into her ribs. Although it growled with a sound that by all rights should have belonged to a dog, Kristin felt her terror give way to pure relief.

David had mentioned a pet named Boy during the briefing. She thanked the heavens that Boy wasn't a Doberman or a Great Dane.

"Boy?" Kristin gasped. "You are Boy, aren't you? There isn't some other monster lurking in the shadows, is there?" The cat cocked its head to one side, the growling fading to a rumbling purr that vibrated against Kristin's middle.

"Pretty Boy," she sighed, wondering if the name was a joke and this creature was really a girl. "Pretty, pretty Boy."

The purring settled into a deep, steady drone, and Kristin moved slowly, pushing the cat back so she could raise herself on one elbow. She took a deep breath before easing the cat off of her and onto the floor. Claws pricked through her Levi's for a second before she managed to get the large animal settled on the throw rug.

She scrambled to her feet with her back to the door, swiping at cat hairs that clung to every inch of her clothes. Her heartbeat began to settle back into a normal pattern.

"You damned cat. You took ten years off my life," she muttered to the animal who fastidiously groomed itself at her feet. "You, my furry friend, just about scared me to death."

A strong hand fell on her shoulder, and the panic of moments earlier came back in a choking rush. Self-defense training she'd forced herself to take last year returned with it. She cocked her elbow and drove it sharply into the middle of the intruder with all the raw strength fear could produce.

A sickening rush of air being forced out of lungs echoed around her, but as she tried to spin around to face her attacker, a strong hand clamped over her wrist. It jerked her hand up between her shoulder blades. Twisting and squirming in a frenzy, she swung wildly with her free hand and kicked blindly behind her. An arm closed around her front just under her breasts, and it pulled her back until she was pinned against a rock-hard body.

Impressions swirled around her—strength, size and overpowering control, then a voice hissed in her ear, "Knock it off!"

"Damn it, *you* knock it off!" Right then she made contact, feeling the satisfying connection of her heel with a leg.

A curse cut through the air, but the hold on her didn't lessen. It never became real pain, but the discomfort in her shoulder and under her breasts remained constant.

"Stop it!"

She kicked back again, but only hit air. "Let me go! Get your hands off me!"

"I'm willing to let go if you promise to quietly take two steps forward. No kicks, no fists. No crazy karate moves. Is it a deal?" When her captor spoke, she froze. Oh, damn, it couldn't be. "All . . . all right, if you quit crushing me," she gasped.

Slowly the hands released her, and the body at her back moved away. Cooler air took the place of heat and strength, and she almost tumbled forward without the support. She reached to steady herself on the oak chest and had to force herself to turn around. When she looked into the face of her attacker, she knew she blushed.

She thought she'd recognized the voice, but she'd hoped she was wrong. No such luck. Alexander Jordan stood just inside the door, as big and disturbing as he had been less than half an hour ago in the store.

Alex felt as off balance as the woman seemed to be. He'd heard the scream from the road and come running. Now he was faced with the same woman he'd seen in the store with Len, and he felt just as unsettled as he had then. It had been a long time since he'd felt such an all-encompassing reaction to a woman. He didn't know her at all, and it went against his reasoning. It felt purely physical, yet it fascinated him the way his whole being seemed to come alive at the sight of her.

He watched her face flush with embarrassment, the way it had in the store. Her incredible lavender-blue eyes widened with surprise.

Slender hands were held in front of her, one a fist, the other wide open, palm out, as if it could be a physical shield for her. "Wh-what in heaven's name are *you* doing here?" she gasped, her high breasts rising and falling rapidly under the loose white shirt.

She looked like a fantasy he might have had, and it shot right through him, hitting him as hard as any physical blow he'd endured in his life. Less than three feet separated them, and the way his body was reacting, he wished it was three hundred. Every soft angle and curve had fit neatly against him, a heady memory, until he recalled the stinging kick at his shins. Laughter crinkled the corners of his eyes and curled the line of his lips.

"You're asking me what *I'm* doing?"

Her full bottom lip, free of any lipstick, wasn't quite steady. "You're laughing at me," she exclaimed hoarsely.

"And you're as white as a ghost," Alex countered, ignoring the stinging that lingered in his shin. He was more concerned with the beauty of her face framed by tousled hair that settled in a silvery cloud around her shoulders. Silvery. The word shimmered the way the cascade of hair did. Without thinking about what he was doing, he took a step toward her.

"Don't come near me!" she bit out abruptly, her hands lifting higher, slender fingers spread and pointing at him. "Don't move."

He'd wondered after he left the store why he hadn't asked her name, why he hadn't found out more about her. Now he understood. If he'd found out even the simplest thing, he would have wanted to know more and more, and he wondered if he would ever be satisfied.

He held up both hands palm out. "I'm not moving."

"Why did you jump me?"

He couldn't stop the disbelieving shake of his head even though he knew it angered her. "Jump *you*?"

More color brushed her cheekbones, a high pink that only emphasized the translucent quality of her skin. "You...you did, sneaking up on me like that."

"I wasn't sneaking," he began in what he hoped was a placating tone. "I was only trying to find out what's going on in here." That scream had torn through the night, combining eerily with the screech of something inhuman. "Who screamed?"

She pushed her hands behind her, her chin lifting. "Me."

"You?"

"Yes, and all you had to do was come in and ask me," she muttered.

He was absolutely certain he'd received more pain from their contact than she had. He'd deliberately watched how tightly he held her, and when she'd been free enough to kick his shin, he'd wished he'd been more in control. "I was trying to ask." He took a breath. "Can we start over?" When she nodded, he asked, "Why are you here?"

She watched him closely, and her hands finally fell to her sides. "I'm house-sitting for the owners."

"I heard someone was coming to stay. Do you have a name?"

"Kristin Delaney."

She didn't ask who he was, and he knew right then that she didn't have to ask. Len must have told her. "Do people really sit for houses?"

Her eyes flickered. "I do."

"And you do it for fun?"

"I do it for money," she said bluntly.

He couldn't stop the next words. "You don't look like a house sitter."

"You don't look like a man who writes those books, either," she countered, without missing a beat.

"I write about violence, and you do violence." When she opened her mouth in protest, he spoke quickly. "Where did you learn to hit like that?"

"Self-defense classes."

"You never said why you screamed."

She motioned toward the gray cat curling itself around her ankles. "That beast scared me."

"Boy made you scream?"

If body language meant anything, the folding of her arms across her breasts showed she was on the defensive. "He's huge, and he jumped out of the shadows at me. I overreacted, I guess. So did you.''

"We both did," he conceded.

"That man at the store just finished telling me about what's been happening around here, and I was a bit nervous."

Len never did know when to keep quiet. Alex didn't want this woman involved in the Restcorp troubles. "Don't believe half of what you hear around here," he murmured.

"He was lying to me?"

He smiled, a smile that was guaranteed to melt the hardest heart. Oddly she didn't react beyond a mere tightening at her eyes and the line of her pale pink lips. "No, just a bit of a gossip." He regrouped. "Listen, I came in to do a good turn, to help whoever screamed. You're obviously in one piece and doing just fine on your own."

Kristin eyed Alex Jordan, wondering why, despite the fact that he had really scared her just moments ago, she didn't feel any threat from him. She sensed a certain laughter in his eyes, a teasing, and it appealed to her.

She never would have guessed that the man who wrote about Jake Warner would have a sense of humor. She needed to readjust. "Thank you. I'm doing fine as long as you promise not to sneak up on me like some crazy Indian."

"I promise. Welcome to Vespar Bay."

He extended a large hand to her, and she hesitated. She didn't want to make any more physical contact with him. But deciding she couldn't avoid it, she quickly touched her hand to his and drew back before absorbing little more than heat and roughness. "Thank you."

The overhead light didn't make his expression any more readable. "Irish?" he asked.

She didn't understand. "Excuse me?"

"Delaney—is it Irish?"

"No, I mean, yes, it is, but I'm not." She wished she could have had this encounter on her own terms, all planned and neat. She stooped to pick up the cat, holding it to her breasts, its warmth some protection from the cold air, its size some sort of protection from the man in front of her. "My husband—my *ex*-husband—his family was Irish. Mine is Scandinavian and French." She was rambling, only the heavy cat clutched to her keeping her nervous hands at rest.

"I hope you won't be uncomfortable staying here alone, after everything Len must have told you."

Kristin shifted from one foot to the other. "No, I'll be fine. I've got Boy."

Alex reached to flick the purring cat's ear, but his gaze never let go of hers. "Your car lights are on," he said as he turned and stepped back out into the night.

Kristin released the cat and hurried after Alex down the steps and into a vaguely chilly wind. "How far is the water from here?" she called after him.

Alex stopped and turned. The houselights played eerie shadows on his high cheekbones. "Go out the back door, head for the garage and go ten paces behind it. You'll fall off the cliff and onto the beach."

"Cliff?"

"This whole area is on a bluff with a drop of twenty to thirty feet to the beach—depending on where you jump from. Be careful when you go out walking."

She glanced toward the back of the house, then turned to Alex. "Is the beach—"

Her words stopped dead when she realized she was completely alone. Alex had disappeared into the shadows of the inky night.

Chapter 3

Alex went around to the back of his darkened house, across the terrace and through the French doors into the study. Silence surrounded him as he walked through the shadows of the book-lined room. Even his steps were soundless on the plush copper-toned carpeting.

He dropped down onto the brown tweed couch, snapped on a small side lamp and reached for the telephone. He dialed a Sacramento number. It rang only once before a man answered in a distracted voice. "Yes?"

"Devereaux?"

Jon Devereaux cleared his throat. "Alex, is that you?"

"Did I get you at a bad time?"

"Very bad." He coughed again. "When I said I'd help you in my free time, I didn't mean my...recreational time."

"Sorry. Are you ever going to settle down?"

"God forbid. What do you need?"

"I need you to find out what you can about a person who just showed up here."

"Just a minute." Alex could hear a woman giggle in the background, then Devereaux was back on the line. "Who?"

"Her name's Kristin Delaney. I don't know much about her except she's house-sitting for my neighbors, the Donaldsons. She's blond, blue-eyed, about five foot eight. She's been married and divorced."

"Where's she from?"

"No idea."

"How old?"

"Twenties, maybe middle."

"Anything unusual about her?"

Alex sank back in the cushions. Nothing beyond his overwhelming response to her. "She's pretty." That sounded juvenile in his ears. "And she's driving a blue Toyota sedan, probably an eighty-five." He recited the plate from memory, then said, "Add her to your list, all right?"

"No problem. I was going to call you tomorrow, but since you're on the line, I'll tell you what's been going on. I've made a contact with the investigation team working on the fires out of the county fire marshall's office." He hesitated. "Not bad, eh?"

"That's why I asked you to help," Alex said. Since he and Devereaux had left the army, they'd gone in different directions, but sooner or later they always got in touch. Over a year had passed at one time, but when they'd contacted each other the time hadn't mattered at all. The connection to a brother couldn't have been more complete for Alex—or more lasting. "It's like waiting for the other shoe to drop up here. You know something's coming, but you don't know what."

"Got any idea who's behind all of this?"

Alex tightened his hold on the phone. "Not really. Just hunches and suspicions."

"There must be a book for you to write in this mess," Devereaux murmured. "You said you wanted to be done with Jake Warner. This could be the book to break away from that series."

"Jess would probably push it for a *Movie of the Week*," Alex muttered. Suddenly he didn't want to joke, and he ended the conversation quickly. "Thanks for helping. Go back to your fun. I'll be waiting to hear from you."

"I'll let you know what I find on . . . Kristin Delaney."

"Thanks," Alex said, and hung up.

He sank back in the cushions of the sofa. Unlike his days in the army, he didn't live around danger anymore. He wrote about it, but it wasn't his intimate friend. That's why he'd called Devereaux for help.

His friend had hired on right out of the army as security chief for an international corporation based in Sacramento. He had contacts. He could find out anything about anyone or anything.

Alex had kept Devereaux abreast of the events since that man's death on the Fourth of July. He ran a hand over his face. He knew why he'd asked Devereaux to check on the others around here, but he really didn't know why he'd asked him to check on Kristin. She'd just come to Vespar Bay. She couldn't have anything to do with the fires.

Then the answer came without any help from Devereaux. Alex simply wanted to know about Kristin Delaney.

Maybe she was a distraction from what was happening around here, a distraction from his problems and his worries. Her impact on him in the store had been something out of the blue, hitting him so hard that he had barely gathered enough control to cross the store to pick up the book. But when she'd turned on him at Charlie's and he'd had her in his arms, he knew he'd never experienced anything like that before.

Physical attraction? Lust? Yes and no. With each encounter he gradually knew it was more than that. He couldn't put a name on it, but it was disturbing nonetheless. The woman touched him on a level he'd never known existed. And it bothered him a great deal—especially when he knew he had to concentrate on protecting this town.

His writing needed his attention, too. Jess was getting nervous, wanting to see at least part of the book. He stood abruptly and crossed to the computer. Snapping on another light, he dropped into the swivel chair in front of the desk and flipped on the machine. He'd thought it would be so easy to kill off Jake Warner, to make it spectacular, but the problems at Vespar Bay had cut into his thoughts. Now the Delaney girl had, too. He called up the file with the book he'd started over and over again these past three months.

Jess thought the book was half done. In reality, Alex had barely begun. He read what he'd done so far.

JAKE WARNER: BOUNTY HUNTER
Final Reward

1865: Arizona

Jake Warner found the camp at midafternoon on his second day in Indian territory.

While the sun, an orange ball of fire in a high blue sky, beat down on the parched land, Jake watched from the security of a brush-covered rise above the camp. A single man, blood caking the back of a torn shirt, lay sprawled facedown by the ashen remains of a camp fire. Dead. No partner anywhere to be seen. And no Emma Forester.

With the only sounds the steady buzzing of flies in the hot air and the cry of vultures beginning to circle high above, Jake took his horse by the reins. Slowly he made his way down the hill, got within five feet of the dead man and stopped. He looked around the deserted camp.

Waist-high brush on three sides acted as a shelter of sorts from the desert winds. No horses. Jake swiped at perspiration that trickled from under his hat, down his deeply tanned skin and into the stubble of a three-day growth of beard.

No girl. No five-thousand-dollar reward. Nothing but the stench of death and the damned heat. He hunkered down by the corpse, a good-sized man, maybe twenty-five, with two shots in his back. He matched the description of one of the men who'd taken the girl from the wagon train.

Jake reached for something caught in the man's hand. He tugged it loose—a torn, bloodied piece of blue gingham. The girl had been here. He stood and scanned the silent land. The shimmering heat made his eyes ache. Was Emma Forester still alive? That's all that her father had asked Jake to do for five thousand dollars: bring her back alive.

Alex stared at the blank screen, then it came to him.

The click of a rifle being cocked merged with a trembling voice ordering, "D-don't you move."

Jake spun to his right and found Emma Forester. The girl was alive but looked as if she'd paid a price for it. Blue gingham, a match for the piece still in his hand, was little more than a blood-smeared rag covering her slender body. High breasts rose and fell rapidly. Long hair the color of cornsilk swirled in the desert wind around a face as delicate as fine porcelain.

Bitterness rose in Jake when he saw the ugly abrasion marring one cheek and puffiness at the corner of her pale-lipped mouth. Eyes so blue they reflected lavender were wide with fear

Alex stopped abruptly. He'd always floundered in his writing when it came to bringing Emma Forester into the story, but not tonight. And he knew why. He was making her the image of Kristin. He almost hit the delete keys to take it all out, but stopped. What difference did it make? If her description fit, it fit. If it worked, he should be grateful.

Five thousand dollars faced him, with a rifle in both hands leveled at his middle.

"I'll kill you," Emma breathed. "Don't you dare move, or I swear I'll kill you."

"If she don't, I will," a rough voice said, and Jake jerked around to come face-to-face with ...

The Donaldson house was spooky to Kristin, not in the traditional sense of ghosts and apparitions, but in a shrouded, empty sense. Everything had been covered by sheets, from the furniture that crowded the full front living room with its fireplace and double-hung windows to the dining room in the middle of the house with chairs turned upside down on a mahogany table, their tapestry seat pads resting on the covered surface.

The only hint of life was a huge water bowl and full dish of cat food on the brown tile floor in the corner of the kitchen at the back of the house. A note was taped to the top can of a huge stack on the white-tiled counter by the sink.

"Sorry we missed meeting you. Boy was fed today but he's very particular." What followed was what looked like a recipe for combining dry food, moist food and canned milk. The note ended with "...and don't forget to hold Boy as much as you can. He'll miss us. Have a good time. The Donaldsons."

"As much as I can?" Kristin muttered as she looked down at the huge animal methodically eating the food in the bowl on the floor.

The supply of canned and dry cat food on the counter looked as if it could feed an army of cats. She left Boy eating and looked through the rest of the house. After opening some windows, Kristin settled into one of the two bedrooms, the one with a note on the door telling her to use it.

Right off the kitchen at the back, the small room done in blue and white and furnished for a child would probably have a beautiful view by daylight. The single canopy bed on the wall facing the windows was framed by bookcases filled with a combination of schoolbooks and storybooks. An old black-and-white television stood in the corner.

After she'd brought her bags in from the car, Kristin kicked off her shoes and sat on the bed while she dialed David's number. It rang four times, then the answering machine clicked on.

"Sorry I can't take your call," David's recorded voice said, "but leave your name and number, and I'll get back to you as soon as possible."

"David," Kristin said after the beep. "It's Kristin. I should have waited to come up here until I had pictures of the suspects. Ben Lewis is up here. Why? Is the government involved in this? If so, why? Call me as soon as you can. We need to talk."

Kristin hung up, stripped, and took a quick shower in the tiny bath between the bedrooms. Then she slipped on an oversize white T-shirt, sat cross-legged on the canopy bed and flipped through the newspaper. Locally the fires were being played down to the point of being nonexistent. A school pageant got more play than arson did.

She closed the paper and saw the Jake Warner book lying on the side table by the telephone. Why had she bought it? She reached for it, scooted under the blankets, bunched the pillow behind her head and opened the book to the first page.

Jake Warner stood by his tired horse at the edge of the mesa, the sounds of the desert carrying on the still, hot air. He knew that he had to kill Webb Tanner, but he didn't know how he'd do it . . .

The next thing Kristin knew it was dawn and she was lying on her back, the Jake Warner book open on her stomach. She couldn't remember falling asleep, but early-morning light was filtering into the room. She pushed herself up and leaned back against the headboard.

The book slid to one side, and she caught it just before it tipped over the edge of the bed. She looked at it a moment, shocked that she'd not only read some of it but had actually almost enjoyed it.

She smoothed her fingertips across the red banner emblazoned in gold. *Jake Warner—The Day of Reckoning*. She could see now why her brother Danny had read the books. The story was well told, and the characters came alive. Even Jake Warner, as insensitive and macho as he was, was a person—a real person.

Poor Webb Tanner, Kristin thought with a shake of her head. He doesn't stand a chance against Jake Warner. She tossed the book onto the nightstand. Later she'd find out what happened to Webb Tanner. Right now she needed to get up.

She looked out the windows across the room and saw the rising sun spread its pale colors into the shimmering sky until they spilled onto the distant water. The house felt cool, almost uncomfortably so, and she finally got out of bed to walk barefoot through the silent rooms, closing windows on her way. Indian summer obviously had run its course.

After donning Levi's and a pink sweatshirt Kristin slipped into tennis shoes and pulled her hair back in a high ponytail. When Boy attacked her at the kitchen door, she placated the constantly meowing cat with a huge bowl of the first food she came to in the kitchen. To hell with special mixing, she thought as he settled in to eat.

She crossed a service porch, unlocked the back door and stepped out onto a small deck with a shrouded barbecue, a redwood picnic table and chairs. She took her time inhaling the freshness of the ocean air. The deep grass rippled in the gentle morning breeze, and Kristin could see that what Alex had told her was true. Ten feet behind the single-car garage the ground fell away and disappeared. She crossed to wooden steps built into the granite cliff and carefully descended, using a wobbly handrail for support. When she stepped down onto the narrow beach and crossed to the tide line, she felt small rocks embedded in the sand pressing at the soles of her shoes.

The coastline curved to the north, blocking any view beyond water and thick forest that grew from the water's edge to the base of the bluffs. Kristin turned to look to the south and barely held her shock in check.

About fifty feet down the beach Alex was striding toward her, one hand raised in greeting. Her strong response when they'd first met at the store yesterday was only the beginning, she realized. She had to concentrate to understand what he was calling out to her because her mind was so consumed with the way he looked in a dark windbreaker, jeans and deck shoes, his dark curls gleaming in the clean morning light.

Alex broke into a loping jog, his long even stride eating up the distance. "Miss Delaney," he called.

Kristin pushed her hands into the pockets of her Levi's and didn't try to speak when he stopped in front of her. "I wanted to make sure you saw me this time," he said in that deep, smooth voice. "I didn't want to take any chances of repeating what happened last night." A smile came suddenly. "I learn fast."

The effect of that smile on Kristin was just as shocking as the fact that Alex seemed to be pleased to see her. "I saw you coming." She looked right at him, his size more imposing now than it had been last night, and she realized how easily he could have hurt her then. Yet his strength had been controlled, and there hadn't been any real pain. "And I learn fast, too."

He cocked his head to one side, studying her from under ridiculously thick dark lashes. "I never expected to get hit in the stomach like that."

"Sorry," she said, shivering slightly as a cool breeze skimmed off the water and brushed across her face. "I'm not very strong, not really, but I worked hard at it after..." She quickly edited her words, shocked that she'd almost let things from her past slip out with this man. "I decided to take self-defense classes," she said. "But I never wanted to use what I learned."

If he noticed her hesitation, he didn't let on. "You didn't waste your time or your money."

She looked away quickly. "It's beautiful around here, isn't it? And a lot cooler than yesterday."

"Yes, it is. Summer's finally gone."

"It's hard to believe that anything bad could happen in a place like this."

"Like anywhere, we've always had our share of problems—but nothing like the last three months."

She saw her opening, but it was hard to figure out where to start. "Len told me a bit, but he didn't go into any details. And the paper..." She turned back to him and was taken aback to find him staring at her. "It...it said hardly anything about the problems."

"How long are you going to be around here?" he asked abruptly.

She shrugged. "As long as the Donaldsons are gone. A month—maybe longer."

"Then you'll find out a lot about Vespar Bay."

"I met a man in the store...after you left. Mr. Cook. He acted as if he didn't want me to know anything."

He didn't look surprised. "That's Dailey's way. He just came back this past spring after being away for a long time. He's very protective of the town."

"I could tell."

He pushed his hands into his pockets. "I didn't expect to find you down here."

The brightness of the morning sun washed over the man in front of her, and Kristin could see a very faint scar hooked over the line of his jaw. "I was looking around, getting my bearings. How about you?"

Alex could have been completely honest and told her that he'd been up since dawn working on his boat because he was having a very hard time figuring out how a woman he barely knew could infiltrate his writing and his dreams. The writing had worked to his benefit, but the dream that couldn't be remembered had left his body with tension that had made more sleep impossible. He didn't think he wanted to be that honest with her. "I was working on my boat."

He watched her studying him and found himself wondering what she was thinking. She looked appealingly fresh, her silky hair pulled back off her face, wispy curls escaping to lie softly against the clean lines of her face and neck. The pink of her shirt reflected in her skin. With any luck Devereaux would call today and he'd find out all about Kristin Delaney.

"How's it going at Charlie's? I thought it might be uncomfortable for you being there alone."

She smiled. "I had the attack cat with me, so I was just fine."

He looked away from the brilliance of her easy smile, needing a distraction. "If you're thinking of going for a walk, you don't have much more than a mile of open beach. We're in a cove, a smaller replica of the one the town overlooks. Restcorp fenced it to the north. You can get to the main cove of the town to the south, but you have to go over private beaches."

"I didn't really think about where I was going. I'm used to city life, and it seemed so peaceful here, so contained and soothing." She shrugged sharply. "Looks can be deceiving, can't they?"

He looked back to her and caught a hint of a light floral scent that seemed to surround her. "I guess so." He turned from her and went across the sand to the base of the cliffs. Dropping down on the sand, he leaned back against the granite wall, bent his legs and circled them with his arms. Only then did he look at Kristin again. He wanted to know all he could about her. Maybe then he could make sense out of his own unsettling response. "It's a bit cool, but if you want peace and quiet, it's as good as it gets right here."

Kristin stayed where she was, seemingly studying him with those incredible lavender eyes. He swallowed hard. "Tell me what you do when you aren't house-sitting," he suggested.

"This and that," she said evasively as she took a few steps toward him. "Whatever comes along."

"You sound like a gypsy."

Maybe she was in some sense of the word, Kristin conceded to herself, willingly going from place to place, wherever her job took her. "That sounds very romantic. And it can be. I spent a Christmas in Rio one year. Crazy to have heat and sun on Christmas day." She shrugged, a bit unnerved by the way Alex had been able to draw that out of her. "I've never had a sense of roots, not like you must have living in a town like this."

He patted the sand. "Sit. My neck's getting stiff. Tell me about Christmas in Rio."

She wondered if she should politely walk away instead of being seduced by the man's voice and sparkling eyes. When he motioned to the sand by him again, she quickly sat down but made sure there was a two-foot buffer of space between them. She moved back against the bluff, nervously pressing her heels into the damp sand while she looked out at the calm water. "Rio wasn't anything great, just a change of scenery." It had also been her first Christmas away from her husband. Ray hadn't wanted to go and hadn't understood why she had taken a job that required her to go there.

"So, you don't have a home base?" he asked.

She stared at the horizon. "Not really. I've got an apartment, but I'm there so seldom that I wonder why I keep it at all." Without looking at him, she asked, "I heard you've only been back here a few years. Why did you come back?"

He didn't speak for a moment, then his answer came softly. "It was time to come home, to put down roots."

She kept her eyes on the waves rising and falling in a strangely seductive rhythm. "Is Jake Warner ever going to put down roots?" She heard his soft chuckle, a gentle sound that seemed to skim over her nerves in the most pleasant way.

"Sure, when they bury him six feet under."

She stared at the waves, watching a large one coming in until it diminished to a soft swell. "It wouldn't be in character for him to settle down, would it?"

"No. How about you? Would it be in character for you to settle down?"

Ray had asked her the same thing, and her answer, even after a few years of marriage, had been "It's too soon." There was too much to do in life to stay in one spot forever. She didn't want to stagnate. It was then that she'd known that though there had been love in her marriage, it wasn't enough to pull her tightly to Ray, to keep her there forever.

Strange that she hadn't seen that clearly until now. "I don't know. I guess everyone comes to a point where he or she wants to stay in one place and put down roots. It hasn't happened to me yet." She lifted a hand full of cool, damp sand and let it drift slowly through her fingers. "My father was in the army, and we moved all over the place. I've lived in Germany, France and all over this country. When I was younger I would look at the ocean and wonder what was on the other side rather than how far or deep it was. I just wanted to keep moving until I knew what was being hidden from me."

She stopped her own words, unsettled to realize how her barriers had begun to slip so treacherously with this stranger. Odd how she and this man could be so different in what they wanted, yet he was the one she was explaining herself to. "I guess I like the idea of seeing new places."

"Maybe it's a condition of the human species, a need for change. I used to need it, but now I do it in my writing, going back in time, making up stories out of thin air."

The pleasing mixture of the sounds of the ocean and the softness of Alex's voice had begun to lull Kristin. She didn't want to move, didn't want to break the spell, but she made herself shift just a bit farther from Alex. Out of the corner of her eye she saw the sleeve of his black poplin jacket, and she could barely see a hint of the small tattoo at the knit cuff. "Did you ever want to write something—" she tried to think of a safe word "—deep?"

"With meaning? With literary merit?"

She shrugged, wondering if it was a constant condition with her to be embarrassed around this man. "I didn't mean to..."

"Yes, you did, and I have. There's a *deep* book sitting in a drawer in my office. It's the very first novel I wrote. I did it while I was still in the army, just after Vietnam."

"You were in the war?"

"The undeclared police action," he murmured. "I spent ten years in the army, the first part of it in Nam." He inhaled with a low hiss. "I wrote the book—well over six hundred pages—and I haven't looked at it since I typed The End after the last word."

Kristin saw his arms tighten around his legs. "Never?"

"Never," he echoed just above a whisper.

"Will you ever get it published?"

"No. I wrote it for me, for what I needed at the time, not for money. Maybe as a catharsis of sorts."

She looked right at him. "What's in it?"

He glanced at her, but his eyes were hooded and unreadable. "I don't know you well enough to tell you that." He stood abruptly and brushed at sand that clung to the rough denim of his jeans without looking at Kristin.

She felt heat rise in her face. "I can see that this talk is over," she muttered, and scrambled to her feet. "I'm going back to watch the house."

Unexpectedly, Alex touched Kristin on the shoulder and she stopped abruptly. "I'm sorry," he said. "I didn't mean that the way it sounded. If I ever think it's time, I'll let you look at it."

She looked up but couldn't meet his gaze, not when she suddenly felt as if her whole existence centered on where his hand rested on her. She knew logically that a bond couldn't be formed between two people by a simple touch, but that didn't stop her from wondering if he could feel each beat of her heart through his fingertips. And it didn't stop her from looking somewhere near his chin instead of into his dark eyes. "What's the novel called?" she found herself asking, not quite able to let the subject rest.

He broke contact and pushed his hands into the pockets of his jacket. For a moment Kristin felt certain he'd turn and leave without answering. But he didn't. When she dared to look him in the eyes, he was staring right at her. "I never gave it a title."

The words were barely uttered before an explosive roar shattered the peace of the cove. Kristin jerked around to look north toward the source of the sound. Beyond the jut of land a huge black plume rose into the heavens, towering over the trees. The cloud of smoke tinged with orange spiraled upward, blotting out the clear blue of the sky.

"What happened?" she gasped and turned to Alex, shocked at the raw anger on his face.

"Damn them all to hell! They've really done it this time," he ground out, and took off at a dead run down the beach toward the noise and smoke.

Kristin didn't think twice about going after him, but he stopped her when he turned and yelled, "Call 911. Hurry! Tell them it's Restcorp again."

She hesitated, then as he took off again, she ran for the stairs. By the time she'd reached 911 and told them what was happening, she knew what she was going to do. Without hesitating she went out the back door, hurried down the stairs and headed in the direction Alex had gone.

The acrid odor of smoke filled the air and burned her lungs as she ran toward the cloud that grew blacker all the time. It spread in a canopy to hover ominously over the land.

At the jutting finger of land where the trees grew to the water's edge, she looked down, saw the prints of Alex's shoes in the damp sand and followed them through the thick growth. She broke into the clear only to be faced with a six-foot chain-link fence. A huge sign hung on the barrier that ran ten feet out into the water: Restcorp, Phase One, Private Property, Keep Out.

Two footprints sank deeply into the sand beyond the wire barrier. Alex must have scaled the fence and jumped down on the other side. As quickly as she could, Kristin climbed the steel mesh, hooking the toes of her shoes in the openings. Then she swung over the top and jumped.

She landed squarely and looked ahead but couldn't see too far because of the irregular shape of the cliffs. Quickly following Alex's footprints around the base of the cliffs, she found herself in a large cove where earth movers sat silently in front of deep gouges they had cut into the granite walls. The huge yellow machines were faced inland, all still, and not a person was anywhere to be seen.

Alex's tracks went out around the machines, still going north. Somewhere in the distance Kristin heard sirens, and she looked up at the smoke that seemed determined to blot out the sun with its ugly blackness.

Around the next curve Kristin stopped. Beyond bundles of drainage pipes and wire she saw stairs—new wood, wide and solid—going up the side of the naked bluff. The smoke was coming from somewhere above.

The sirens were closer now, loud wails that cut through the air, and fine ashes drifted down like snowflakes. Kristin

ran for the steps and took them two at a time. When she got
to the top, she stopped to gulp in air.

The area in front of her had been stripped of trees for at
least the length of a football field in either direction and
probably just as far straight ahead. The charred skeleton of
the burned condominiums to the right looked stark and
ugly, a scar against the cleanness of the forest beyond. To
the left, foundations for new buildings had been laid, the
cement still mottled and drying with stacks of new lumber
by the forms. But what was happening directly ahead caught
and held all of Kristin's attention.

Just off center in the bare earth clearing an orange fire-
ball billowed black smoke thirty feet into the air, but she
couldn't even tell what was burning so furiously. Men were
running everywhere; ten-foot gates on the far side were open
and fire trucks roared through, their sirens and lights going.

Kristin spotted Alex running toward three men huddled
by the charred remains of the condos. She recognized Dailey Cook with his long hair loose around the shoulders of a
heavy navy sweater. The other two were strangers to Kristin, one of them heavyset, balding, middle-aged and incon-
gruously wearing slacks and a sport coat. The other man
was as tall as Alex but more slender, with shaggy gray hair
and a deeply lined, mustached face. He wore a plaid work
shirt and Levi's.

Alex shouted something as he ran toward the men, and
they all turned to look at him. Kristin couldn't hear anything over the sound of sirens, roaring fire and shouting
people. But she could see that the heavyset man looked
stunned, the older man stared at Alex and Dailey Cook
looked furious.

Ashes and smoke swirled around the men, and as Alex got closer, Dailey Cook yelled something, his face contorted with anger. The next instant Alex stood in front of the long-haired man, his hands clenched into fists at his sides.

Chapter 4

Kristin ran toward the men but slowed when she could finally hear Alex's words. "My God, this is like a holocaust!" he was yelling. "I told you before that someone's going to get killed!"

The older man reached out and tried to restrain Alex with a hand on his arm. "Restcorp is the only one hurt so far. And you're getting way too upset. You can't change a thing now, so calm down, boy."

Alex jerked away from the touch as Dailey stepped closer to him. "This is insanity. I never wanted it to—"

He stopped abruptly when he saw Kristin coming up by Alex's left shoulder. "What's she doing here?" he demanded.

Kristin felt as if her left side was being scorched by the heat of the fire, and a strange wind that seemed to originate at the blaze swirled around the group. A vibrant anger crackled in the air.

She looked up at Alex, but he didn't spare her a glance. His gaze, intent and angry, went from man to man, then he moved behind Kristin and around until he was between her and the fire. Right then she understood what was going on. He knew, or thought he did, that one of these men was responsible for the fire.

"What happened?" she gasped.

"Restcorp's been stopped in their tracks," Dailey said, and his expression held an annoying smugness. "An earth mover and the new lumber they just received to start rebuilding the condos is burning."

His attitude repelled Kristin, and at the same time she took a step back, she heard a thundering roar. Everything blurred for her except the fact that Alex seemed to be jumping right at her, hitting her squarely with all of his weight. She tumbled backward, and with Alex over her she hit the hard ground. The air rushed from her lungs in a sobbing gasp.

His cotton jacket pressed over her face, and her voice came out in a muffled choke. "What . . . are you doing?"

It took Alex a full heartbeat to understand what had happened, that there had been another explosion—but he didn't need any time to realize that he was on top of Kristin. Her ponytail tangled around his face, its freshness at odds with the acrid air, as at odds as her softness was with the hard ground. Dreams and writing were one thing, but being against her right now was too much. He pushed back quickly and took Kristin by both arms, pulling her up to stand in front of him.

Dirt streaked one cheek, and tendrils of hair had been loosed from the clip. "I'm sorry," he breathed, meaning to pull back and be free of her, but his best intentions died when his hand lifted and swept along her jaw, brushing at the strand of hair that clung there.

He heard the other men getting to their feet, muttering curses, but he didn't look away from the lavender-blue eyes in front of him. "Are all of you all right?" he tossed over his shoulder to the others.

"Great," Dailey muttered. "I love getting blown off my feet."

Alex lowered his hand but didn't break the contact. He let it rest on Kristin's shoulder, and it unnerved him to feel her trembling under the dirt-smeared sweatshirt. "This is about all I'm going to take," he breathed.

"Let's hope it's enough for Restcorp to throw in the towel," Dailey said.

Alex turned, anger at Dailey's words choking him, but he felt Kristin move close to his side and no words came. Instead it seemed natural to put his arm around her and hold her against him—tightly. Maybe they both needed support.

Kristin felt uncomfortable being stared at by the two strange men and Dailey, and she forced herself to speak up. "I'm Kristin Delaney, the house sitter for the Donaldsons."

The bald man nodded tightly, his face grim. "Charles Overton. I'm the mayor of Vespar Bay, or what's left of it."

The other man glanced at Kristin from deep brown eyes under gray brows. "Bob Lipton," he muttered in a gravelly voice.

"Bob does logging north of here," Alex said.

No one else said a thing. They all stared at the destruction in front of them, the deadly black smoke rising from a combination of the second earth mover that had exploded and more stacks of raw lumber being torched. Kristin didn't fight the pressure of Alex's arm holding her to his side.

"Dailey, Dailey!" someone screamed, and Kristin looked in the direction of the gates. A woman in a baggy blue sweat suit was running toward them. She skirted the fire trucks, pushed her way through a group of firemen and never broke stride. As she came closer, Kristin could see that at any other time she would have been pleasantly pretty, with curling brown hair framing a round face dominated by wide-set eyes and a small nose dusted with freckles. But right now she looked horribly pale, her eyes filled with fear.

"Thank God you're okay," she gasped as she threw herself into Dailey's arms. "I saw you falling and that ball of fire and Alex flying forward—" She gulped in air, and Kristin could see a plain gold wedding band on her hand as she clenched the heavy knit of Dailey's sweater for support. "Y'all could have been killed," she sobbed.

"Gwen, sweetheart, I'm fine."

"What were you doing here?"

He held her tightly as the ashes showered down around them. "I saw the smoke when I was out walking. Someone must have put explosives in the machines. We just happened to be here when it went up."

Before anyone could do or say anything else, firemen came running toward them. "Get out of here!" the first man to reach them yelled, and he pointed to two more huge machines and piles of lumber near the fire. "They might go at any second!"

Alex didn't argue. He simply shifted his hold on Kristin and led the way through the maze of fire-fighting equipment. He headed toward a row of trailers to the left of the open gates and well out of the way of the fire.

At the trailer closest to the gates Alex stopped and looked down at Kristin. "Stay here with Gwen." He let her go and turned to Dailey. "Come on. We can't just stand here and watch this. Let's see if there's anything we can do."

"You have to be kidding," Dailey muttered.

"No, I'm not," Alex said, and headed off toward the fire trucks. Kristin stifled an urge to yell after him, to warn him to be careful, that he might be hurt. But she kept silent and looked at Dailey. The long-haired man hesitated, then with a shrug, jogged off after Alex.

Kristin sank down on the wooden steps dampened by the drifting water being sprayed from the hoses. But she never lost sight of Alex, who had begun to help maneuver cars and trucks to the far side of the clearing near the bare foundations.

Kristin watched, her hands balled into fists on her thighs, as policemen and firemen hurried all over, yelling orders, directing the fire-fighting effort. Only when the blazes began to die, when the lumber had been reduced to mounds of smoldering debris and the two machines to scorched, twisted metal, did Kristin feel an easing in her. She spread her hands, relieving the cramping in them. Then she remembered the other woman sitting silently by her on the steps.

She spoke, never looking away from Alex. "I've never seen anything like this in my life."

"Most of us haven't," the woman said in her soft drawl as she nervously twisted her wedding band.

"Thank God," Kristin whispered, watching Alex help some firemen recoil a water hose. It took a real effort for her to look away from the man and turn to Gwen. The woman's hair and clothes were filmed with ashes, and sooty streaks marred her face. Kristin looked down at her own arms and hands, and when she swiped at the soot on them, it turned to greasy smears. She grimaced then rubbed her hands together hard.

"Here we've gone through all of this," Gwen said when Kristin looked up at her, "and we haven't met."

"Kristin Delaney."

"I'm Gwen Cook. Are you a friend of Alex's?"

Kristin sat back, her eyes skimming the crowd until she saw the large man with dark hair again. He was talking to several firemen who stood near the farthest engine. "We just met yesterday, at the store in town. I didn't know who he was, and I said some things that weren't too nice about his books." Her eyes followed Alex as he wandered over to help disconnect the last hose hooked up to the water tanks. "He doesn't seem...well, exactly like I thought anyone who wrote those books would be."

"He's tough enough. He was in some special group in the army, but he doesn't talk about it too much." Gwen shifted on the stairs. "You just met him yesterday?"

"Seems like a lifetime ago." She rested her elbows on the step behind her and leaned back, suddenly very tired. "I'm watching the Donaldsons' house while they're on vacation."

"You're the house sitter?"

"Yes."

"That's a really unusual occupation."

"I guess so." She shrugged. "You don't sound like you're from around here."

"I'm from Georgia. I came here when Dailey decided to come back to teach at the high school. He was in Atlanta on vacation, and I was working at the hotel where he stayed. I never guessed he was a teacher, what with his long hair and all. He's actually a great teacher; the kids love him. If this wasn't Saturday, he'd be in school and wouldn't be around here." Dailey looked up right then, as if there was some sort of invisible connection between him and this woman. "He can be difficult and opinionated, like he is about the Restcorp situation, but he means well. He's just very worried. And I couldn't live without him." She stopped talking when her voice began to shake, and she looked back at Kristin. "Sorry."

"He's lucky to have someone who cares as much as you do," Kristin said, and meant it.

"Doesn't staying alone at Charlie's worry you?"

"I'm fine. I'm used to being alone. That's the nature of the business of house-sitting." She watched a fire truck drive slowly out of the gates. But before it could turn onto the paved road, a sheriff's car followed by another car marked Fire Marshall came inside. Both had their lights flashing.

"Are you from the city?" Gwen asked.

"I've lived in San Francisco off and on."

"I wouldn't mind living there."

"You don't like it here?" Kristin asked.

"Oh, sure I do, most of the time, but now it's all so unsettling..."

"This fire..."

"Not just this one. There've been a bunch of little ones—stacks of wood, old buildings, that sort of thing. But the big one, it was awful. Dailey and I could see it from our place. It lit up the sky like the Fourth of July." She shivered expressively. "It scared me to death. And who knows when whoever's doing it will begin to burn other places in the town?"

Cook was with his wife when the big fire took place. Kristin filed the fact away but knew that it didn't mean a lot, not with delay timers available. Not any more than it meant anything that Alex had been with her when this one started. Her stomach knotted at the thought, then settled. Something in her couldn't believe he'd done this. She suddenly remembered his shouted words to Cook, Overton and Lipton: *I told you before that someone's going to get killed!* No, he didn't do it, but chances were good that he knew who did. And he was angry about it.

She watched Alex crossing to meet Dailey by the police car, and she rubbed her hands on her jeans without looking at what she was doing. "How long have you been married?" she asked just to keep talking.

"Eight months. How about you? Married or lookin'?"

"Neither. I'm divorced and on my own." That sounded so simple. "I like it that way." Kristin didn't want to talk about marriage, so she diverted the subject to Restcorp. "It's hard to believe that someone is doing this deliberately just because they don't want Restcorp to build here."

"Someone is." Gwen sighed. "The old residents are the worst in protesting this thing. The mayor hates it, the old logging people hate it, the fishermen hate it, and the way Bob, Dailey and Alex feel, I was really worried they'd bomb this place."

Kristin's mouth dropped. "What?"

"Don't look so horrified. I was just joking." She grimaced. "Sorry. That's a very bad joke under the circumstances."

"Kristin!"

She turned at the sound of her name and saw Alex striding toward her. Dailey was a few paces back, his long hair held back by a yellow strip of material. Black soot streaked Alex's skin, and gray ash lay thickly on the shoulders of his dark jacket. She stood as he came closer, overwhelmed by everything that had happened, but mostly by the sheer presence of this man.

She could see the ashes clinging to his curls, and when he brushed at his hair she saw small red dots on the back of his hand—burns that were rapidly blistering. "Oh, no," she gasped, and took a step forward to reach for him.

Her fingers tangled awkwardly with his when she tried to turn his right hand palm down to look at the back. It had been less than twenty-four hours since she first met him, yet a staggering pain hit her when she saw watery blisters on the dark skin and a welt that zigzagged from his knuckles to his wrist, almost to the tattoo. "You're hurt."

He shrugged. "It's nothing." He moved, but instead of breaking contact he turned the tables and caught her hands between his. His thumb made slow sweeps over the back of her hand, a curiously intimate contact under the circumstances. "You've got streaks all over your face and ashes in your hair."

"I've been around a fire," she said in a soft, unsteady voice, so aware of his touch that she couldn't move.

"Are you up to speaking to the sheriff?"

"Why?"

"We saw the explosion, and you called it in. They need to fill in some forms."

"Can't they come by her house later?" Gwen asked Alex. "She's gone through enough for one day."

Alex drew back from Kristin, pushing his hands into the pockets of his soiled jacket. "I can ask them, but it's up to you."

She looked up at him, focusing on sable-colored eyes filled with concern. "I'm really tired." And actually her legs felt drained of the power to stay standing. "I didn't expect anything like this when I left the house." She forced herself to take a deep breath at the same time the door to the offices behind her opened.

She looked back and barely covered her surprise at seeing Ben coming out and down the steps. She'd completely forgotten he seemed to be with Restcorp. "You folks all right?"

"We're fine," Alex said. "Too bad this happened."

Kristin glanced at Ben as he paused at the bottom of the stairs. "One of your people around here must be pretty pleased," he muttered, and walked off toward the gates.

"A bit testy, wasn't he?" Dailey asked.

"He's got every right," Gwen countered. "The guards must feel pretty stupid to have this happen right under their noses. Let's get out of here." She grabbed her husband by the hand and looked at Alex and Kristin. "How about you two? Want a ride? I've got the truck."

Alex glanced at the sheriff then back to Kristin. "He can wait. He knows where to find me if he needs me. Would you like a ride back?"

She knew she lacked the strength to go very far. "Yes, I really would."

Kristin and Alex sat in the back bed of the truck, their legs dangling over the lowered tailgate. Side by side, they rode in silence, with Kristin inordinately aware of every sway and bump that brought Alex's arm against hers.

By the time the Donaldson house came into view, her nerves felt raw and she asked the one question that wouldn't go away. "Do you have any idea who's doing this?"

Alex glanced at her fleetingly before looking back at the road behind them. "There's no point in making any guesses until they can be proven."

"If it's someone from around here . . ."

His look was back on her suddenly, sharp and penetrating. "Who mentioned that to you?"

"No one. I was just thinking about how angry everyone seems about this development—although for the life of me I can't see what it can hurt." She was babbling now, and she knew it. "Lots of money would come into the community, and it's so far from the town. It seems stupid—"

"You said you're used to the city," Alex interrupted.

"Well, these people are used to the country, and they don't want it changed."

I don't fit in at all, and you'll tell me about your "literary" book when you're damned good and ready to, she thought. Frustration tasted bitter on the back of her tongue.

When Dailey drove onto the driveway of the Donaldsons' house and stopped behind the rental car, Kristin jumped down quickly. Inhaling a deep breath, she turned to

look at Alex. With him sitting on the tailgate and her
standing, they were at eye level. "You should see a doctor
about those burns."

"They aren't anything."

"Are you trying to be as tough as Jake Warner?"

That brought a welcome smile, a cracking of the tension
as his dark eyes crinkled at the corners. "I never could be
that tough," he said softly, and tapped her on her chin. "See
you."

She nodded and hurried around the back of the truck to
the steps. When the truck had backed out onto the street and
headed south, she went up the stairs, reached for the door-
knob and stopped. She could have sworn she heard her
name called, softly, no more than a brushing whisper on the
cooling air.

She looked around but saw nothing and thought that the
growing wind was playing tricks with her nerves. Then she
heard it again—low, soft, almost indiscernible. She looked
to the north, to the press of redwoods and pines on the far
side of the driveway, and caught a flash of movement. Then
her name came again, this time clearly.

As she watched, a shape took form and she released a held
breath when she recognized Ben emerging from the dense
greenery. She hurried down the steps toward him.

"Not too close," he said quickly, not coming out into the
open. His green uniform blended with the colors of nature
behind him—a perfect camouflage. "Just come forward
about ten feet then look back toward the garage."

Kristin did as he said, stopping within five feet of where
he stood. "I didn't even see you there," she admitted,
looking right at Ben before she turned toward the garage.

"It's me all right, kiddo." When she glanced back at him,
he took off his hat to smooth his thick hair with the flat of
his hand. "Don't stare at me like that. I might be getting

older, but I'm not a ghost." He put his hat back on and motioned south. "Yesterday I didn't know if you were passing through or staying here. Then I heard you telling that Cook woman about house-sitting here. I've got to get back, but I thought we needed to talk for a minute. Walk slowly back to the garage, and I'll follow."

She took off, walking very slowly. "What are you doing here? What's going on?"

"It's good to see you, too," he said smoothly, his voice drifting out from the trees near her.

"It's good to see you, Ben. Now what's going on? What's the government doing up here?"

"They aren't. I quit them last year—retired, about a month after I saw you in New York. I was with them twenty years, and it was nineteen too long."

She slowed even more, looking down at the long grass pressed flat under her sneakers. "Why are you up here?"

"Would you believe that I'm a simple security guard with a company that has a big problem?"

"No. I can't see you doing anything so..."

"Mundane?"

"Or so boring." She let her eyes roam over the locked garage.

"You're too smart for your own good, kiddo. And you're right. I wouldn't do this unless I was starving, which I'm not. And even if I were, I'd look around for something else."

The sound of a car coming down the road stopped Kristin, and she turned toward the road. A police car drove slowly down the rutted lane heading south toward town. When it was out of sight, she slowly turned back to the garage, her eyes barely skimming over Ben in the trees. "So?"

"I've gone private, just like you. Only I'm my own company. I don't have a David Allcott to account to. I suspect that you and I are up here for the same reason."

"Which is?"

"Restcorp and arson."

She nodded, seeing no sense in hedging with Ben. "You're right."

"House-sitting is a good cover and less work than mine."

"Why are you doing this?"

"It's a living, kiddo. Restcorp's got a big reward offered, and now that this has happened, the amount might go up."

Kristin turned and found Ben leaning against a giant redwood. "Big bucks?"

"Six figures." He lifted one brow. "If we work on this together, share what we find, what we know, maybe we can help each other out a bit."

"And the reward?"

"We'll split it fifty-fifty. Agreeable?"

She managed a smile. "The money's all yours, Ben."

"No, half-and-half, or the deal's off." He stroked his mustache with one finger. "Fair is fair. All right?"

"All right."

"Now can I ask you a question?"

"Sure."

"Why did you let Allcott send you up here after what happened before?"

An unwelcome but all too familiar tightness clutched at her middle. "David needed me to do this."

"You told me that if your job with Allcott ever got tangled up in violence, you'd quit."

She shrugged. "I will. I don't intend to get involved in anything up here but finding the truth. This isn't the shoot-out at the O.K. Corral, Ben."

"You were just at a fire...."

"It isn't the same as...as before. You know that. You were there when Jerry was shot."

"Yes, I was." He studied her intently. "You've got to get over what happened sooner or later, kiddo."

"I am over it." She wished she sounded more convincing. "It just isn't something you forget easily. To see your partner shot then stand there with a gun in your hand and not have it in you to shoot the man who did it..." She took a deep, shaky breath. "He got away, and Jerry didn't."

"I was there. I didn't get him, either."

Kristin shrugged. "Maybe because you were in the restroom and didn't get out until the guy disappeared."

"Government agents know when to get out of the way," he said with a grating smile. "Insurance investigators don't get off so easily, I guess. Do you keep in touch with Jerry Rule?"

"Of course." She tightened herself to stop a shiver that seemed to be getting ready to slide up her spine.

"Are you still sending him money?"

Her heart lurched. "How did you...?"

"A good guess. I know how guilty you felt about what happened. God, you were at the hospital for days waiting for word on him." He studied her for a long moment then asked, "Hasn't anyone ever pointed out to you that you weren't responsible for a quirk of fate? That you don't have to take the guilt of the world on your shoulders?"

"When did you get into psychoanalysis?" she asked tightly.

He stood straight. "It comes with the job."

Kristin didn't want to think about the past, about mistakes that she knew couldn't be righted no matter how much money she sent Jerry every month. "How did that fire get started today?" she asked abruptly.

"You've got me." He shrugged. "But it looks pretty damned professional. Whoever is doing this, they never miss a beat. They wait long enough for Restcorp to feel as if they're safe, then they strike. Damned scary, if you ask me."

The air had cooled considerably, and Kristin felt the breeze chill her skin. "If it's professional, do you think a local is involved?"

"Sure, it has to be—a local resident with the ability to blow things sky-high and set fires." He exhaled and buttoned the jacket of his uniform. "Next time we meet, let's make sure someone introduces me. Then I won't have to tromp through the woods like some Boy Scout."

"You'll never be taken for a Boy Scout, Ben," Kristin said with a weak smile.

"Let's hope not, kiddo. Let's hope not." He began to move back. "Keep in touch."

"How?"

"Call the Restcorp number. It's available through Information. If I'm there, fine. If not, leave a message. Say that..." He thought. "Say that my watch is ready. I'll understand and get back to you as soon as possible. In a pinch, I'm staying at a cottage north of the construction site. They provided it with the job."

"We need to talk some more...."

"Later, kiddo," he said, and turned, melting into the shadows and colors of the forest.

After staring at the blinking cursor on the monitor for well over an hour without an idea coming to him, Alex was vaguely relieved when the telephone on the computer table rang. He reached for it. "Hello?"

"Alex, it's Sheriff Lane. I need to get in touch with that woman you were with today. Have you got a number for her?"

He almost recited Charlie Donaldson's number to the sheriff, but stopped. He'd already showered and pulled on clean jeans, and he wasn't getting anywhere with his writing. The diversion of seeing Kristin again seemed very appealing. "I'm just heading over to the Donaldsons' place where she's staying. Do you want me to bring her by your office so you can talk?"

"No. I'll drop by Charlie's place to see her. Just tell her I'll be by in about half an hour."

"Sure," Alex said. "I'll see you there."

Quickly he slipped on a white cotton shirt, pushed his bare feet into deck shoes and reached for his jacket. When he saw the ashes still staining the black cotton, he thought better of it and slipped on his navy-wool pea coat.

The drive to Kristin's took about three minutes. He pulled into the driveway behind her car, flipped off his lights and engine and got out.

In two quick strides he was at the porch and going up the steps. He rapped on the door twice and heard movement inside the house. The full force of how much he wanted to see Kristin again hit him when her shadow appeared on the frosted glass of the front door.

Chapter 5

Kristin jumped when she heard a knock on the front door and almost spilled cat food all over the kitchen counter. Quickly pushing the half-full bowl at the cat at her feet, she turned and hurried through the house into the foyer.

"Who's there?" she called with one hand on the door-knob.

"Alex."

With annoyingly uncoordinated movements she managed to pull the door open. Alex stood in front of her, his size emphasized by a heavy wool jacket he wore. Would she ever get used to the zing that seemed to shoot through her every time she saw him? No, not any more than she could stay calm as his dark eyes skimmed over her, taking in her loose hair, the thigh-length T-shirt and her bare feet.

"I didn't think I'd see you so soon," she said a bit breathlessly.

"The sheriff called and wants to talk to you tonight. I offered to meet him over here."

Kristin shifted, trying to ignore his strong legs encased in faded denim and the sensuous line of his lips. "Did he want to talk to you, too?"

"I *was* there at the fire."

She nervously tucked her hair behind her ears. "When's he coming?"

"Any minute."

She motioned Alex in, backing up so there was no contact as he came through the door. "In here," she said, and hurried ahead into the living room. She tugged the sheet off the couch, letting it slide to the floor in a pile to one side. Smoothing the cushions of the maroon sofa, she turned to look at Alex not more than a pace behind her.

Right then she realized the only thing between her and being naked was the skimpy piece of turquoise cotton. "I— I'll be right back," she stammered, and hurried to the bedroom.

When she walked into the room five minutes later in pleated corduroy slacks and a white silk shirt, Alex was on the couch, his jacket discarded. He was staring into the empty fireplace. The soft light of the two side lamps near the couch touched him with a gentle glow. His shirt exposed the strong column of his neck, and she could see the steady beating of a pulse in the hollow there. She felt a now familiar stirring, as if she'd known him forever. Silly notion, she told herself. She cleared her throat.

Abruptly he turned to her and exhaled. "Sorry. I was thinking."

"About what?" she asked as she came into the room.

"Fate."

A quirk of fate, Ben had said earlier. She stopped in the middle of tugging a sheet off the chair to the right of the couch. "What about fate?"

He sat forward, resting his elbows on his knees and letting his hands hang loosely, his fingers laced together. "How long have you been here?"

She shrugged as the sheet fell in a mound by the chair. Sitting down, she tucked one bare foot under her. "A little more than twenty-four hours."

"Is that all?" he asked.

And she remembered her statement to Gwen. It was as if she'd known Alex a lifetime. This didn't happen in real life. It shouldn't. From what little she knew about him, it was obvious that he had roots here. He belonged, and he wanted it that way. No matter how she looked at it, she was temporary, the way she'd always been in life. A few weeks one place, a month in another, a year at the most. And she liked it. She was never bored. Tired, worn out, but never bored.

"A lot has happened," she said, and avoided looking right at him. "How long did you say it would be before the sheriff gets here?"

As if in answer to her question, a car drove into the driveway, its lights sweeping across the windows, then going out at the same time the sound of the engine died.

"He's here now, I think," Alex said as he stood and went to open the door.

The sheriff, a middle-aged, painfully thin man in a very neat blue uniform, walked into the living room and nodded to Kristin. "I'm Boyd Lane, sheriff in these parts."

"Kristin Delaney," she said, scrambling to her feet.

He took off his cap and began to nervously run a finger back and forth across the crown. "Thanks for seeing me tonight. I need to get the reports straight on the fire."

Kristin motioned the man to the couch. "It's no problem. Have a seat."

The sheriff kept standing, obviously waiting for Kristin to sit first. When she did, he finally sat. Alex came back into the room and settled near the other man.

Boyd Lane laid his cap carefully on the cushions between himself and Alex, then turned to Kristin as he ran long fingers through salt-and-pepper hair that had receded from a high forehead. "First I want to tell you that Vespar Bay is really a very nice community. We've just had some problems lately. These fires..." He shook his head. "Terrible things. Alex understands about this place. He's been giving me trouble since he was a boy. It's his home, but you being a stranger and all..."

An outsider, Kristin amended mentally, his words only emphasizing what she'd been thinking a few moments ago. When she saw the man and Alex exchange knowing glances, an understanding that came only from years of friendship, she felt even more separate. "I understand."

"You'll be leaving soon, and I hate to think you'll take these bad memories with you." The lamplight sharply highlighted the sheriff's face, emphasizing a hawkish nose and long chin. He seemed obviously agitated, as if he had trouble dealing with what was happening in Vespar Bay. She glanced at Alex, who was staring down at his feet, then she looked back to the sheriff. "What exactly do you want to know?"

He took a small notebook and a pen out of his breast pocket and looked at Kristin. "Start at the beginning and tell me what you remember."

Kristin talked, Alex listened and the sheriff wrote constantly in his little book. When she'd said everything she could remember, she sat back in her chair. "Was it deliberate?"

Lane glanced at Alex quickly then back to Kristin. "No idea, yet." He pushed the notebook into his pocket and set his cap back on as he stood. "I'll be in touch," he said to Kristin, then he turned to Alex. "You come on by the office when you can, and we'll do some serious talking."

Alex nodded, then showed the sheriff out. When he came back into the room, he sank down onto the sofa with a sigh. "That's over."

"The poor man," she murmured, settling back in the chair. "He's out of his league, isn't he?"

Alex leaned forward, his elbows resting on his knees. "We all are with the fires."

"Too bad Jake Warner isn't here," she said, hoping to lighten the mood.

"He'd just be shooting people." He looked at Kristin for a long moment, then sat back again. "Lane's a good man. He'll do just fine for now."

Kristin looked down at Alex's hands resting loosely on his thighs. The burns. She scrambled out of her chair and went to him, dropping down on the couch and reaching for his left hand. "You didn't do a thing for these, did you?" she asked, almost flinching at the rawness that marred his skin.

"I told you they aren't too bad."

The small burns had faded, but the welt stood out vividly. Without arguing, Kristin got up and went to the bedroom. In the bathroom she rummaged through the medicine cabinet until she found antibiotic ointment. She turned to go back into the living room but stopped when she saw Alex standing in the bedroom doorway. He was watching her from across the room, and it made it difficult for her to think what to do.

"I found some ointment," she said, raising the tube in her hand.

He stared at her, the bed separating them, and didn't speak.

Nerves bunched in her stomach. This wasn't the place to be with Alex. She knew it, yet she seemed incapable of moving. "Did...did you need something else?"

"You said today that you wanted to know what was beyond the obvious."

She touched her tongue to her lips and nodded. "Yes."

"How far does that curiosity go?"

"Why?"

"I was just wondering."

Kristin moved abruptly, crossing the room. When she reached Alex, he moved back to let her pass. Once in the living room she knew she'd be able to settle and think clearly. She turned when she got to the couch and almost ran into Alex behind her. One hand went out to stop a collision, and she dropped the tube. It fell unheeded to the carpet as Kristin stared up at Alex.

"I have my own curiosity," he murmured, and before she understood what he meant, he was reaching for her.

His hands closed gently on her shoulders, and he drew her body against his. The motion was fluid, almost gentle, and she didn't think of resisting, not even when Alex bent over her. Certain he was going to kiss her, she braced herself but was taken off balance when his lips touched her forehead. Slowly he found the pulse at her temple, then tasted her eyelids, trailing down her cheek.

The searching contact stunned her. Softness mingled with roughness as his lips and coming beard skimmed over her face. Finally he found her mouth with his. Heat. His hips moving ever so slightly against hers, creating dangerous explosions deep in her being. Fire seemed to fill her, and her blood soared with unbidden need. Reason fled in that instant, and Kristin knew that she'd been looking for this all her life.

Hesitantly she held to Alex, his effect on her shattering. How completely natural to open her mouth to his, to let him enter and explore her and find the secrets of her taste and scent.

A delicately slender thread began to grow between herself and this man, a bond she'd felt earlier. It intensified as his kiss deepened, then she froze. A bond? No, that couldn't be. Not here, not with this man, not now in her life. She spread her hands on his chest, felt the hammering of his heart under her palms. Reluctantly she pushed back and free.

His hands fell from her, and space separated them, yet her troubled spirit didn't calm. Only inches separated them physically, yet a whole life-style separated them emotionally. She looked at Alex, at his eyes darkened with passion yet filled with the same shock she was experiencing at their response to each other.

"No," she managed.

And he didn't question her, as if he knew that no amount of talking could make sense out of what had just happened. He simply touched her cheek, a fleeting contact that all but scorched her skin. Then he turned and scooped up his jacket on his way out of the room and out of the house.

The telephone rang at ten o'clock that evening, and Kristin stopped her agitated pacing in the living room to hurry to the bedroom. She almost tripped over the cat at the kitchen door, and the gray fur ball squalled before darting under the table.

She got to the telephone on the third ring, reached for the receiver and sank down on the bed. "Hello?"

"Kristin? David here."

"What do you have for me?"

"Nothing on the fire, except that they found traces of what might be a timing device in both machines. No one admits to having undercover investigators in that area, certainly not the government. Ben Lewis retired ten months ago, a bit earlier than most agents, and no one's saying why he retired."

Kristin scooted back, letting her head rest against the headboard. She closed her eyes. "He's probably doing just what he said he is—making a living."

"A good one with the reward to be had—and the amount might go up since this latest blaze. They lost a half-million in machinery today. God knows how much in lumber. I'm sure there will be others going after the reward, maybe even people from the town."

An impatient squall drew her attention to the cat sticking its head around the door. It eyed her with a gleam of hunger. "I just don't understand these people," she said as she tossed a pillow in Boy's direction and watched him scramble back from the room. "They almost take glee in the company having problems, yet they risk their lives trying to help. It doesn't make sense."

"You'll figure them out," he said.

She hesitated, then touched her tongue to her lips before she asked, "What did you find out about Alex Jordan?"

"He looks clean. Special services in the army. Went right from that to writing. Married, divorced and pretty private. I'm still looking into Dailey Cook."

"He was in Atlanta, Georgia, this past spring, and he got married there. Her first name's Gwen. She worked at some hotel."

"That's what I like—specifics," he said on a chuckle. "Take care of yourself."

She uttered a simple, "Of course," before saying goodbye and hanging up.

In the silence she stared out the windows at the night. Without thinking, she touched her lips, then her hand fell. She looked left and picked up the open Jake Warner book that was lying facedown on the side table. The story was becoming almost as addictive as the writer.

Pushing her legs under the covers, she found the spot where she'd left off the night before.

Webb Tanner didn't see Jake until it was too late to do a thing to avoid the dark-haired man who was coming down the middle of the main street. Dust swirled around Jake's black boots, his eyes narrowed, and his large hand hovered over the gun in the holster strapped to his thigh.

Webb Tanner didn't want to die, not now, not like this, and not with Jake Warner on the other end of the gun.

If he hated anyone, it was Warner, and he didn't want that man to be the one...

Alex was up until past midnight, sipping brandy and staring out the French doors of his study at the dark night and the ocean. He sat very still, thinking about what was happening to his hometown—and about what a slender blonde with lavender eyes could do to him with a mere look.

Finally Alex stirred. He rose, crossed to the bathroom, splashed water on his face and came back into the study.

For over an hour he worked at the computer, and the story came with frightening ease. He finally got Emma Forester and Jake free of the second man who had kidnapped her. And they rode off into the desert, deeper into Indian territory.

It seemed too pat to let the Indians kill Jake off. Not flashy enough. So he had to get them out of Indian territory and let someone else, or something else, be the executioner. He hesitated, then the story began to come, his fingers flying over the keys.

Jake and Emma rode double on his pinto across the open valley. He felt her at his back, her arms clamped around his middle so tightly that he was having trouble breathing.

She was terrified. Rightly so. Her abductors had been working for Cochise for over a year now getting white women for camp slaves. And there was a two-day ride to get out of Cochise's ring of power. Jake dug his heels into his horse's sides.

"Please, hurry," Emma whispered in a small voice near his ear. "Please."

Jake glanced over his shoulder at her, into lavender-tinged eyes. "We're going as fast as we can," he said, his heart hammering in his chest. He looked ahead toward the canyon opening and headed for its protection, hoping for fresh water. They could make camp there before they made their final run to the border in the morning.

In less than a minute they were through the arched opening and in the shelter of the high walls. Jake pulled the horse up, stopped and jumped down. He reached up to help Emma, then heard a sound at his back.

He caught a flash of movement partway up the wall, on an outcropping near the entrance. He saw the glint of a gun, and he didn't stop to think before he threw himself between it and Emma. Using his body to keep Emma safe, he blinked into the glare at a single figure.

"Webb Tanner," Jake rasped. "Damn it, I thought you were dead."

Alex sat back. He'd protected Kristin just hours ago with his own body, a bit involuntarily, but he'd done it nonetheless. He wasn't as tough as Jake, nor as quick on his feet, but he couldn't have done otherwise, he realized.

Had he ever felt that protective of anyone before? He doubted it. Damn, he never should have kissed her. The impulse should have been denied or controlled. Alex tipped back and ran a hand over his face. He'd been drinking too much brandy since he'd come home, and his mouth felt cottony, his thought processes slow.

He stared at the monitor and realized that he didn't know where to go from here with the story. He concentrated, filling himself with Jake Warner, but it didn't help. The flow of the story had stopped as quickly as it had started.

When the telephone rang, Alex jumped. He stared at it for a long moment then reached for it. "Hello?"

"It's just me," Devereaux said over the line. "I saw the fire on the news tonight."

"So did half the state."

"Did I disturb your writing?"

Alex sank back in the swivel chair and stared at the computer. "I was just staring at the monitor." Alex fingered his tattoo and felt the discomfort of a tiny burn that touched it. "What do you have for me?"

"Some good stuff. The man who died on the Fourth wasn't named Franks. He was Ronald Fletcher. And he wasn't a retired mailman, he was a small-time con man, burglar and—" Devereaux paused, giving the dramatic extra beat before he finished "—better-than-average torch."

"An arsonist?"

"He's been inside two times for setting fires in the wrong places. He's got an apartment in San Francisco. His rent's paid up to the end of the year, and his landlord still doesn't know he's not coming back. Ronald Fletcher. Fifty-five.

M.O.—rob and burn. Fire covers what he's done. It's any-body's guess what he was doing up here, but the fires..."

Alex absorbed the information. The man had died be-fore the fires began. It didn't make sense. "How'd you find this out?"

"By accident. I had a drawing the police artist had done when they were trying to find any relatives after his acci-dent, and it was sitting on my desk. An old friend from San Francisco, a P.I. there, saw it and recognized him. Seems he had a run-in with him a few years back."

"Lucky," Alex murmured. "But the guy was dead be-fore the fires up here began. This really confuses things."

"Sure does. About as much as that girl you wanted me to get information about."

Alex felt an annoying heaviness in his body just at the mention of Kristin. "What are you talking about?" he muttered.

"At first I drew a blank on her. Nothing. There's very little background. She looks like a drifter, moving around and trying to get a job any way she can. What did you expect me to find out about her?"

That someone cared about her, Alex almost said, but didn't. How could she be in this world and not have made a deep impact? "What about the license number on her car?"

"A rental in that name, using a cash deposit instead of a credit card. Very anonymous. Yet that's where I hit pay dirt. I went to talk to the counter girl who made the rental at a downtown agency. She knows Delaney. Are you ready for this? Kristin Delaney is an investigator." He let that sink in before he added, "She worked as an insurance investigator for quite a few years. Now she's with one of the best pri-vate investigation companies in the Bay area—Allcott In-vestigations. But they usually deal in white-collar jobs. I don't know yet why they're involved in this case."

Alex stared at the monitor, the letters blurred and unfocused. "What about her private life?"

"Twenty-eight, divorced for three years from a guy named Ray Delaney. He's in insurance sales, remarried and lives in Santa Barbara. She's still single and just back from Spain. She's been all over with her job, never one place too long, but she keeps an apartment in San Francisco."

Alex felt numb. "Anything else?" he asked in a voice he could hear had become a bit flat.

"You might give me a big thank-you and tell me how wonderful I am."

"Thanks, you're wonderful," Alex repeated by rote. "Anything else?"

"I saw her picture when I checked out her P.I. license. She's a beauty."

Alex felt a stirring that he couldn't begin to understand at the mere thought of her. Maybe the experts were right about the most potent aphrodisiac coming from one's own mind. His mind seemed to be all tangled up with the story, the problems of the town and a woman whose image wouldn't leave him alone. "She's attractive," he said brusquely. *Yeah, and the Grand Canyon is a hole in the ground.* "Keep up the good work."

"I'll be in touch," Devereaux said, and hung up.

Alex sat in the silence. A private investigator? She wasn't like any investigator he'd met. No wonder she'd known self-defense. He touched his stomach where her elbow had robbed him of all the air in his body.

Her lips had gently robbed him of more than that.

With a soft curse, Alex crossed the room to lie on the couch. Sleep came quickly, a heavy deep sleep that began to expand into a dream.

Alex could feel heat on all sides, but he didn't know the source of it. His whole attention focused on a blond woman standing by the water. Desert seemed to surround him, yet the water sparkled turquoise in the brilliant sun.

The woman dipped one foot in the water, and her silky hair drifted around her shoulders, ruffled by a gentle breeze. Slowly Alex moved toward her, knowing the heat had to be coming from something other than the sun. He couldn't feel the coarseness of the sand under his feet.

His whole world centered on the blonde, and he couldn't look away from her or from her slender body clearly defined by a skimpy T-shirt. The soft cotton emphasized high breasts and the gentle curve of her hips. Legs, long and lithe, seemed to go on forever.

Then she cast him a slanting look from under lush dark lashes, and his world stood still. But the heat increased. Kristin. Lavender eyes invited him. She began to back up and at the same time beckon to him to go with her, motioning with her slender hand. One step, then another, and she was on the water without sinking, all part of the sparkling jewellike quality of the turquoise expanse.

"Come," she whispered in a throaty voice that ran quivering awareness across every nerve in his body. "Come and see what's on the other side."

And he went to the edge of the water, reaching out until just the tips of their fingers touched. Yet the contact carried him up and to her. Her eyes held his hypnotically as he drew closer, much closer, and the heat grew. It became scorching, yet there was no pain—just a sense of impending pleasure and completeness.

In one easy movement, he had Kristin against him. He felt her curves, every angle, and the flimsy barrier of her T-shirt was gone. Her naked breasts swelled against his bare chest, and her hips moved seductively on his, pulling responses from him that made his whole body ache. The water was

gone, lost to a softness that held the two of them sus-
pended above reality and time in an all-encompassing heat.

Kristin was under him, naked, inviting and waiting to
consume him as surely as if she was fire itself. And he joined
her, tumbling backward, over, around, swirling out of con-
trol. Out of this world. All knowledge of any other woman
he'd ever known fled, and Kristin was everything to him.
She was his beginning and his end, his completeness.

Possessing her seemed as important as his next breath,
and she smiled, a knowing smile, as if she understood
everything about him. Yet she wanted him. He teased her,
caressed her with his lips and hands. When he felt ready to
explode with desire, when the fire reached the point of
blotting out everything, Alex knew he could have her just by
entering her....

The dream fragmented.

Alex moaned, a low, guttural sound of rage, and it echoed
all around him. He abruptly threw a forearm over his eyes,
and in that moment, he knew the dream was over. Frustration consumed him.

With a deep, ragged breath, he dropped his hand to his
stomach and forced his eyes open. It took him a full heartbeat to realize that Kristin hadn't been here at all. He'd
never touched her like that nor come close to possessing her.
A dream, all a dream. Yet his body throbbed at what might
have been.

He pushed himself to a sitting position, braced his bare
feet on the softly carpeted floor and ran careless fingers
through unruly black curls. His hair felt damp and his scalp
hot, yet he knew that outside the heat was gone and in no
way responsible for his discomfort.

The dream. He rubbed at his eyes then hunched forward, his elbows resting on his knees. A damn dream. But

so real. He'd only lain down for a moment, closed his eyes to relax and try to concentrate on his writing. And the dream had come. It had robbed him of a quiet time to escape from his problems. The problems—Kristin and the fires—had followed him into his dreams.

"Damn them all," he muttered. He rose and paced quickly across the floor to his computer. He'd get another chapter done and prove to himself that he could do it— prove it to himself and to Jessie. She'd call soon, he knew, and he wanted to be able to tell her that he was well on his way to finishing.

Alex dropped into the swivel chair in front of the computer, ignoring the discomfort lingering in his body and started to read what he'd written before he fell asleep. After the first few lines he saved the file and flipped off the computer. He needed to be out in the fresh air, to move and to stop thinking of a woman he barely knew.

Quickly he showered, dressed in navy corduroys and a blue polo shirt, slipped into his wool jacket and headed outside in search of answers to the questions that plagued him.

When Kristin woke around dawn, she felt the chill in the house. Curled up in the warm bed with the cat lying on the open Jake Warner book at her side, she watched the sun spread its pale colors through the sky. She felt pleasantly groggy and snuggled further under the soft covers.

The next thing she knew, she was opening her eyes to bright sunshine, the cat heavy on her chest, the book on the floor and the clock by the bed showing ten minutes to noon. Pushing off the sheets and the cat, Kristin scrambled out of bed, the cool air brushing her bare legs and arms. She pulled off her T-shirt and dressed quickly in Levi's, a white sweater and tennis shoes. Leaving her hair loose, she brushed it and finally went into the kitchen to feed the complaining cat.

Within minutes, Boy was ecstatically devouring a huge dish of chopped liver, and Kristin was heading out the back door. She crossed the damp grass to the wooden steps, looked out at the ocean, then turned. She wasn't going to go down the beach as she'd planned, she decided. Instead she'd walk up the road to the north.

She recrossed the lawn, passing the garage and the house and coming onto the driveway. At the road she looked right and left but saw nothing. Turning north, she walked along the side of the rutted road, the coarse gravel and dirt crunching under her feet. Despite the clear sunshine, a cold breeze whipped her loose hair around her cheeks and neck.

She walked quickly until she saw the border of Restcorp property and the sound of an approaching car drew her attention. Moving backward into a thick stand of pines, she watched a construction truck pass. When it was out of sight, she stepped back onto the road and continued north. Finally reaching the Restcorp entrance, she stepped off the road and into the forest again.

From the protection of the trees she saw the gates open and the sheriff's car drive out. Boyd Lane drove past her, heading south. Kristin waited until she was certain no one else was coming then walked silently through the trees, staying parallel to the road. The sounds of machinery and motors were loud in the air, mingled with the shouts of voices issuing orders. Cleanup from the fire had begun.

Kristin stayed in the trees until she was well past the gates, then she cautiously approached the road. When she saw nothing, she stepped into the clear.

The end of the Restcorp fence was in sight, and a huge sign stood on the overgrown land beyond the fence: Restcorp, Private Property, Phase Two, No Trespassing.

Kristin stayed to one side but kept walking north until the road narrowed and the trees branched more densely overhead. Finally she saw an overgrown path that cut into the Restcorp land heading toward the water. She crossed the main road and followed the path.

Deep in the forest she stayed with the trail until she finally saw buildings ahead. Going toward them she realized they were deserted and falling apart. Sagging roofs, splintered siding and weeds gave a feeling of total abandonment. She moved along the side of the first building and stepped out into a brushy clearing. From what she could see, it looked like the old logging camp David had told her about in the briefing. This land was where Restcorp would expand when the first phase was completed.

And David had told her a man called Franks had died here three months ago on the Fourth of July. She crossed the open area, stopped and listened, but nothing stirred beyond the growing breeze. Security was supposed to be tight, yet she hadn't spotted one person to stop her from crossing this land. She frowned, then looked up at the sky, which was beginning to cloud over, the sun dimming in the grayness.

She turned, walked to the cliffs and saw steps, old and rotten, in the granite wall. Carefully she descended to the beach below, a strip of sand littered with wood and the remains of some old burned-out sheds. Franks had died there. She turned away, tucked her chin in the collar of her sweater against the growing cold and faced the water's edge and a dock that looked like a caricature of what it once must have been. Pieces were falling off into the water, pilings broken and rotting, and a single boat was tied to it.

Walking closer, she saw the boat was small—ten or twelve feet long—and open, with an outboard motor and a canvas tarpaulin over the bow section. The name had been painted in a flourish of black script—*Jenny Lee*.

Kristin stopped by the steps that led up to the dock, their broken boards hanging awkwardly because of missing supports. When the dock had been in good repair, it would have been heavy enough and wide enough to support a large car or a truck. Now it seemed barely able to hold the boat secure.

Turning, Kristin looked to the top of the bluffs, at the dark shapes of trees and the vague outlines of pitched roofs against the darkening sky. Here there was no movement, no life. She looked back to the dock and carefully stepped up onto the rotting structure. Surprisingly, despite its appearance, it felt solid under her feet. Avoiding gaping holes, Kristin made her way to the boat and stooped, fingering the heavy knot in the looping anchor rope. Someone must be here.

She straightened and turned from the water and its choppy waves aggravated by the growing wind. In pale, thin light as clouds continued to blot out the sun, Kristin saw movement near the bluffs, a stirring in the blurred shadows at the foot of the old steps. Squinting, trying to make out what was there, she moved cautiously along the dock, jumped onto the sand and stopped.

Nothing moved now. She took a step forward, putting one foot in front of the other until she could see the area at the foot of the stairs. Shock seared through her. A man in dark clothes, a very large man, lay facedown on the sand, a knit hat covering his hair. Completely still, his legs and arms were splayed at crazy angles from his body.

Chapter 6

Sickening, wrenching horror tore through Kristin as she broke into a dead run toward the man at the foot of the stairs. She reached him in seconds, bent and grasped the shoulder of his heavy wool jacket. "Oh, God, Alex, be all right," she breathed as she tugged at his leaden weight.

When she finally managed to roll him over so he flopped limply onto his back, she felt giddy with relief. Bob Lipton. It wasn't Alex at all. But her relief lasted only a moment before the horror surged back with renewed strength. The older man's face held little human color. The eyelids looked like mottled parchment, and a bloody abrasion ran from his temple into his thin gray hair.

Kristin swallowed real sickness and looked at the stairs, noting two freshly broken rungs near the top. He must have fallen the full length to land here. "Mr. Lipton?" she said as she dropped weakly to her knees beside him.

His eyes fluttered and his mouth moved, but no words emerged before he groaned and stilled.

A memory tore through Kristin—that moment of total helplessness when Jerry Rule had crumpled at her feet, his blood puddling on the green tile floor of the café. Don't think about that, not now. Not ever. "I . . . I'll help you," she managed to say through chattering teeth, hoping she was telling the truth. "I'll get help. I promise."

If she could only stand. If only the strength-sapping weakness weren't permeating her whole being. *Stand,* she told herself. *Get up and run.* But she couldn't move.

"Fall...help...m-me..." the man mumbled, and his eyes fluttered open, the dilated pupils almost obliterating the dark color. "Police..."

"You need an ambulance."

The man jerked violently, and his hand fell heavily on her sweater sleeve. "Police...help..."

"Yes, sure," Kristin responded, and forced herself to stand.

The first drop of rain touched her skin, and Kristin began to shake uncontrollably. She hugged herself as the scattered drops developed into a light misting rain. Glancing at the angry heavens, she knew she couldn't leave the man out in the open. Yet she couldn't move him. If he had a broken back or internal injuries, she might just make things worse.

Protection. She looked around frantically, then spotted the boat again. The tarpaulin on its bow. "I'll be right back," she called as she took off at a run toward the dock.

When she came back, she had the heavy canvas and two thin boards she'd ripped off the side of the dock. She knelt down by Lipton and saw his eyes were still open, but she knew that he wasn't focusing on her at all. "Police...please..."

"Yes, yes," she said, and with shaking hands poked the boards into the sand a foot from each side of his head. Then she pushed with all her weight to get them as deeply imbedded as she could.

"I'm going to try and make a cover for you—a tent," she said, speaking rapidly, needing the sound of her own voice in her ears. "It's going to rain, and . . ." She pushed the last board in a few more inches, then reached for the canvas.

"It's the best I can do," she kept saying to the man as she draped the canvas over the two boards and angled it back above Lipton's head. She pulled the edges to the sand and quickly piled on heavy earth to keep it in place.

She sat back shakily and looked down at Lipton. He shuddered suddenly, and his mouth worked. "Police . . . p-pushed . . ."

"Yes," she whispered. "I'll get the police."

Another tremor gripped his entire body, and a small trickle of blood showed at the corner of his slack mouth. "Pushed," he muttered weakly, and his head lolled to one side.

Kristin swallowed back the sickness again and made herself touch the base of the man's neck. The pulse under her fingertips was fluttery but there. She stood. She had to go back the way she'd come.

She ran through the light rain, heading toward the steps. Avoiding the broken ones, she made it to the top just as the rain changed from a mist to needlelike drops being driven by a gusting north-east wind. With narrowed eyes, she took in the forlorn and shadowy buildings blurred by the rain and failing light.

Kristin took a step, stumbling on a projecting rock and looked down at the soft ground by her feet. Her heart lurched and the sickness came again. There in the muddied earth was a confused pattern of footprints. This had to be where Lipton had stood before he fell.

She stood frozen for a second, staring at the prints being filled by rainwater, and Lipton's last words finally sank in past her fright. He had been pushed! Had whoever had done it stood here after Lipton had fallen, watching to make sure he didn't get up?

Kristin spun around in the rain, her gaze darting over the empty buildings. He'd fallen only moments ago. Could someone be watching her now? Would she know if they were?

Her hands began to tremble uncontrollably, and she pushed them into her pockets as she headed out at a slow jog across the open expanse in the middle of the buildings. When she found the trail, she broke into a dead run. The rain was coming down in earnest now, plastering her hair to her face and chilling the clammy clothes that clung to her skin. She gulped air into aching lungs, never slowing her pace until she spotted the road.

She headed south, ducking her head to keep the stinging rain out of her eyes. Finally she could make out a light off in the distance, a murky glow through the sheeting torrents, and she ran toward it. The trailers and the gates.

She stumbled, righted herself by reaching for the metal webbing then tugged at the gates with all her strength. But they were firmly locked, and she couldn't see a person in sight behind the wire. "Help! Help! Please, I need help!" she screamed, shocked at the hoarse cry that seemed to be her voice.

Almost immediately, the door to the nearest trailer opened, and Kristin thought it was Ben until the man looked out at her. "What's going on?" a guard called, squinting out into the storm.

"I need help. A man's been hurt!"

The door closed then opened again, and the man emerged in a yellow rain slicker. He hurried down the steps and ran across to the gates. "What'd you say, lady?"

Kristin knew tears of relief were mingling with the rain on her face. "A man f-fell on the beach," she gasped, "and he's really hurt." She swiped at the water coursing down her face. "Please, he needs help."

The man hesitated.

"Please," Kristin begged, "please, hurry."

The man fumbled with the lock on the gate and pulled it open just enough to let Kristin through. "Get inside," he said, motioning to the building he'd just come from. "We'll talk in there."

Kristin felt weak, drained of the strength that had taken her this far, and she had to make a great effort to walk the short distance from the gate to the stairs. She forced her feet to take the two steps, and finally she was in dry warmth that surrounded her like a smothering blanket. For a minute she couldn't feel the air going into her lungs, then the heat began to seep into her being. Hugging her arms around herself, she turned as the man followed her into the tiny room.

"Please, you have to get help," she said hoarsely.

The guard closed the door and crossed to a desk that took up half the space in the eight-by-ten room. He tossed his slicker hat on a small filing cabinet to the right and reached for the telephone. He stopped with his finger poised above the buttons. "Where is this guy?"

Kristin barely recognized her own voice. "He—he's on the beach near the old logging camp. He—" She edited her words for some reason she couldn't begin to fathom. "He fell down the stairs there." Her teeth began to chatter as cold rain ran in rivulets under her collar and between her breasts.

He punched some numbers. "We've got an emergency out at the Restcorp site. Someone's been hurt." He looked back to Kristin. "Any idea what's wrong with him?"

"No, he's just hurt. He fell down the stairs." Had she told him that or had she only thought she had? She didn't know. Her mind didn't feel right. "I made some cover for him, but he's hurt badly."

"He took a bad fall on the beach below the old lumber mill." Pause. "I'll wait for you by the gates and go with you to find him."

Kristin licked her cold lips as the man put the receiver back in place. "When will they be here?"

"As soon as they can get here."

Her legs were getting more unsteady with each passing second. "I—I should get back...and help them find..."

The man came around to her. "No, you aren't going anywhere." For the first time Kristin noticed that his eyes under shaggy gray brows were a soft brown and filled with concern. "You're soaked to the skin." He took her by the arm to gently lead her around the desk and ease her down into the chair. "Sit. Try and catch your breath. If anyone shows up here, tell them where the guy is. I'll be outside." He started for the door, grabbing at his hat on the way. He turned back to Kristin. "Did you say who this guy is?"

"Bob...Bob Lipton, I think." She held so tightly to herself that her fingers were digging into her upper arms, but the trembling wouldn't stop.

He frowned. "Damn it, Lipton's been around here before, but I thought he'd given up." He pushed the hat on his head. "He's got himself into a real mess this time."

She closed her eyes, but opened them quickly when a vision of the hurt man came back full force. "I—I made a tent of sorts for him, but this rain..." She shuddered and looked back at the guard. "It's so cold out there."

"You're pretty upset," he said softly.

Her fingers dug in more. "I found him half-dead." She shuddered.

"Will you be all right alone?"

"I should come with you," she protested once more.

"No, stay here. You've done enough."

She wanted to go back, to make sense of everything, but she didn't have the strength to argue. So she merely nodded. "Just help him."

"Sure," the man said as he turned and opened the door.

For a moment, the cold and dampness stormed into the room, then the door closed and warmth surrounded Kristin again. It should have been a comforting gentleness after the past half hour, but she seemed unable to absorb it. Her body felt alien to her—cold yet flushed, stiff and filled with a fear that almost stopped her heart. Fear? Why?

Then she knew. Through the fog one word jumped out at her again—*pushed*. It circled around and around in her mind. *Pushed*.

She trembled violently. What had the men said yesterday, that at least no one had been hurt? Had Lipton said it, or Cook, or the mayor? Had anyone even said it? She couldn't remember. She took in deep breaths, letting go of herself to spread her hands on the desk. Dirt had pushed under her nails, and a scrape marred the knuckles on her right hand. She didn't remember doing it, but it ached now, the abrasion raw and bruised. Clenching her hands into fists, she hunched over them, pressing her forehead against them.

Bob Lipton. She forced away the image of his shattered body on the sand. Had he really been pushed? Or was he a victim of his own deceit? Had he been the one to start the fire, or had he come upon the person responsible for it and been pushed over the edge of the bluff?

She closed her eyes tightly. At least this time she hadn't frozen. This time she'd looked at the hurt man and done something. She'd done what she could for him; she'd run blindly through the rain, and she'd found help. She bit her lip hard, only vaguely aware of the metallic tinge of blood on her tongue. Enough, enough.

The Hunter was cold and wet, but he didn't dare move from the cover of the forest—not yet. Well back, partially hidden by the now-steady downpour, he had a clear view of the gates and the guards' shed. He hadn't lost sight of the girl from the moment she'd found Lipton until she'd entered the shed. Moments later the guard had reappeared, come out to the gates and waited until an ambulance and police car drove up. After talking to the driver of the ambulance, he'd gone back to climb into the police car, and they'd driven off to the north. As the red lights were absorbed into the rain, still the Hunter didn't move.

If Lipton wasn't dead, everything could explode. Stubborn man. Couldn't leave well enough alone. Coming back like that, sneaking up on him, forcing a confrontation when he should have known better. Damn him! He'd been so certain no one had seen him messing with the earth movers yesterday.

The Hunter sank back against the tree to his left. Even if Lipton didn't survive, the girl had found him alive. She had been with him for more than two minutes making that damned contraption to cover the upper part of his body. But had Lipton been conscious and able to talk?

Fletcher had died instantly and gone up in flames, and the memory of watching the fire consume him stirred nothing in the Hunter beyond lingering irritation. Why had Fletcher tried to double-cross him and then hide everything? The Hunter stopped his own thoughts with a soft chuckle, absorbed by the sounds of wind and rain. Fletcher hadn't been as easy as he'd thought.

He swiped at the rain on his face but felt strangely impervious to the cold. He'd have the jewels sooner or later, one way or another. He'd have them, and he'd have the last laugh. He wasn't going to stop—whatever it took. He didn't mind staying in the town a bit longer. It wasn't all that bad. As long as Lipton died.

He stiffened. If Kristin Delaney didn't catch on. He'd have to take care of her if she began to figure things out. He felt a degree of sorrow at that thought.

Alex got out of his truck just inside the gates and hurried to the guard shed. He took both steps in one long stride and pushed open the door. He stopped when he saw that the only person in the tiny space was Kristin, her head down on her hands, her blond hair spilling in wet tendrils and tangled curls over her hands and onto the desk. Her shoulders moved with each faint, shuddering breath she took. He hated the way his stomach tightened at the sight of her, at the sight of such vulnerability.

He swung the door shut and could barely keep his hands from reaching out to touch her bowed head. "Kristin?" he whispered. "What's going on?"

No response came at first. Then ever so slowly, her head lifted. Smeared mascara under her unfocused eyes only made them seem large and haunted in the paleness of her tense face. "You...what are you doing here?" she asked in a raspy, weak voice.

"I heard the sirens and came to see what was wrong. The gate was open, and the guard—" He looked around the trailer. "What's going on?"

She sat back, a shuddering sigh lifting her slender shoulders under a sweater that looked heavy with rain. "Your friend. He got hurt on the beach."

Every inch of his being tensed as he moved closer and leaned forward. Swallowing hard, he pressed his fingers to the smooth wood of the desk top. "Who?" he demanded, almost not wanting to know.

Her tongue darted out to touch pale, unsteady lips. "Bob... Bob Lipton."

Oh, God, not Bob! His heart lurched in his chest, and Alex reached to touch Kristin's hands clenched on the desk. "Are you sure it's Bob?" he asked hoarsely.

"I think so. I only saw him once, but—" she nodded once "—yes, it's him."

His hand tightened on hers. "What happened?"

She moved abruptly, pulling away from his touch, and nervously pushed back her damp hair. The movement was jerky, as if a camera were snapping the sequence a frame at a time. "I'm not sure, but he's hurt. I don't know how badly."

Enough! Enough of this! he wanted to scream. Instead he tightened himself from the inside out and straightened, moving back, keeping some distance between himself and Kristin. He was confused enough without touching her again. He shivered without being able to stop the action. "Just tell me," he demanded in a still-hoarse voice. "Is Bob alive?"

Her eyes closed for a fleeting moment. "I think so. He was when I left him."

"What happened?"

Kristin hated remembering, but she could feel the tension in Alex. "He tumbled down the stairs. I—I found him on the beach by the old lumber mill. He was sprawled out, his legs and arms all twisted, and I thought..." She stopped her words on a gulp as sickening pain tore at her middle. She pressed a hand there and made herself focus on what had happened—on how and why it could have happened. "Does he have a boat called *Jenny Lee*?"

"A skiff."

That would be a perfect way to get to the Restcorp site and not be seen by any guards. She'd seen clearly enough yesterday how easy an approach from the water side was.

"You know Mr. Lipton pretty well, don't you?"

"I've known him all my life."

Rain beat against the small building, and Kristin decided to face this thing head-on while she had the strength to do it. "Do you think he could have...did he start those fires?"

The silence between them all but crackled, and she could see the increased paleness in Alex's complexion. Then the denial came, but a breath of a second too late. "No."

Alex knew, and he wasn't about to tell her. And right then she knew she wouldn't tell Alex about Lipton saying he was pushed. She didn't quite understand why, but she wouldn't. She took a breath into tight lungs. "Who's doing this to Restcorp, to this town?" she asked.

Alex had wondered about Bob for over a month—Bob, among others—but he almost hated Kristin for voicing his fears. Almost, but not quite. Then he remembered she wasn't an innocent victim here. She was a private investigator, a professional who knew the questions to ask. But he wasn't going to give her answers yet. Maybe never. So he hedged. "I don't know for sure."

She watched him intently for a full heartbeat, as if she could read his mind, then she seemed to sag. She sank back in the chair and exhaled on a soft sigh. "I'm sorry. I didn't have any right to ask you that. But this is so scary. First the fire, then finding him..." She shuddered. Suddenly she didn't look like a professional who surely dealt with life-

and-death situations as her job. She simply looked vulnerable, her mascara streaking across both cheeks when she wiped her face with an almost childlike sweep of her trembling hands. And the longer he stood across the desk from her, the more endearing she became.

She sniffed softly, and whispered, "I really am sorry."

Alex straightened, getting more distance and needing it. Cold rain ran under the collar of his heavy jacket to invade the warmth of his skin. "Maybe I should go and help them with Bob."

She stood slowly, holding on to the edge of the desk as if she needed the support. "The guard got help," she whispered unsteadily.

"I'll wait here to see how Bob is." He couldn't take his eyes off Kristin, off the line of her cheek and the delicate sweep of her throat. How unexplainable that a perfect stranger could touch a person in a way that was entirely unique, entirely new, and at a time when horror seemed to be all around. "I need to know."

Kristin trembled violently, her eyes closing in a grimace, and Alex moved immediately, his actions not thought out at all. He simply did what he'd wanted to do since he walked into the trailer. He unbuttoned his jacket, then pulled Kristin inside it against his chest, and she all but collapsed against him. He held her, tugging the jacket around her, trapping her effectively against his body.

"Body heat," he murmured. "You need heat."

His arms tightened around her, willing her body to stop shaking. He could feel her hands in fists pressed against him, and he inhaled the scent of wet clothes mingled with a delicate flowery perfume that clung to her. Every curve of her slender body fit to the angles of his taller frame, just the way he'd felt her in the dream. He cautiously absorbed the fact that he'd known her less than two days, yet she stirred him fiercely, in body and spirit. She set her own sort of fires in him, deep and intense.

He stood very still with his chin resting on the top of her head, and he closed his eyes against the rush of feeling. He wouldn't think about his responses right now, not when he couldn't even name them. She didn't even trust him. The thought came from nowhere even as he realized how true it was. She kept to her house sitter cover story. She never let that slip, and knowing she wasn't telling him the truth made it easier for him to keep some emotional distance. "Are you feeling better?"

She nodded, the action rubbing the dampness of her hair against his chin. "I'm okay."

A private investigator? Why wasn't she someplace safe and warm, anywhere but Vespar Bay in the middle of this horror? When her small hands spread on his chest and her face pressed into the sweater he wore under his jacket, he spoke his thoughts softly. "You shouldn't be involved in this mess."

She took an unsteady breath and moved back just enough to look up at him. Her bottom lip trembled, and her eyes met his.

Kristin had never felt this sensation of need for one person, a stark, all-encompassing need to stay as close as she could to him. It seemed a natural outcome of that staggering awareness that she hadn't been able to deny since the first time he'd kissed her. At least she knew a small victory in that she didn't reach to hold to Alex again. This man stirred and frightened her, drawing her as surely as a flame could draw a moth. Maybe the results would be as devastating.

That thought brought Kristin up short, and she turned, ducking her head and resting her unsteady hands on the cold

desk top. *It's shock,* she assured herself. The shock of seeing
a man lying on the sand and thinking it was Alex.

It was a rational thought meant to soothe, to justify her
response—but instead it made her whole being knot as she
vividly relived the moment she'd first seen Lipton on the
beach.

Kristin turned with a jerk when the door opened at the
same time a man called out, "What's going on?" She kept
her eyes off Alex and looked past him to see a drenched
Dailey Cook stamping into the trailer. Behind him stood the
mayor, his round face flushed from hurrying, his black
slicker gleaming with moisture. Behind the mayor came
Ben.

"There's been trouble on the beach below the old mill,"
Alex said. After a quick glance at the men he looked back
to Kristin. "Bob Lipton's been hurt."

Kristin heard the surprised exclamations and curses and
watched the scenario in front of her while she trembled from
the cutting cold coming in the open door. The men crowded
into the tiny space, words tumbling over words, then Overton and Cook left together. Ben closed the door with a
muffled slam and turned. He took off his uniform hat,
shaking the rain from its plastic cover, then slid off his
slicker.

"What a damn mess," Ben muttered as he carefully hung
the wet coat on the rack by the door.

Kristin wanted to tell him just how much of a mess
everything was now, but she held her peace by biting her lip.
She didn't want to talk in front of Alex, not when she
couldn't get rid of the feeling that he knew who had done
this.

"Miss Delaney found Lipton on the beach near the logging camp," Alex said.

Ben looked at Kristin. "What happened?"

"I...I don't know," she lied, wishing Alex would leave.

"How bad is it?"

"He...he might be dead by now." She tried to take a breath and found her ribs so tight the air wouldn't go in. "He looked awful."

Ben shook his head. "Just what this company doesn't need now is someone slipping and falling on rotted steps. Bad thing right now."

"A fall like that doesn't do anyone any good," Alex muttered.

Kristin backtracked in her mind, confused. Her eyes darted from Ben to Alex. She sensed that something important was evading her, but damn it, she couldn't think. When Alex touched her shoulder, she jerked back. "What?"

"You need to get home and dry off," he said.

Kristin didn't want to leave. She wanted Ben to help her figure out what was going on, but she didn't know how to do it until he came to her rescue.

"I'll take the little lady home. I've got to go into town, anyway. Where do you live, Miss Delaney?"

Before Kristin could respond, Alex cut in. "She lives right next door to me, so I'll take her. There's nothing I can do around here but get in the way."

Ben didn't push. He nodded, his eyes meeting Kristin's to let her know that he would make sure they talked later. He reached for his slicker and motioned to the others there. "Use one of these and keep dry." With a nod, he slipped his back on then pulled back the door and left.

"I could have gone with him," Kristin said as soon as the door shut. She didn't want to be anywhere near Alex. She didn't want to inhale the scents that clung to him nor listen to his deep voice speaking with a seductive gentleness.

"You're going with me," Alex said. "Unless you have your car somewhere around here?"

"No, I don't," she admitted tightly.

He crossed to pick up a slicker and brought it over to drape it around her shoulders. His fingers brushed her chin, sending shock waves through her as he snapped the top fastener. "Let me help you," he said softly.

In Alex's pickup truck, Kristin curled up in the farthest corner, her hands hidden by the long sleeves of the clammy slicker. She flexed her toes in her soaked shoes. The heater began to blow warm air as soon as Alex drove through the Restcorp gates, the comfort deliciously welcome. She stared at the slapping windshield wipers and beyond to the sheeting rain that was beginning to turn the road into a sea of mud. All of the day's light had been absorbed by the storm.

"How are you doing?" Alex asked without taking his eyes off the treacherous road.

"All right." She turned to look at his profile in the dimness. "You said you knew Mr. Lipton all your life?"

"Yes."

"I'm sorry I said what I did back there. But I can't help wondering why he was there." She could feel her heartbeat increasing with each word as once more the image of Lipton the last time she'd seen him rushed at her.

Alex drove in silence before speaking in a low, tight voice, "This isn't your town. Don't worry about it."

"I know, but I seem to be getting involved in what's going on."

He shot her a slanting look. "It's too bad you have to get in the middle of all of this, that you can't stay clear of what's happening around here."

Have to get involved? Can't stay clear? His choice of words struck Kristin, and she frowned at him, a niggling uneasiness coming from nowhere. "It's too bad everyone around here is getting involved," she countered.

He rubbed the steering wheel with his right hand and spoke totally out of context. "Bob once dated my mother. When my father died, Bob was the one who took me out on his boat and showed me how to make it go. He was the one who asked me to come home when...when my life was falling apart."

"He means a lot to you." He did, she could tell, yet she could almost swear Alex had his suspicions about Lipton. She shivered in the slicker. "I'm not going to ask how your life was falling apart."

"Obviously the rain didn't shrink your sense of tact," he said with a touch of humor. "So someday I'll tell you."

And she found herself looking forward to that time, as if another piece of the puzzle to understanding this man would unfold. "How long have you lived in Vespar Bay?" she asked, seeking neutral territory.

"Not long enough."

"Does that translate into years?"

He controlled the truck when it hit a slippery spot, then flashed her a crooked smile. "I'm sorry. I was born and brought up here, then when I was drafted, I left. I was gone for years, living in San Francisco for a while. One day I woke up—"

"When your life was falling apart?"

"Exactly. I woke up and realized that I could write Jake Warner books here as well as anywhere. So I came home. It was a good place to be." She could see his jaw tighten, a muscle jump. "Until now."

Kristin sat back, the events of the day hitting her with such force that she felt sick. "Where will they take Mr. Lipton?"

"Probably down to Santa Rosa. Their hospital is a lot better equipped than anything around here."

"How do I get there?"

"What?"

"How do I get there?" she repeated, needing to see the man and find out if he was still alive. She felt that she owed him in some way she didn't quite understand.

"You aren't family, and if he's hurt as badly as you think, he'll be in the ICU." He looked at her again, his face set, his gaze intent. "Why do you want to go?"

She couldn't begin to explain it. "I want to see him." She nibbled on her bottom lip as she turned to the storm-smeared glass and the distorted trees that lined the road. "I *have* to go and see him."

Alex drove slowly to the right and onto the driveway of the Donaldson house. He stopped by the porch steps, and at the same moment the rain began to ease, changing to a fine mist that let the rays of a low sun drift through. Floating rainbows scattered in the sky, and the wind turned to a breeze. "If you're so bent on it, I'll take you. You'll never make it out there in your car, let alone get in to see Bob."

"No." The word came before Kristin could stop it.

Alex put the truck in neutral, leaving the engine running to keep the heater blowing warmth into the cab. Shifting sideways on the seat, he looked at Kristin. "I've got this four-wheel drive truck. It can get out of here easily."

Kristin studied Alex in the strangely ethereal light that came through the mist. "I don't want to bother you anymore."

"I offered, and I want to be there."

"Why?" she asked, her nerves beginning to prickle in the strangest way. Something was wrong, and the worst part was, she didn't have any idea what it could be.

"Because—" he reached to touch her chin with warm fingers "—I want to be there when you see Bob again."

Her reaction was pure instinct, a sharp jerking back and away from the contact. "Don't."

His hand withdrew to rest on his thigh. "You're right. Do you want to talk?"

She pressed harder into the corner. "About what?"

"Whatever's going on here. About what happens between us whenever we're in close proximity to each other."

He felt it, too—it hadn't just been her. But she couldn't figure it out, not now. "I don't think..."

"Yes, you do. I just wondered if you understood it any better than I do." His exhaled breath echoed in the closed cab. "I've been trying to remember if anyone like you has been in my life before." His hand moved to touch her shoulder and didn't withdraw when Kristin tightened. "And I don't know. I really don't remember. I want to make some sense out of this."

She felt suspended in time, her heart bouncing crazily inside her rib cage. "After what happened today, nothing makes sense, does it?" she whispered.

"Nothing?" Alex prodded softly.

She bit her lip hard, trying to ground herself in some reality, even if pain was what was required to do it. "I don't know," she said, speaking in a rush. "You said your life had hit a spot in the past where it was falling apart, well, so did mine. This, everything that happened today, it brought it all back to me."

"Tell me about your life," Alex said with a gentleness that almost brought tears to her eyes.

She looked at him, and she could almost feel his concern. A man who wrote about violence, yet this sudden tenderness seemed an innate part of him. Right then it seemed such a seductive idea to tell him everything about Jerry. But her throat felt tight, and she knew she couldn't begin to put it into words now. "Maybe later."

"Whenever you're ready to tell me about yourself—" he shrugged, his fingers tightening on her shoulder "—just let me know."

"I will," she whispered unsteadily.

Alex cupped her chin with one hand and tasted her lips quickly, fleetingly with his, then moved back before she had a chance to do more than gasp. "I'll be by for you at six-thirty."

Not trusting herself to do more than nod, Kristin scrambled out of the truck cab. As soon as she was in the house and the sounds of the truck had died in the distance, she knew that the time would come when she would tell Alex about Jerry. But before that she'd have to be able to tell him that Bob Lipton had said he'd been pushed.

Chapter 7

Kristin shifted on the seat of the pickup and felt thankful that the shadows of night minimized the details she took in about Alex. He drove in silence, not more than a foot from her, and she watched him. She knew he could help her understand this town, its people and what they were capable of doing. And he cared so much about what was happening here. While she'd been showering then dressing in beige linen slacks, an ivory silk shirt and a thigh-length brown cardigan, she'd tried to figure out how much she should tell him.

They'd been driving for almost fifteen minutes, and she still didn't quite know what to say. She rubbed the toe of her pump back and forth on the rubber floor mat. Finally she spoke up. "Alex?"

"Yes?" he said without taking his eyes off the road.

"This thing, whatever's happening up here, has to be stopped."

In the glare of oncoming headlights she could see his face tighten. "Yes, it does."

"After meeting the sheriff, I don't think he can do it. He may not even understand that it's beyond him."

Alex glanced at her. "Why don't you just tell me what you're getting at?"

"You said that we needed to talk. I want to talk about what's going on up here. I think it's time for us to trust each other."

She almost held her breath until he reached over and covered her hand that was resting on the seat between them with his. His voice was soft but intense. "Thank you. I want to trust you, Kristin." His hand tightened on hers. "It's important to me."

The simple words almost brought tears to her eyes. She turned her hand over until her fingers laced with his. She held to him. "You can. I swear, all I want is to make this stop."

He slanted her another look and kept hold of her hand. "Give me something on good faith."

"What?"

He exhaled, and his thumb began to move slowly, drawing circles on the back of her hand. "Your choice. Tell me something about yourself. Anything that's important, that you haven't told me yet. Trust me."

Everything fit right then. *He knows who I am,* she realized, and said it out loud. "You know who I am, don't you?"

His thumb stopped its movement. "Tell me."

"I'm a private investigator," she said without hesitating. "But I don't want people to know. They'll clam up. They'll close ranks, and no one will be able to find out what's going on up here."

He stayed silent for so long she was afraid that he was the one who would clam up. Then he exhaled. "Thank you for trusting me with that."

Right then she knew that she could trust him. Although there wasn't any one thing that let her know, she suddenly had the overpowering sense that Alex was the one person she could trust with more of the truth. "There's one more thing."

"What?"

"Bob Lipton told me he was pushed."

The car lurched slightly, and Alex released her hand to grab the wheel. "Oh, my God." He slowed so much that she was certain he was going to stop, but then he sped up again. "Are you sure?"

"That's what he said when I found him."

He looked back at her, and even in the dimness she could see his eyes held pain. "Someone pushed him." A statement, not a question.

"I think so." She touched her tongue to her lips. "Your turn."

"What?"

"You tell me something, anything important."

He didn't hesitate, but what he said wasn't what she expected to hear. "Do you know about the man who died here on the Fourth?"

"Yes. Franks?"

"His name wasn't Franks. It was Ronald Fletcher. He came from San Francisco, and he wasn't a retired mailman. He was a small-time con artist, a burglar, and he covered his burglaries with fires."

"I didn't know any of that." This was nothing she'd expected, and she shivered spontaneously, a product of the cold and the bunching of nerves in her shoulders and neck. "I don't understand."

"I don't, either, but it all has to be tied in."

"You're right, but how?"

He looked right at her. "It has to have something to do with the logging camp."

"Are we in this together?" she asked.

He reached out for her, and she took his hand again, the strength and warmth in it just what she needed. "Yes, we're in it together," he said softly. "After we see how Bob is doing, we'll figure out where to go from here."

"Can I ask you something?"

"Sure."

"How did you know about me?"

He cast her a long look, then said, "You're not the only investigator in the world. I've got friends." He gently squeezed her hand. "We could make a very good team."

"Very good," she echoed, and knew she'd done the right thing in telling him the truth.

"Nothing," Alex said as he turned from the desk in the intensive care unit of the hospital. He spread his large hands in helplessness. "He's holding on—barely."

Kristin tried to ignore the odors peculiar to a hospital, fighting back memories of that long night while Jerry had clung to life. He'd made it, partially paralyzed but alive. Kristin had often wondered if one compensated for the other. "Will he make it?"

Alex shrugged, his broad shoulders moving under the heavy jacket he was wearing with gray slacks and blue jogging shoes. "Who knows?" Deep lines cut from his nose to his mouth. "He's tough, but things don't look too good."

Shivering, Kristin turned and walked out of ICU into a gray-tiled corridor where she couldn't hear the beeps of the life-support system behind the glassed-in cubicle.

A flash of movement down the hall caught her eye, and she looked up to see Gwen Cook hurrying toward her.

"Kristin, what are y'all doing here?" she asked, tension clear in her eyes and the tight line of her mouth.

"I came with—"

"She's with me," Alex said as he came up behind Kristin. "She found Bob, and she wanted to come and see how he's doing."

A tiny red-haired woman came running up behind Gwen. "The car's parked," she said in a breathless voice as she shook her jacket clear of the clinging rain that had begun to fall just as Kristin and Alex had arrived at the hospital. One hand touched Gwen's arm, and the eyes, behind round glasses, stared at Kristin.

"Louise, this is Kristin Delaney," Alex said. "She found Bob." His hand fell firmly on her shoulder, a comforting support through her light cardigan. "Louise Overton, our mayor's wife."

Kristin never would have paired this slip of a woman with the mayor. Louise nodded to her and looked past to Alex. "What's happening with Bob? I couldn't get any information over the phone, so Gwen and I decided to drive down."

"He's holding his own." Alex never let go of Kristin. "If she hadn't found him, he wouldn't be here now."

Kristin clutched her purse, unable to smile as Louise touched her cold hand on Kristin's wrist. "We're all grateful to you," the little woman said. "So very grateful you found him in time." She drew back. "Charles is upset. He wants me to call him as soon as I find out what's going on here. He wanted to come, but I couldn't wait for him to dry off and get dressed. So I called Gwen and came with her."

"Where's Dailey?" Alex asked. "I saw him at the Restcorp site, then I couldn't find him."

Gwen shrugged sharply, a bit of tightness at the corners of her mouth. "He's driving around, thinking. It's Sunday, and no school, so he's taking one of his little excursions."

Gradually Kristin realized that she was using Alex's touch for support. That wouldn't do at all. A partnership to end this madness was one thing, but that was all there could be. Moving from under his hand, she mumbled, "We could all use some coffee. I'll go try to find some."

The odors of sickness filled her head with suffocating dizziness, and she turned to hurry off down the gray-tiled corridor. She needed to be alone, needed time to think and try to sort out what was happening.

As Alex and Kristin headed home later that night the rain suddenly stopped, giving way to a night filled with brilliant stars, a partial moon and clouds skittering across the darkness.

"It's so beautiful tonight that no one would ever guess what a horrible thing happened today," Kristin said softly as she watched a small cloud cross in front of the moon.

No response came from Alex. He kept driving and turned onto the ocean road, slowing to let the lugged tires find traction on the thick mud. Finally, he asked, "Did you say something?"

"Not really. Just how awful today has been."

"At least we got one thing settled. We're going to try and stop this insanity... one way or another." He shifted to a lower gear and turned onto the road that ran parallel to the water. Passing his entrance gates, he drove on until he turned left onto the irregular brick driveway of the Donaldsons' house.

Kristin glanced at the shadowy man in the truck cab with her. "Do you have any ideas?"

"I wish I did," he sighed.

Kristin touched the door handle, the metal cool under her fingers. "Maybe we should sleep on it and talk in the morning."

"We might have a better perspective."

She hoped she would. "Thanks for giving me a ride."

Alex touched her arm to stop her from getting out into the night. "Kristin?"

"Yes?"

"I need to know something."

She didn't let go of the handle, but she stayed. "What?"

She could feel his eyes on her through the darkness, and she wondered if he could see as little as she could. "Why are you taking this so hard about Bob? This is a job to you. You hardly knew him."

She held tightly to the handle, pressing the metal into her fingers. "No, I didn't know him." A piece of a long-hidden truth came out. "I hate being impotent, seeing someone needing help and being unable to do anything."

"If you hadn't done what you did, Bob would have died alone on the beach."

"So now he'll do it in the hospital," she muttered tightly. "Is there such a great difference?"

"Yes, a great difference."

"If I had been there a few minutes earlier or turned when I should have..."

"What? What do you imagine you could have done to stop someone from pushing him?"

She closed her eyes tightly for a moment before looking back through the night at Alex. Could she have stopped Lipton from being pushed? She'd never know. "I don't know. Maybe that's it—I don't know what I would have done if I'd had the chance to change things."

"None of us knows until it confronts us. Only Jake Warner knows and can do what needs to be done before it happens. And he can only do it because I spend hours figuring out what he's going to do in the first place and then editing it to death."

He let her go, and settled back in the darkest corner of the cab. "My agent tells me that Jake's my alter ego. Maybe she's right. I thought I'd left that part of me behind when I left the army. Maybe I didn't. Maybe I just put it on paper now."

Kristin thought about the parts of the Jake Warner book she'd skipped, the parts involving torture and mayhem the man had performed on an enemy who wouldn't tell him the location of Webb Tanner. She couldn't have read them. It was hard for her to believe that Alex had actually written them. "You aren't anything like Jake Warner. If you were you wouldn't give a damn what goes on up here."

"I do care. And I hate it when someone I care about is hurt."

His words drew memories out of some deep part of her being, ripping them into the present. She had to swallow twice before she could ask, "Have you ever watched someone being hurt, and everything in you wanted to strike back, but you couldn't?"

"Hasn't everyone?"

"Have you?" she persisted.

"I had a friend in Nam, and I was right beside him when he died. I stayed awake for three days and nights, slogging through the mud and stench of the jungle until I found the enemy who killed him. In the end, I had revenge, but it wasn't very satisfactory."

"War's different," she breathed.

"No, it's not. Killing just becomes legal when you wear a uniform." He didn't touch her, but his voice drew her out. "Do you want to tell me what happened with you?"

She shocked herself by nodding. She wanted to speak about Jerry. "I was in a coffee shop, a regular everyday coffee shop, with a friend of mine, taking a break from working on a case. We met another man there, and he'd gone into the restroom." She took a breath but couldn't stop the words that suddenly wanted to spill out of her. "So we were drinking coffee and talking. Then a stranger came in, this man with stringy hair, and the man I was with knew something was wrong."

She clasped her hands tightly in her lap. "Before I knew what was happening, he was getting up, going to check on the guy, and then there were shots and—" she took an unsteady breath "—h-he fell. And the gun was there, and I— I tried to pick it up and fire it at the stranger. But I couldn't do it." She pressed the palm of her hand to her middle where the pain always centered. "Damn it, I couldn't do a thing. I froze. I tried. God, I tried, and I couldn't pull the trigger. I couldn't—"

She stopped abruptly, hearing the pain in her words and the edge of burning tears. "I'm sorry, I didn't mean…" She tried to pull air into her tight chest. "He didn't die. That's a blessing, I suppose."

"You think you should have shot the man who shot him?"

All she could do was nod.

"Why do you blame yourself for being human?"

"Human? Ineffective. It could have been different," she finished flatly. "It should have been different."

"Do you think it should have been *you* who got shot?"

She stared at him in shock. Was that it? Had that been the reason she'd never been able to assuage the guilt she felt about Jerry? Alex's words dug into a deep, hidden place in her soul. "Maybe. Either way, I know I should have been able to stop that creep."

"You couldn't have done that any more than you could have kept Bob from being hurt."

"How would you know?"

"I know. I went through the war, months and months of feeling that I should have died instead of the one beside me, that I should have been able to protect the others." He turned and rested his hands on the steering wheel. "I wrote a whole damned book before I finally figured out that it wasn't up to me. What happened, happened. That's it. I couldn't change it, not any more than I suspect you could have changed what happened. Guilt gets so twisted at times."

"War is different," she mumbled, but she knew that it wasn't. What she had faced was a war of sorts. And she had been left standing when Jerry fell.

"This isn't a novel that you can end happily ever after. Life is war," Alex said. "That's something I've been certain of for years. And people like Bob Lipton are the casualties."

Kristin sank back in the seat, weakened by talking. "Casualties?"

"Mistakes, maybe that's a better word."

Kristin felt strange inside, almost peaceful, as if talking about Jerry had taken the edge off it all. How could Alex reach so deeply into her being without really knowing her? Maybe the same way he could get under her skin and make her feel things she hadn't for a very long time. "Yes, mistakes," she breathed.

"Poor Bob," Alex said softly.

Kristin reached out to Alex. When she touched the sleeve of his jacket, she could feel the tension in his muscles. "I hope he makes it," she said softly. "I really do."

"Whether he does or doesn't, it's not your fault."

She knew that rationally, but she couldn't hide from that remembered image of the man sprawled on the sand. "Sure," she said, and drew back.

He looked at her for a long moment. "The person you were talking about—the man who got hurt—was he your husband?"

The question didn't make sense to her at first, then his words settled in. "No, no. Not Ray."

"No guilt over your marriage failing?"

"What?"

"You're divorced, and I was wondering..."

"Oh, I see. Sure. There was guilt about failing, but we weren't married long enough for me to get tangled up in the guilt. We met, got married the next year and got divorced three years later." What an awful summary of something she had once thought would be for the rest of her life. "We're friends still—sort of." When had she seen Ray last? She made an effort to think and only came up with a vague memory of running into him at a friend's house when she'd visited Santa Barbara months ago.

"He's married again and seems happy." The words came out flat. Kristin frowned. She was unemotional about a part of her life that seemed like a sliver from someone else's past. "I wasted a lot of time and energy going in the wrong direction," she admitted without rancor. Then she turned the tables on him. "How about you? Aren't you divorced?"

"You checked?"

Kristin nodded.

"I married because my life had never been what you would call stable, and marriage seemed so *very* stable. Kaye and I were together five years, some good, some bad. The bad just started to outweigh the good. It was hard to let go, but I did. Now there's only lingering regret for what I didn't find with her." He exhaled. "I found it myself by moving home. I've got roots, a foundation, stability. For the first time in my life, I'm settled."

Kristin felt herself withdrawing from the picture he painted of his life. That was good, wonderful—for him. But it only left her confused by what she could feel for him.

Alex moved closer to Kristin, and she tried not to retreat. She could feel the seat move, the brush of his thigh against hers, and she held her breath.

"How about you?" he asked. "What are you looking for?"

"I don't know," she said with all honesty. "I'll know it when I see it, I suppose."

His fingers touched her throat, gently circling it, the pulse in his thumb pressed to the hollow under her ear. He didn't say anything, then his mouth found hers with an ease that should have only come after years of knowledge.

She absorbed the soft heat of his lips, faintly dazed that his touch could be so encompassing, that it could stir a long submerged passion, a searing explosion of her senses that burned past reason. Why? she wanted to scream. Why does it have to come with this man who wants small-town roots, stability and sameness? But the cry never materialized. His searching mouth stopped it. Don't move. Don't inhale his essence, she warned herself.

Unlike the first kiss between them, this time she kept still, certain that if she showed no response it would die, that the feelings would evaporate. She pushed away an urgency that she didn't understand in herself and concentrated on the pain where the gearshift pressed into her hip.

His touch was pure fire on her, catching at a hard knot forming in her middle, an ache that hurt more than anything she'd experienced, yet gave pleasure at the same time. Explosive currents chased through her, pulling her closer to the edge of reason. If she gave one bit of herself right now, if she let go of one more shred of control, she knew she'd be lost.

The safest thing to do was to stop it now, and with all the strength of soul she could muster, she jerked back, free in one sharp movement. Her hand pressed to her throbbing mouth, and she refused to acknowledge her loss—or what Alex could draw from her. She couldn't begin to comprehend her response, not any more than she could put a name to what she felt.

Running seemed terribly logical right then. She fumbled for the door handle. "I have to get in," she muttered, and scrambled out into biting cold that hit her like a slap on her face. She ran up the steps to the door and almost made her escape before Alex caught up with her.

His hand closed on her upper arm, and he turned her to press her purse into her hand. "Don't run away without this," he said softly.

"I'm not running away," she lied, all but crushing the purse with her fingers.

"Oh, weren't you?"

"No, I'm tired, that's all." She wouldn't admit fear to this man—not ever. "Today's been a drain, and I just want it to end."

He let her go, but he didn't leave. "We'll talk tomorrow and figure out what to do. All right?"

Kristin felt as if she'd been ready to topple over all day, and one more contact with Alex would surely bring her crashing down in a pile of disjointed thoughts and needs. "Yes, tomorrow," she murmured.

Alex stared down at her as she fumbled in her purse for her key. He could almost feel her fear, but he didn't know why it was there. Surely what had happened in her past couldn't linger with that much strength. And what was going on between them shouldn't have bred fear. Shock at how quickly it had developed, maybe. Wonder at its strength. He could barely understand it himself, but it held no fear for him.

He watched her hand tremble as it pushed the key into the lock. Then she turned her lavender gaze on him. If he did what he really wanted to do right now, she would probably run and never stop. He touched her lips ever so gently with the tips of his cool fingers, a very poor substitute. He couldn't think of another thing to say, so he turned and left.

Kristin watched until the red taillights faded into the night, then released a shaky breath. An ache lingered in her, a sensation that had been forming since her first contact with Alex, and she wanted it gone. She wanted peace and quiet away from a man she didn't understand. She wanted escape from ugly violence.

When this job was done, she'd ask David for work in New York or in Florida. Someplace far away from California.

She rubbed her knuckles over her lips, then turned the doorknob and entered the darkened house.

"I've been waiting for you," a voice said out of the shadows in the living room.

Chapter 8

Kristin spun around, a light flashed on in the living room, and she saw Ben as he straightened from turning on a small lamp. Pressing a hand to her chest to contain the thundering of her heart, she gasped, "What are you doing here?"

Ben grinned from under the thick mustache. "Didn't mean to give you a fright, but I figured you'd know I'd be around real soon." Dressed all in black from his pullover to his pants to his crepe-soled shoes muddied and wet, he looked the part of a cat burglar. "I didn't want to wait out in the cold, so I found a back window that wasn't fastened." He chuckled. "It's hard on the nerves sneaking around like that."

Her fright and annoyance fled under the glow of his good humor. "Hard on my nerves, too."

"Sit down," he said, motioning her into the living room where the sheets had been removed from the furniture again. A half-full glass of milk sat on the undraped coffee table beside the easy chair facing the fireplace. "After what happened, I knew that I needed to talk to you." He crossed to the easy chair and picked up the milk. "Don't mind that I got myself a drink, do you?"

"Not if the cat doesn't. That's his milk." She took off her sweater and tossed it onto the chest in the foyer before following Ben. "You can have some of his kibbles to go with it, if you want." She sank down on the sofa, smiling at Ben as he sat in the chair. "We've got a year's supply in the kitchen."

"I met the little monster. He jumped on me from the dresser in the back bedroom." He sat back, smoothing his mustache, a habit of his that hadn't disappeared over the years. "I'd like to make a cat coat out of him."

"He grows on you." Kristin tugged her legs up Indian-style on the soft cushions of the sofa.

"You look all dressed up for these parts."

"I went to the hospital to see about the man who got hurt today." That brought back everything in a rush. "Today was just terrible."

Ben sat forward, letting the glass dangle from his fingers while his elbows rested on his knees. "How's the guy doing?"

"Barely holding his own."

"What happened, kiddo?"

"I was out walking, getting the lay of the land, and when I was at that old dock, the one that's falling apart, I turned around and saw him lying on the beach. When I got to him, he was rambling, saying strange things."

Ben watched her intently. "Like what?"

For some reason that she didn't understand, she didn't tell Ben about Lipton being pushed. It was there, right on the tip of her tongue, yet she held her peace. Maybe it was enough to have told Alex, to have shared the horror with another person. "Just ramblings." She fingered the crease of her linen slacks at her knees. "I've been wondering if he might be the one behind the fires."

Ben's eyes narrowed. "You think he got caught in his own trap?"

"Silly, huh?"

"No. Anything's possible."

She pressed her fingertips on her knee and shrugged sharply. "Ben, whoever is doing this isn't fooling. This isn't a game or simple harassment."

"Maybe you're right about Lipton—that the firebug might pay with his life." He stroked his chin. "Any other ideas?"

"No, not really." She studied Ben for a moment, then asked a question she'd been wondering about. "Why did you leave the Agency?"

He sat back, slouching low in the chair until his chin rested on his chest. "I got tired of being told what to do and how to do it. I wanted to be on my own for a while."

That made sense to her. "No more orders?"

He rested the glass on his middle and stared at Kristin. "Wouldn't you have liked to tell David Allcott that you wouldn't come up here, that you didn't want any part of fires and accidents and bombings?"

She tightened. "Sure. But—"

"He needed you up here, right?"

"Yes, and I'll do what I can to help him."

"I found out that other investigators have really messed up, and Hammon is getting paranoid." He drank the last of his milk and held the glass up to the light. "That's something else I don't miss—all that stress. Too much tension and too little pay." He put the glass on the table, but didn't get up. "Have you talked to the police yet?"

"Not about Lipton. Just about the fire yesterday."

"The sheriff is an insignificant sort, all tied up in small-town thinking."

Ben had Boyd Lane pegged perfectly. "I know."

"You'd better follow Ben's number one rule—don't expect the police to do anything except foul things up."

"What's your second rule?"

"Keep your mouth shut around small-town people." He grinned. "Never, never let the enemy know what you're thinking."

"How right you are." Maybe she'd tell Ben later about Lipton being pushed. In some way the right time to tell him tonight had passed.

He studied her. "How about the local celebrity who brought you home? Did you tell him any secrets?"

"Alex?" She smoothed her pants again with the tips of her fingers. She hadn't intended to tell Ben about Alex at all. "He just drove me to the hospital to check on Lipton."

When Ben stood to reach for a black coat lying over the back of his chair, Kristin got slowly to her feet.

"Take care, kiddo," Ben said, and left by the front door.

Alex drove slowly, his hands gripping the steering wheel tightly. Even when he pressed the button for the gates to his property and they slid open, he didn't hurry. He took his time driving into his compound, along the darkened driveway lined with pines and into the clearing where his truck lights caught his home in a flash of light.

In the center of a sea of rich grass, the adobe structure, the only real home he'd ever known, was little more than a low shadow. He stopped the truck by the sweep of steps leading up to the tiled terrace that wrapped around the ocean side of the house. But he didn't get out.

Things weren't adding up anymore. Not with his writing, not with the other areas of his life.

He sat back in the seat, slipped the cigar case out of his pocket and methodically lit one of the slim brown cylinders. He let the smoke trickle slowly out of his mouth as he closed his eyes. When he'd left the army, it had been because he'd had enough. He'd seen enough and been through enough.

Alex drew on the cigar again. Burned out. That was what it had been, and he'd wandered around, ended his marriage and finally realized that he wanted to be home. He opened his eyes to the night. Home. He knew where it was, and that it had always been here. But there wasn't anyone to share it with. He shifted in the seat. A piece of the puzzle of his life wasn't in place. A hole gaped, yet he had never missed that piece before... until Kristin.

His hand smoothed the steering wheel. Kristin. He hadn't planned on what was happening between them. He certainly didn't want to deal with it now. He could use Jake Warner now. Cool, collected, so sure of himself.

He sat for over an hour in the silence of the truck cab until the chill began to seep into his bones. Finally, he got out and walked alone toward his house. He stopped at the door. He knew once he opened it and stepped inside, he'd be completely alone. Suddenly the idea made him feel uneasy and empty. With an abrupt movement he turned on his heel and walked away from the shadowed house toward his boat.

"If you want out, just say so," David said, his voice filled with shock over the phone line.

Alone in the darkened bedroom, Kristin sat at the foot of the bed and stared out the windows at the night. The offer should have been a relief, but she shocked herself by not even considering it. It might be the best thing to leave, but she couldn't do it. Not yet. "This place grows on you, David. It's small and peaceful. I need answers for what's happening.'' She saw lights out on the blackness of the water, a flashing red-and-blue glow that must have been from a boat cruising slowly northward.

"Is small-town life starting to appeal to you?" he asked softly.

What appealed was a tall man with rich brown eyes and a touch that could stop her heart. All she said to David was, "I don't understand small towns—how people can dig in and live their whole lives in one place."

"Every wanderer has to settle sooner or later."

"Maybe." Before David could say anything else, she added quickly, "I've got some new information. The man who died here three months ago, the man called Franks..."

"Yes, Ronald Franks."

"That's not his name. He was Ronald Fletcher, originally from San Francisco. He did time for burglary and arson."

"What are you talking about?"

"No mailman, no retired civil servant. I just can't figure out how he fits in with the fires up here."

"How'd you find this all out?"

"Alex Jordan found out. He hinted that he heard it from some investigator." She watched the boat lights until they were out of sight in the blackness of night. "I'll try to find out who he talked to. And I'll try to find out what else he knows. He seems ready to cooperate to find out what's going on up here." She exhaled. "I just hope Lipton makes it."

"If he doesn't, it's not your fault." David had read her mind over all that distance. "From what you've told me, you did everything you could."

"It still doesn't make me feel any less helpless."

"Are you sure you want to stay?"

"Yes." She closed her eyes to shut out the sight of the trembling in her free hand. "I'm staying. But when this is over, send me someplace far away. All right?"

Alex made himself wait until seven o'clock the next morning before calling Kristin. And it wasn't easy. The whole night hadn't been easy, with his sleep torn by dreams and thoughts of her. So he'd stayed on the boat, spending most of that time cruising up the coast and back. Finally he'd docked, walked to the house and sat on the terrace waiting for dawn.

He dialed Kristin's number on the cordless phone and heard it ring seven times before he finally hung up. She must have gotten up early and left the house. One thing he'd accomplished during the long hours of the night had been to settle on a plan of action. And he wanted to talk to Kristin about it. Abruptly he stood, zipped his black windbreaker, jumped down the steps and headed away from the house.

Kristin woke up thinking about what was happening. And she realized that if Bob Lipton wasn't at the bottom of the fires at Restcorp, something had drawn him to the logging camp, something that had brought him face-to-face with his attacker. And a man named Ronald Fletcher had been drawn there on the Fourth of July.

As Kristin walked out the back door she heard the phone ring, but by the time she made it back to the bedroom and picked up the receiver, all she heard was the dial tone.

She waited by the bed, staring at the phone, waiting for it to ring again. When it didn't, she put out her hand, almost ready to call Alex and tell him what she wanted to do, but she stopped. She could see him later to explain.

She turned and left the house. Wearing a white corduroy jacket over black chino slacks and a red shirt, Kristin stood a moment, enjoying the coolness of the morning, then she headed out across the back lawn. She stopped at the top of the stairs, looked out over the water and steadied herself. She had to go back to the logging camp.

She descended the stairs to the beach and headed north. When she came to the chain-link fence, she stopped. Someone was on the other side of the barrier, a man who didn't belong. He was facing away from her, on his haunches, looking under one of the silent earth movers. Slowly he got to his feet, looked around and moved north, keeping close to the bluffs. His long, loose hair drifted around his shoulders.

Kristin didn't breath until Dailey Cook was beyond the machinery and out of sight.

She leaned back against the granite wall, her chest hurting with tension. It was Monday—a school day. Why would Dailey be out here now, alone? Lost in her agitated thoughts, Kristin didn't hear anyone approaching until her name was called out. "Kristin?"

She spun around. Alex strode toward her, and her chest constricted even more. He came within five feet of her before he stopped. Clear sunlight caught at the highlights in his wind-ruffled hair, and his dark eyes skimmed over her from head to foot, coming back to meet her gaze.

He hesitated, then came closer and, without touching her, stooped and touched her lips with his. "Hello," he said softly as he stood back. "I called you, but you weren't there."

"I heard it ring but didn't get to it in time." Was that her voice sounding so even? It shocked her that she could appear calm when that mere brush of his lips had set her heart beating so erratically in her chest. "I was going to call you."

"What about?"

She pushed her hands into her pockets and shifted from foot to foot on the gritty sand. If he could look at her like that and not touch her, she could do it, too. But she had to narrow her eyes a bit to minimize the details she took in. "I think we need to look over the logging camp."

"Yes, we do," he said without hesitating.

And she didn't argue. The idea of him going there with her was infinitely comforting. "Let's go."

He looked right at her. "You think Fletcher is at the bottom of this, too, don't you?"

All night she'd gone over and over what she knew about the case and had kept getting the same answer. Ronald Fletcher might be dead, but he was involved in some way, either by his life or by his death. "Yes."

"I like the idea of being partners," he said unexpectedly. "How about you?"

"Yes, partners in finding out what's happening to Vespar Bay." That spelled it out as much for her sake as for his.

He held out his hand. "Partners."

She met his handshake, and when she felt the strength and warmth in it, she found herself reluctant to let go. "You and me," he said softly. "And the first thing we have to do is take a look at the camp."

"Something else," she said, and hated to tell him. "Dailey Cook just went that way."

His lingering hold on her hand spasmed. "How did you . . . ?"

"Weren't you following him?"

There was no attempt to evade the question, just a sad resignation in his eyes. "Yes. I saw him come into the cove south of my dock."

He thinks Dailey's involved in this, she realized, and it's killing him. She kept holding to him, partly for her comfort, partly for his. Over the hammering of her heart she said, "Let's go."

The spot where Bob Lipton fell had been wiped clean by the rain, but all Kristin had to do was look at it and the whole scene replayed in her mind with painful clarity. She and Alex had come to the spot in silence, lost in their own thoughts. When Kristin told Alex it was where the fall had taken place, he nudged her away from it.

He pointed up the bluff. "Let's look up there."

Cautiously Kristin climbed the steps, taking a large step over the broken stairs. She stopped at the top and looked down at the place where the footprints had been. The rain had completely washed them away.

She walked away from the edge and crossed to the central area. Both she and Alex silently went through one after another of the dilapidated, vacant buildings. Any doors were long gone and whatever contents the buildings had held had been taken away over the years by scavengers and souvenir hunters. She stopped in the last cabin, a single-room building with part of its roof gone, its only fixtures a crumbling fireplace and a toilet with a cracked bowl and no tank.

A rat scurried past Kristin, darting out from a hole in the fireplace to disappear under a loose plank in the warped floor. She stared at the rodent until it was out of sight then exhaled, her breath curling on the cold air in the run-down building. "Rats. Ugh," she muttered.

She backed up abruptly and bumped into Alex. He steadied her from behind with both hands on her shoulders. Right then she realized how easy it was to lean on him, figuratively and literally, just the way she had at the hospital. And that truth made her straighten quickly.

"Let's get this over with," Alex said.

She turned to look at him, less than six inches separating them. "But what are we looking for?"

He touched her cheek, then his finger trailed heat along her bottom lip. Gently he traced the fullness, then stilled. "Anything, everything."

She stood very still until his hand fell from her. "All right, let's keep looking," she said in a rush and ducked past him.

Back in the open, she looked at the last two buildings, the mill closest to the bluffs and a mess hall behind it, backed on to the forest. Two stories high, the mill had a stone path leading to its door and a crude fountain outside filled with a thick layer of rotting needles and leaves. The mill was in better condition than the other buildings, probably because the logging company had put more money into it. The roof still looked solid despite warped and cupped shingles, and the walls were only missing a few boards here and there. What glass still remained in the windows was clouded and obscured with dirt and grime.

Kristin walked by Alex's side up the stone sidewalk and stepped through an entry door that had been propped open by a twisted pine branch. She found herself in a reception area of sorts, a square space with three doors leading off of it. The doors to the right and left were gone, but the one right in front was in place and closed. She stood very still next to Alex, sniffing at the damp mistiness touched by odors of rotting wood and rusting metal.

"Alex?" she asked in a whisper.

"What?" His voice echoed strangely.

"Where do you think Dailey is?"

"I don't know." She heard his exhaled breath. "I hope to God he's not around here or at the other Restcorp property."

She did, too. She looked down at the floor then dropped to a crouch. "Look, Alex."

He dropped down by her, his thigh pressing against hers. In the thick dust there were recent footprints. One the pattern of lugged boots, the other made by smoother-soled footwear. They could have been like the ones she'd glimpsed at the edge of the stairs in the rain. She pointed to them. "They're really fresh, aren't they?"

Alex pointed to the lugged set. "Bob wore boots like that."

"After I found Bob, I saw footprints at the top of the cliff. I had an awful feeling whoever they belonged to was still around... watching me."

She trembled at the thought and stood. As Alex straightened beside her he touched her arm and motioned to the doors. "Let's look around here, then you can figure out what to do next."

She looked at him. "Me? Why me?"

"You're the professional investigator." He cupped her chin gently. "You tell *me* what to do."

One thing you can do is not touch me like that, she wanted to say in self-defense. Instead she said, "That has possibilities," attempting a lightness of tone that she didn't feel. As soon as the words were out, she knew she shouldn't have said them.

Alex grinned, an endearingly crooked expression. "I'm glad you finally realized that."

She looked away quickly. No snappy answer miraculously occurred to her, so she moved away from Alex to look in the door to the right. She found what must have once been the office and looked back at Alex turning from the opposite door.

"A storage room," he said, and strode to the closed door in the middle. It creaked loudly in protest when he pushed it open.

Kristin came up behind Alex and looked past him into a vast space that filled both stories and held monsters of machines, rusted and silent. Light that filtered in through high, dirty windows caught at dust hanging in the stale air. Shadows and strange shapes in the space set the hair at the back of her neck on end, and Kristin backed up. "We can look around here more later on."

Without waiting for Alex, she left the mill and walked out into the fresh air. She inhaled deeply and glanced at Alex as he came to her side. "What else do you know about Fletcher?"

Alex pushed his hands into his pockets. "Not much. He rented a small place north of here—lived there alone. He walked a lot in the woods. I saw him myself quite a few times when I was on the boat. I would see him near the cliffs. He never looked up, never waved."

She tried to concentrate on what to do, but being this close to Alex was fogging her reasoning processes. She asked the first thing she could think of. "Do you know exactly where he lived?"

Alex nodded. "Sure."

"Maybe we should go and look."

"We can walk from here. He did often enough."

Alex led the way along the side of the mill onto a dirt path narrowed by weeds. After a ways it formed a Y, one branch going into the woods, the other going to the front of the mess hall.

"While we're here, let's look inside," Kristin said, and led the way into the low building with warped siding and a sagging, shingled roof. They simply glanced inside, into a huge empty room with a kitchen to the left through double doors. Back outside, Alex and Kristin waded through weeds and grass to the other fork of the path.

This part of the path looked well traveled, going around the side the building, past empty barrels and old machinery parts and finally into trees. "It seems Fletcher went this way a lot," Alex said as he walked along and casually reached for Kristin's hand.

The contact seemed as natural as breathing, and Kristin laced her fingers in his and kept going. "Someone has," Kristin agreed, and kept walking ahead of Alex.

They went about half a mile through the thick forest, then walked out into a narrow clearing, not more than a hundred feet wide. A small white bungalow sat near the edge of the cliffs with a few small bushes at the base of the walls. It looked stark and vaguely forlorn but well-kept. An older car was parked at the back, and the porch light was still on.

"This is it," Alex said. "They're using it to house Rest-corp employees now."

Kristin remembered something Ben had said about living in a cottage provided by the company. She moved forward, letting go of Alex with a degree of regret. "Let's see if any-one's here."

They circled the house, walking on its neatly mowed lawn, then Alex went up the narrow steps to the door. He rapped sharply on the solid wooden barrier and waited then turned to look down at Kristin. "No one's home."

He looked both ways then tried the knob. The door clicked, but before he could open it, someone called out, "Help you folks?"

Alex turned sharply at the sound of a man's voice, but Kristin didn't have to look. Ben. She turned slowly. It was Ben, all right, with his gun drawn and pointed at them.

Alex held up his hands. "Sorry, we weren't going to break in or anything. Just looking."

"I recognize you now, Mr. Jordan." Ben nodded and lowered the gun. "What do you need?"

Kristin spoke up. "We heard the man who died on the Fourth of July used to live here."

"Don't know about that. I've only been here for a couple of months." He slipped his gun back in the holster. "Don't know anything about that guy except his name...Mr. Franks. Some sort of retired civil servant."

Alex came down the steps and stood by Kristin. "Did he leave anything around here?"

"No, nothing. They cleaned out the house really thoroughly before I got it." He stroked his mustache. "They got in professional cleaners. They even painted the inside."

Alex dropped an arm around Kristin's shoulder. "Thanks. We'll be going."

Kristin eyed Ben, then motioned back to where the car was parked. "The company gave you a car?"

Ben shook his head. "No. It's been here as long as I have. Never used it at all. I don't even think it runs."

"Thanks again," Alex said, and urged Kristin to start walking. "See you around."

Ben nodded and went past them up the steps and into the house. The door clicked firmly shut as Alex and Kristin walked back toward the woods and the path. But as soon as they were in the shelter of the trees, Alex stopped abruptly. "I just remembered about the car."

"What?" Kristin asked in a low voice.

"I think I remember seeing Fletcher in it once or twice driving through town."

"Are you sure? You said that he always walked."

"I'd forgotten. Twice he was in that car. I'd swear he was. Maybe you could run a check on it?"

Kristin looked back at the house through the trees. "That would take too much time, don't you think?"

"And we don't have a lot of time," Alex said softly. He motioned Kristin to follow, and he went back through the

trees but didn't break cover. Instead he kept behind a large
trunk and looked through the foliage.

Kristin followed his gaze and saw Ben step back outside.
The uniformed man stood at the top of the steps, looked
around then headed down the driveway toward the road.
When he was well out of sight, Alex turned to Kristin. He
touched her shoulder. "Let's take a closer look at the car."

Cautiously stepping clear of the trees, Alex glanced at the
road then motioned for Kristin to follow. Quickly they
crossed to the car, and Kristin could see it hadn't been
moved in a very long time. Weeds had grown around the
tires, and the windows were filmed so thickly that she
couldn't really see more than shapes inside. While Alex tried
the doors and found them locked, she rubbed at one of the
windows.

"Kristin," Alex said softly. "Look."

She turned and saw that he had the trunk open. Hurrying around to the back, she looked inside, but there was
nothing except a fairly new-looking spare tire and a jack. "I
guess that's that," Alex murmured.

Kristin reached inside the trunk and stretched forward to
press at the back of the rear seat that made the back side of
the trunk. It moved. "Do you want to get into the car?"

Alex looked back at her. "Of course, but..."

"All right." Carefully she climbed into the trunk and
pushed hard on the seat back. It fell forward into the car. A
hole about three by two was opened between metal supports, and Kristin had no trouble slipping through it. Once
inside she scrambled over the front seat, slipped into the
driver's seat and pulled the lock up. Alex opened the door
and smiled down at her. "Quite a little thief, aren't we?"

"No, just a trick my brother Dan used to use when he got
locked out of his car. He'd have me climb in because I was
smaller than he was."

"I'm impressed. I certainly couldn't have made it," he said, and motioned for her to slip across the seat.

When he settled in beside her, she pointed to the odometer. "Almost a hundred thousand miles, but look at the trip-mileage counter. Two hundred and five miles."

The gas gauge was the type that registered even when the power was off, and it showed less than a quarter of a tank.

"I wonder what kind of mileage these cars get?" Alex asked.

"I had one sort of like it when I was a teenager, and it seemed to go about two hundred and fifty miles on a tank. I don't know what that works out to at miles-per-gallon. I didn't worry about that sort of thing then. My brother did."

"He's got less than a quarter of a tank left, and he's put two hundred and five miles on the car." He looked around the car. "This is neat to the point of being bare. Just like the trunk. I guess the police looked through this when he died. But I don't understand why it's still here." He looked in a side pocket. "Nothing. The man looks as if he was very particular. I've heard that some people who've been in prison get obsessively orderly when they're on the outside."

Kristin twisted the handle on the glove compartment and pulled down the door. "Nothing in here but a small stack of paper kept together with a rubber band." She took the bundle out. "Receipts. The top one's from July 3."

Alex took them from her, and looked closely at the white slips. "They're from Len's store."

Without saying anything else, he dropped them into his pocket and turned to push the back seat into place. He got out, waited for Kristin to do the same, pushed the lock down and slammed the door shut. Quickly he went around to the back, and as he snapped the trunk shut, he looked at Kristin. "Let's go talk to Len."

* * *

They arrived at the store just before ten o'clock. Alex stopped the truck and got out, and Kristin followed him inside. Len looked up as they entered, his eyes widening at seeing them together, but he didn't comment on it. He simply smiled and nodded. "Hey, there, Alex. Miss Delaney."

"Kristin," she said as she walked with Alex to the counter.

"Kristin," he said agreeably.

"Len, I need a couple of answers and no questions," Alex said without preamble.

Len didn't hesitate. "Sure thing."

Alex took out the receipts, slipped off the rubber band and spread them out on the counter. "These are receipts from this place, aren't they?"

Len picked up one. "Uh-huh. Got my name and code right there," he said, pointing to the top of the slip. "This one's for gas." He looked at one, then another, then another. "Gas." He looked up at Alex. "I can even tell you who they belonged to."

"You can?"

"Sure, that poor mailman who got himself killed at the loggin' camp last Fourth of July."

Alex leaned forward. "How can you tell?"

"The guy never bought anything here except gas. Once a month or so, he'd come in, fill up, then leave town for a day or two. Then he'd come in a month or so later, fill up again and leave again." He put the receipt back on the stack. "Reason I remember, he always got nearly the same amount—about sixteen, seventeen gallons. Wanted to ask him about it but never did. I figure he went someplace pretty regular, then came back and parked the car until he went again. Maybe to get his checks. You know how the government sends out retirement things once a month? He prob-ably went someplace to get them and cash them. Maybe where he used to live.''

Alex stood back and reached for the receipts. Without rebundling them, he put them in his pocket. ''San Francis-co's about a two-hundred-mile round trip, isn't it?''

''Right about that.'' Len looked right at Alex. ''You said no questions, but somethin's going on.''

''I'm going down to the city,'' Alex murmured. He took Kristin by the arm. ''Thanks, Len. I'll see you and explain when I get back.''

''You goin' right now?'' Len called as Alex reached the door.

''Yes. I'm going to run the boat down. Thanks again.''

Alex hurried Kristin out of the store and into his truck before he spoke. ''Are you coming with me?''

''On the boat?''

''Yes.''

''Why don't we drive?''

''I think better on the boat. Will you come with me?'' he repeated.

''Yes.''

He touched her hand for a fleeting moment then started the car. ''Good.''

The sound of an approaching car caught Kristin's atten-tion, and she looked away from Alex just as an old Volks-wagen drove into the parking lot. She could see Gwen driving, and she lifted a hand in greeting.

The woman got out into the clear morning light, the breeze ruffling her brown curls. ''Alex, Kristin!'' she called as she hurried toward the truck. ''I'm glad to finally find you two.''

''We're heading for the *Dream's End*,'' Alex said.

"Going for a cruise?" Gwen asked as she reached the truck door on the driver's side.

"I'm going to show it to Kristin."

"I'm trying to find Dailey. Have you seen him anywhere?"

Kristin let Alex talk because she simply didn't know what to say. "Wouldn't he be at school?" he evaded.

"He called in sick, and a substitute took over for him today."

"He's sick?"

She shook her head. "Not physically, but maybe sick at heart. Bob's accident really shook him up. He took off this morning without telling me where he was going, and he never came back."

Kristin could feel the worry in the woman. "You said he likes to drive and think. Don't you have an idea where he'd be?"

"Anywhere, Kristin. Sometimes he'll take off for San Francisco or Santa Rosa. Or off into the back country. He says driving gives him solitude, the way Alex goes out on the boat." She looked at Alex. "Did you hear about the town meeting tonight?"

"No. Who arranged it?"

"Charles Overton, Dailey and a couple of others. That's part of the reason I'm out—to tell people—and I thought I'd look for Dailey while I did." She looked past Alex at Kristin. "Will you come to the meeting?"

"I—I might."

"What time?" Alex asked.

"Eight at the high school."

He put the truck in gear. "See you then. I hope you find Dailey."

Gwen moved back and stood watching as the truck backed out of the parking lot. Then she turned and went into the store.

"I can get Fletcher's address from my contact," Alex said. "Then we'll take a look at his other life."

Chapter 9

At one o'clock Kristin and Alex drove up in front of a run-down boarding house in the Bowery section of San Francisco. The address Devereaux had supplied Alex with looked bleak.

Gray-shingled and clapboard-framed, the house was a wide, squat, three-story structure with shuttered windows and a sagging wraparound porch. Alex checked the address again, then got out of the rental car and held out his hand to Kristin.

She took his hand and continued to hold it as they walked up the broken cement walkway. The stairs creaked under their feet as the two of them stepped onto the porch. Somewhere inside a television was going. Alex pressed the button labeled Ring for Manager.

Nothing happened, so Alex rang again. The television's volume lowered, and the door swung back. A young girl of maybe sixteen stood in front of them, her flowing black hair framing a thin pale face. She wore a threadbare bathrobe, her feet were bare, and she blinked in the sunlight. "What do you want?" she asked in a nasal voice.

"We were looking for the manager," Alex said.

"Mrs. Dixon's out, but if you was looking for a room here, we're full up."

"No, we aren't. We're looking for Ronald Fletcher."

"Popular man," she muttered under her breath. "Ronnie never got company much, then two in one day. He ain't been around here lately, not since..." She shrugged. "I ain't seen him since before the Fourth of July."

Kristin stepped forward half a step and smiled at the girl. "He's had company today?"

"Yeah, about an hour ago when Mrs. Dixon was leaving for her sister's. The guy's been here before, so Mrs. Dixon let him go up to leave a message. I offered to let him in, but Mrs. Dixon, she says, 'Lillie, just let me do for the nice man,' then she took him up."

Kristin felt her whole being tense. She'd never expected to run into anyone at Fletcher's. "Is he still there?"

"Naw, he left fifteen minutes ago." Lillie pulled a key out of her pocket and dangled it by a tag from her fingers. "Brought back the key, though."

"He came to see Mr. Fletcher?"

"Yeah. Said he didn't know Ronnie was gone on one of his trips."

"Trips?"

Lillie looked at Kristin. "What's Ronnie to you?"

She thought fast. "He's my uncle." She felt Alex squeeze her hand, but she kept talking. "My husband and I, we wanted to surprise Uncle Ron. Do you know where he is now?"

The girl shook her head. "No." She frowned, scrunching up her forehead. "If you're family, how come you don't know where he is?"

"I guess we should be honest with you, shouldn't we?"
Alex squeezed her hand again, and she tightened her own
grip on him but kept her eyes on the girl. "I think we can
trust you."

Lillie looked over her shoulder then stepped farther out,
leaning toward Kristin. "Sure you can. I won't say nothing
to no one, not even Mrs. Dixon. What's going on?"

Kristin lowered her voice. "Well, Uncle Ron, he's sort of
strange, you know." When Lillie nodded, Kristin kept talking. "He loaned me some money last year, and yesterday I
got a call from him. He didn't say where he was, but he said
he needed the money real bad. Well, he said to come here
and just leave it in his room…in a special hidden place. He
said that a pretty young girl, Lillie, would know enough to
let us in."

The girl looked pleased, but still asked, "Where'd you
two come from?"

"Los Angeles."

"You want to leave money?"

"Not much, but he needs it."

"We all do, don't we," the girl said with one eyebrow
cocked.

And you aren't too stupid, Kristin thought at the same
time Alex let go of her. Out of the corner of her eye, she saw
him taking something out of his pocket.

"How about this money?" he asked, holding a twenty-
dollar bill to the girl.

She took it quickly and shoved it in her robe pocket.
"Yeah, no problem." She dropped the key in Alex's hand
then motioned along the porch to the right. "Around the
corner, top of the stairs. Don't forget to bring the key back
down."

"Thanks," Kristin murmured.

As the door shut, Kristin looked at Alex. "That was fast thinking, giving her money."

"Thanks. But not as quick as that story you told her."

"It's part of the job," she said. She motioned to the stairs. "By the way, you could have given her five dollars and had the same results."

"Now you tell me," he muttered.

Kristin headed off along the porch and around the corner. The flight of wooden stairs had two landings. One partway up seemed to service a second-floor apartment. The top one was for the third floor.

Alex came up behind Kristin as she climbed the stairs. "Do you really think five would have been enough?"

"No," Kristin admitted. "She probably would have held out for ten."

Alex chuckled. "I'll remember that."

On the top landing Alex reached past Kristin and put the key in the lock of the only door. It swung back with a faint protesting squeak, and Kristin and Alex stepped into Ronald Fletcher's apartment.

The big living room in front of them looked as if a bomb had hit it. The cushions of the single couch had been torn and split, spilling their stuffing out onto a worn braided rug. Two chairs had been reduced to stuffing and torn fabric, the drawers of the end tables were out and spilled into the mess, and a small desk to the right had been ransacked. A three-shelf bookcase had been emptied, its books dumped in piles on the floor. The television and compact stereo system to the left hadn't been spared, either. They lay facedown on the floor, their protective backs ripped off.

Straight ahead Kristin could see part of a small kitchen, its drawers and cabinets in total disarray. Even the old refrigerator stood open, its contents tossed and broken on the tile floor.

The place smelled of a horrible mixture of mustiness, disuse and spoiled food.

Alex gave a low whistle. "Either Fletcher had a temper fit or his visitor was looking for something." He swung the door shut behind them and looked at Kristin. "What now?"

She shrugged. "I guess *we* look around. See if we can find anything. Just be careful what you touch."

Alex shot her a questioning look.

"Fingerprints," she explained. "The police will be taking some. We don't need to have ours mixed with the others, do we?" She stepped over the scattered books and crossed to a closed door to the right. Kristin carefully nudged the door open with her elbow. "His bedroom looks just about the same," she called back over her shoulder. "I'll look around in here."

Methodically she searched around a bed with a gutted mattress, slashed pillows and a closet that seemed disemboweled, with clothes spilling out into the room. A metal chest sitting under a window that overlooked the street seemed to be the only thing left in one piece. She looked at the padlock that fastened it shut. "Come here for a minute," she called to Alex.

He hurried into the room. "What did you find?"

She motioned to the lock. "Nothing yet, but I can't get into this thing."

He looked down at her with a smile. "You can't pick locks? I thought that was a prerequisite for being a private eye."

"We're called private *investigators*, and I've never been able to get past locks," she muttered. "But from the look of this room, we could probably bludgeon it with a rock and not make a bit of difference."

He dropped to his haunches, reached for a loose sock on the floor and wrapped it around the lock. With one tug it clicked open. "There you go," he said. "First rule of thumb, Kristin: make sure something's locked before you try to break into it."

He used the sock to lift the lid. It fell back with a muffled thud against the wall, and Kristin felt a surge of disappointment as she looked over Alex's shoulder into the empty trunk. "Nothing," she muttered then raised her eyebrows as Alex reached inside.

He stood, letting the sock fall to his feet, and held something out to her. In the center of his palm was something that looked like a piece of Silly Putty. "Well, well, well," he said softly.

She shook her head. "What is it?"

He sniffed the putty. "Plastic explosives—a classic." Alex frowned. "I haven't seen anything like this since Nam. Could be very effective for blowing up things like . . . earth movers."

Kristin looked up at him. "Alex, how can this have anything to do with that? Fletcher's been dead three months."

He touched her cheek, his fingers cool and lingering. "I know. But there's got to be a connection." He put the explosive back where he'd found it and turned toward the door. "I'll finish out here."

Carefully Kristin searched the closet and a tiny bathroom. When she'd finished she stepped back into the living room but stopped when she saw Alex on his knees methodically looking through each of the books that had been tossed off the shelves.

"I just thought of something. What if Fletcher's friend who did this had something to do with Fletcher being in Vespar Bay? And if . . ." Her voice trailed off when Alex looked at her, his eyes bleak.

"A partner?" he asked flatly.

Dailey, Kristin thought. She could see in his eyes that he thought the same thing—that his friend had been doing it all. That one friend had tried to kill another. "It's just...just an idea," she said quietly.

Alex dropped the book in his hand and straightened. Without a word, he stepped over the piles of books and over to the desk. Kristin crossed to him, wanting to ask about Dailey, yet not able to. What would Alex do if it was his friend? Would he protect him or turn him in? Would it destroy Alex? She had no idea, but the thought of the pain it would cause him squeezed her heart. Nervously she looked down at the desk and fingered the only thing that seemed to be untouched, a clean blotter on the top.

"I wonder who he wrote letters to?" Alex asked, looking at what she was touching.

"No one," she said without thinking.

"How do you know?"

She ran her fingertips over the blotter, a two-foot-square absorbent surface—a completely smooth surface. "No indentations. No impressions. People usually put the paper on top of the blotter. When they write it leaves images."

"You're good." Alex shook his head.

Kristin looked at the blotter again and wondered how good she really was. Why couldn't she even begin to figure out why Fletcher had been in Vespar Bay, who he'd been with and how he was connected to the fires and Restcorp? What if Fletcher had been pushed the same way Bob Lipton had? She stopped the thought, not willing to think that Fletcher might not have slipped, either.

"I wonder why the person who destroyed the room didn't look under the blotter?" she asked, and looked underneath it herself. Strangely, someone had laid out newspaper clippings in the exact shape of the blotter, butting the cut edges together, one after the other to form a large rectangle. "Oh, my..." Her voice was breathless as she slowly lifted the blotter and set it on its side against the desk.

Alex looked over her shoulder and murmured, "Our little fire bug."

Kristin scanned the clippings, all neatly arranged by date. One after another talked about robberies and fires. Jewels. First small robberies, then larger ones. The last two had been important enough to earn front-page coverage. Kristin stared at the dates, then turned sharply, almost hitting her chin on Alex's shoulder.

Before she could say a thing, Alex reached into his pocket and pulled out the gas receipts. One by one Kristin and Alex matched the receipts beginning nine months ago with the robberies. One day the gas receipts, the next day, a robbery. The pattern was clear. When all the receipts had been matched with corresponding clippings except for the July 3 receipt, Kristin stood back.

"He was using Vespar Bay as a hideout, a place to stay between jobs."

"Why Vespar Bay?" Alex asked softly. "How would scum like Fletcher even know about the town?"

From Dailey Cook, the activist, the angry young man. The man who took off for the city at odd intervals. Where did Dailey meet a man like Fletcher? And why would he bring him to Vespar Bay? Or had he met him in Vespar Bay and struck up a deal? But Fletcher had died before the fires had started. Kristin's head began to hurt from trying to make everything match up.

Alex ran a hand over his face then began to stack the receipts and clippings in a pile. "Let's get out of here."

"What about this?" she asked, motioning at the ruins around them.

He shrugged. "What about it?"

"We have to report it, and the police will keep us here forever. That's assuming that they don't think we did it."

"No one will know about this until we report it or until the landlady comes up snooping. Whoever did it won't be back. And Fletcher certainly isn't going to come home. From what Devereaux told me, this place is rented until the end of the year." For a moment Alex stared at the clippings, then he quickly pushed them into his pocket. "December's a long way off."

It made Kristin uneasy to walk away from the mess, but she understood his logic. "All right, but we can't take those clippings. They could be evidence."

"We'll take good care of them," Alex muttered, and put the blotter back in place. He reached for Kristin's hand. "Let's get out of here."

They went in silence out and down the stairs. Alex rapped on the manager's door. Lillie answered it right away. "Did you leave it?"

Alex took a deep breath. "No, we changed our minds. We'll wait until we see her uncle." He hesitated. "I was wondering about the man who just came here."

"Wondering what?"

"What did he look like?"

"Don't know. Mrs. Dixon talked to him. I only talked to him on the phone once. All I know is he talks real fancy."

"What do you mean?"

"He speaks good. That's why Mrs. Dixon is so impressed with him."

"Did she ever say what he looked like?"

"No. She just said he was good-looking, but that don't mean nothing. She thinks a lot of guys are good-looking, and they turn out to be dogs."

Kristin had an idea. "If we leave a number, do you think Mrs. Dixon could call us—collect, of course?"

"I suppose."

"We're going up north for a few days. I can give you the number there. Do you have a piece of paper I could use?"

Lillie sniffed hard before turning to disappear back into the apartment. She came back with a torn piece of notepaper and a stub of a pencil. Quickly, Kristin wrote her name and the number of the Donaldsons', then handed it back to Lillie. "You'll make sure she gets this, won't you?"

"I suppose," Lillie said, pushing the paper into her pocket without looking at it.

Alex hesitated, then reached into his pocket. He took out the key and handed it to Lillie. "Almost forgot to give you this." He dropped it in her hand along with a five-dollar bill. "We would appreciate you seeing that Mrs. Dixon calls us soon."

The girl looked from Alex to Kristin. She nodded. "Sure." With that she went back inside and closed the door.

Alex took Kristin by the hand, and they walked away from the house.

They settled in the rental car, but Alex didn't start the engine. Finally he turned to Kristin. "You were right. Fletcher is—was—involved with someone else. A partner of sorts, probably. Someone who knew about Vespar Bay and who either brought him there or sent him there."

Say it, Alex, say it, Kristin pleaded silently. But he didn't. "Alex?"

"Uh-huh."

"We have to find out who his partner is."

"I know," he muttered as he started the car. "I know."

Kristin and Alex didn't talk all the way back to the docking area. They were still silent as they cruised under the Golden Gate Bridge, away from the city and out into the open coastal waters.

Kristin watched Alex at the controls of the *Dream's End* and found she was becoming overwhelmingly aware of each little detail of this striking man. She watched his large hands grip the wheel, his dark eyes narrow on the distant horizon, his strong legs flex to maintain balance with the rise and fall of the rough water.

She didn't want it to happen. Everything within her screamed against it, yet sometime during that trip she knew that Alex was treacherously close to sneaking into her world. There shouldn't be a niche there for the man, and Kristin tried to ignore her feelings.

For two long hours silence prevailed on the gleaming white thirty-foot cabin cruiser. Unlike the trip down to the city when they had talked nonstop, the trip home was silent and strained, Alex and Kristin lost in their own thoughts. Finally, as they neared Vespar Bay, Alex was the one to break the silence.

"What we have is a firebug and thief, who happened to die at Vespar Bay—who evidently used Vespar Bay as a hideout. But how does that tie in with Restcorp? How could harassing a big company tie in with San Francisco robberies?"

Kristin stood by Alex at the wheel. "Good questions. I don't know."

The boat moved through the increasingly rough blue-gray waters with ease, and Kristin hunched a little against the wind that carried a chilling spray. She watched Alex squint into the bright sunlight.

"Alex. Who's Devereaux? You mentioned his name earlier, and I heard you talking to him before we left for the trip. He was the one who got you Fletcher's address, wasn't he?"

He glanced at her and rubbed his tattoo with his free hand. "Yes, he did. He's a friend. We were in Nam together, and he's the only one I've kept in touch with over the years."

"The tattoo..."

Alex pushed back his jacket sleeve until the mark was clear—an oval shape with the letters *S* and *F* entwined, the number 85 in the middle. "He was in my unit. We all got drunk one night and had ourselves tattooed." He tugged the cuff back over the mark. "A part of my life I've tried to put behind me. A part that's gone...the way some of the men are."

Kristin could hear pain creeping into his voice, and she asked a question as a diversion. "Why did you call Devereaux for information?"

He shrugged. "He's in security now, and he's been getting information for me when I need it."

"And he told you who I am, didn't he?"

"Yes." He gave her a long look before turning back to the water. "You're quite an investigator. Very inventive."

Kristin glanced at the land gliding by, at the cliffs and trees set against a sky growing heavy with clouds. The sun had slipped behind a cloud more than an hour ago and had never shown itself again. A northeast wind robbed the air of what little warmth it might hold. "I can think on my feet."

"So I noticed." He flipped a button on the bank of gauges that meant nothing to Kristin, then attached a rope to the wheel. He tied the other end to a metal loop on the floor, then turned to Kristin. "Automatic pilot—my version."

"You're very inventive, too," she murmured, suddenly very aware of his nearness. "About Fletcher..."

Alex held out his hands toward her. "Can I hold you for just a minute?" he asked, his voice edged with roughness.

Kristin didn't think twice about going to him and cuddling close to the warmth of his body. It felt wonderful. Too wonderful. She could almost feel his pain, his uncertainty over Dailey. She drew back just a bit to look into his eyes, and spoke softly, "Are you all right?"

"Life gets pretty rough sometimes, doesn't it?"

"Yes, it does."

His deep brown eyes studied her intently, and heat rushed into her face. Slowly his gentle lips descended and found hers. The sudden kiss became deep and searching, an exploration that seemed to touch every hidden part of Kristin's soul.

Completeness. That was all Kristin could think of. Missing pieces that finally fit. Rightness. But just when the word *insanity* began to surface, Alex drew back. He gently framed her face with hands as unsteady as Kristin felt, his body heat penetrating her clothes. He looked into her eyes. "Tell me about you," he said, his voice raspy. "I want to know more—everything."

The wind blew all around them, but its chill didn't reach Kristin. A fire couldn't have been any more warming than this man so close to her. She wanted to know everything about him, too, she realized. How she wished it was that simple.

She covered his hands with hers and touched her tongue to her lips. "We've known each other such a short time, haven't we?"

"It seems a lot longer," he murmured. "I can almost feel your heartbeat, each breath you take." He chuckled softly. "I'm writing my last Jake Warner book, and the strangest things have been happening."

Kristin couldn't look away from him, though she was almost losing herself in the velvety-brown depths of his eyes. "What strange things?"

"You're in it. You're the heroine. I got this call from my agent, Jessie Moss, and she was furious that the book wasn't done. Then when I gave her a brief synopsis, she said, 'That sounds like some damned romance, Alex.' I have to agree with her.''

Kristin thought he was joking. "Oh, sure. I'm some fancy dance hall girl with crinolines and low cleavage.''

His hold never faltered, and he didn't smile. "No. You're Emma Forester, gentle and strong, smart and quick, soft and...'' His thumbs moved slowly on the lines of her cheeks. "Very endearing.''

Endearing. That's exactly what he was to her. Endearing and growing more so with every passing moment. If things could only be different. If life could be simple and written like a novel for a happily-ever-after ending.

"And you're Jake Warner?''

"Take away the macho image, and I suppose everyone has the same needs.''

"Needs?'' She felt as if every inch of her was being consumed by her needs at that moment—needs that she was trying desperately to control. "Alex, we don't—'' she took a breath ''—I don't know...''

"Know what?''

"You're so rooted, settled. I'm not. I never have been.'' Her hands lowered slowly but didn't break contact. She couldn't seem to do that, so she rested them, open palmed, on his chest. "My father was in the air force, and we moved all the time. People used to say how awful it was for me and Danny. Maybe it was hard on my brother, but I loved it. New places, new situations. I've never lived anywhere long. And roots...'' She sighed. "I don't know if I even want them.''

Strangely, Alex didn't withdraw, but she could feel his heart. Its rapid, strong rhythm against her hands seemed as familiar as her own heartbeat. "It took me over thirty years to realize that *I* wanted them,'' he said.

"Then I have a few years to go," she countered nervously, trying anything to break whatever was growing between them.

The boat lurched, and Alex bumped into Kristin, pinning her between his body and the hard rail. Fire flared deep in his eyes for just a moment—then his mouth possessed hers. And she let him. The need was there, a complete, all-encompassing need, and Kristin wasn't at all certain she could fight it anymore. Or that she wanted to.

She felt Alex tangle his fingers in her hair, capturing her, and she melted against him. Her arms went around his neck, and she arched toward him, her mouth open, as searching as his. She felt desperate for his taste, to know it and keep it in her memory. The cold wind whipped around them, making choppy waves and sending the boat up and down with the swells, yet Kristin felt a peace that was so sweet it was painful. She felt a sense of homecoming, an end to a searching that she didn't understand at all. One person shouldn't be that important in so short a time—if ever.

And she felt frightened.

The chill came, making itself known to her, and she tried to draw back. She framed Alex's face with her hands, gently easing him away from her. Frightened? She was terrified. Whatever was coming was beyond her comprehension, yet she knew to fear it.

"Alex...please," she whispered. "This is all moving too fast for me. I don't know what's happening."

"I can tell you what's happening." He might have stopped kissing her, but his body still pinned hers against the rail, and she could feel his response to her—as complete as hers to him. "There was something right from the first, wasn't there?" he said, his voice still rough with desire. "Right from that time in Len's store." He brushed at her hair gently with unsteady fingers. "You felt it. I felt it. And

I'm not just talking about the physical thing. There was something else there, something very special."

Kristin shook her head, but she couldn't say anything out loud to deny the truth. Instead she turned awkwardly from him and clutched the rail with her hands. The limitless ocean in front of her blurred. "That's . . . that's crazy."

"Is it?" he asked softly right by her ear.

"Yes . . . no . . ." How could she think when he persisted in touching her. She could feel every line, every contour of him, and it made her thoughts scramble. To feel the strength of his arousal made her ache. Tears burned at the back of her eyes. "I don't know."

Then Alex was gone, and only chill touched her back. She closed her eyes tightly, trying to absorb the loss. She heard the engines die. Alex moved past her to the back of the boat.

Something hummed, there was a splash then Alex spoke from a distance. "I'm anchoring here. Home is just around the point, and I want to talk to you. A captive audience."

"Alex, I . . ." She turned. Wrong thing to do. Seeing him coming toward her only deepened the ache. "Alex . . ."

Then he was within inches, so close she could feel the heat of his breath when he spoke. Yet he didn't touch her. "Listen. Don't talk. Let me say something."

She shoved her hands into her pockets, hoping that would control her need to touch him. She licked her lips nervously. "All right."

"From the first moment I saw you staring at me in Len's, I haven't been able to forget about you. This fire thing, Bob being pushed, my book that New York is screaming for . . . nothing blocks you out of my mind, out of my thoughts or out of my dreams."

He reached out then, and with one finger gently stroked the line of her unsteady lips. Back and forth. Back and forth. His eyes never left the work his finger was doing.

"Believe me, even if I could shut you out until this is all done, I wouldn't. But I can't. And I don't want to. Maybe that's the bottom line. I've shut things out for so long...." He drew back, took an unsteady breath and met her gaze. "Do you understand?"

She did and wished she didn't. "Yes, I do. But we're strangers. You know that."

"Everyone is until you get to know them."

"But, Alex..."

"All I'm saying is give us time. When this is done, stick around. Don't run off on some job. Stay here."

"And then what?"

"And then we'll worry about 'then,'" he said softly, and pulled her into his arms.

Kristin knew "then" would come faster than she wanted it to. But until it came and hit her head-on, she wanted to be like this, to be held in Alex's arms against his heart, feeling as if she'd found her own special niche. *Until then,* she whispered in her heart. She tipped her head back.

She knew that the fire in Alex's eyes must be echoed in her own. This man touched her so deeply that it took her breath away. He snatched away reality and traded it for a fantasy world where anything was possible. Out on the water, not anchored on solid ground, dreams could be made and lived.

"Alex," she whispered against his searching mouth.

"Hush," he said, and in that moment swept her high in his arms. "Please, hush."

Bracing himself against the pitch and roll of the boat, Alex carried Kristin down the three steps into the small cabin and laid her on the single wide bunk. Then he was by her and over her, all-encompassing. Kristin tasted Alex, absorbing his scent, and realized how inevitable this moment had been all along.

She fumbled with his jacket, trying to push it aside, then she felt the contained heat on his chest, the soft sweater over his muscles under her palms. She pressed her lips to the hollow of his throat, where his racing pulse vibrated wildly. She had known him forever and had wanted him forever. He'd always been there, and she had always been looking.

Alex groaned when she tugged up his sweater and ran her fingers across his hair-roughened chest. His hands worked on her clothes, pushing them aside, then his hands spanned her middle, stroking her soft abdomen.

The rising and swelling of the ocean seemed to echo Kristin's feelings, the sensations coming, then ebbing only to come back even stronger. As his hand moved higher, her breath caught in her throat, her whole being contracting in the most delicious way.

"Kristin," he whispered by her ear. "You feel wonderful. I knew you would."

She looked up at Alex over her, his face inches from her, his breath sweet on her face. "How did you know that?"

"I'm a writer," he smiled. "I've got a wonderful imagination." His expression faltered as her fingers moved over his skin.

His head dipped, and Alex kissed her exposed throat. Kristin closed her eyes, absorbing sensations, then she trembled as Alex's hand grazed the underside of her lace-covered breast. She swelled at the merest suggestion of his touch, and when his hand covered the warm mound, a groan of pure desire broke from her throat.

Explosive pleasure rocketed through her. His touch was exquisitely gentle yet demanding, and her nipple peaked in response as his fingers gently worked their magic, drawing, tensing, searching her. She arched toward the experience.

Her world could be this man, she realized, the thought shocking her as it came. No, that couldn't be. She wouldn't let it be, not with Alex or any other man. Damn it, she couldn't reason with Alex touching her like this! She knew she needed to think, but she was incapable of stopping what was happening right now.

All she knew was his touch, his irresistible demands. Life wasn't like this, it shouldn't be. Falling in love should be gradual, over time, getting to know each other, to see if— Her spinning thoughts stopped dead. Falling in love? Oh, God, no. Not that. She couldn't love Alex.

With a muffled gasp she tried to push back, to free her hands of his sweater, to make him stop touching her. She could imagine anything with his hands on her, with fire shooting through her and sensations rocking her. Awkwardly she scooted back until she was sitting on the bed and Alex was facing her. Her breathing came in rapid gulps, and she tugged at her clothes, trying not to meet his gaze, unable to meet his penetrating eyes.

"Kristin?" he asked in an emotion-roughened voice.

"No, I—I'm sorry." She scrambled off the bunk and would have run back onto the deck if Alex hadn't caught her by her shoulders and stopped her.

He forced her to turn and face him. "What's wrong?"

She closed her eyes so tightly that colors exploded behind her lids. "I-it's all..."

"Look at me and tell me what's wrong with this...with us."

She tilted her head back slowly. When she opened her eyes she almost flinched under the intensity of his expression. "Us...you...me. There is no 'us.'"

"Can't there be?"

She licked her lips and forced out words. "This...this sounds like a line from a bad B movie, but we want different things in life, different spaces in this world."

"Do we? How can you be so sure?" he demanded, his fingers tightening on her.

"Because this town, it's everything to you. I know that. I can see it. These people, they're your past, your present and your future."

"Does that exclude you?" he asked.

"I don't know. I've never lived in a place like this. I don't have friends that I've had for years and years. You and Dailey . . ."

"What about us?"

"You're so close." She realized what she needed to know. "He's your friend. How far would you go for him?"

"To the limit," he said without hesitation.

And if he was trying to burn down your town? She didn't voice the thought. Instead she asked, "Without hesitating?"

"We were brought up together, went to school together, got shipped to Nam together. But he came back in four years. I didn't. He started teaching and I started writing. I came back here, he left for a while. But we're friends. Maybe more like brothers. I don't know. Why?"

She had to know. "Alex, if Dailey was the one behind the Restcorp thing, what would you do?"

He released her suddenly, and the isolation tasted bitter on her tongue. "Where did you get the idea he could do all this?"

"He's been sneaking around. He hates Restcorp. He's been going into San Francisco. Alex, he could have brought Fletcher here. He could be the partner of Fletcher's that we're looking for."

Alex stared at her, his withdrawal from her complete even before he turned to climb the stairs to the deck.

"Alex?"

He stopped on the last step but didn't turn. "What?"

"Is Dailey the one?"

He stood absolutely still. "If he was, what would *you* do?"

She swallowed hard. "This isn't something like a ransacked room that can be ignored until someone finds it. I'd have to turn him in."

He glanced back down at her. "Would you?"

"Yes."

He turned and left her completely alone without saying another word.

Chapter 10

Tension was palpable between Alex and Kristin as Alex raised the anchor and started the engines. But as Vespar Bay came closer Alex began to point out spots of interest—superficial conversation to skirt the issues of Dailey's possible involvement and what they had found in San Francisco.

Finally Kristin broached the subject in the broadest way she could think of. "What are we going to do now?" she asked tentatively.

Alex stared at the water ahead for a long time before he answered her. "I guess we need to get in to see the house where Fletcher stayed."

"It's been cleaned, painted and redone. Remember?"

"Still, something might have been overlooked. Maybe we can talk that guard into letting us look around."

Kristin hesitated then impulsively decided to put all her cards on the table. "I know the guard."

"So do I."

"No, I mean I really know him—from before I came here. Before *he* came here."

For the first time in many minutes Alex looked right at her. "What?"

"He used to be an agent with the government. He retired."

"What in the hell is he doing at Vespar Bay?"

"He's after the Restcorp reward."

"Damn," he muttered. "I suppose he thinks he knows who's been doing this."

"He hasn't said." She shook her head. "Ben's pretty closemouthed."

"Has he made any connection between Fletcher and the fires?"

"No, I don't think so. But he could be of help to us."

"No," Alex bit out. He eased his tone a bit. "No. It's just you and me, or I'll do it myself."

She nodded. "All right. We'll do it together. We can go to the cottage and see what's there."

When the town was behind them, Kristin looked at the line of towering bluffs and rolling clouds over the land. "Can I ask you something, Alex?"

"It depends," he said softly, carefully steering the boat to keep it a safe distance from the jut of land.

"You found Fletcher after he died, didn't you?"

"Yes."

She fingered the smooth dampness of the side rail, its brass gleaming under her fingertips. "What happened?"

"I had gone down to the boat to watch the fireworks being shot off from town. Right after the fireworks started at midnight, I saw fire in the other direction. I went to investigate. At first I didn't know someone had died—not until the fire department came and found Fletcher."

"Who came first ... after you?"

He looked at her. Hard. "Dailey. And don't say it, Kristin."

She felt her heart lurch. "He was there?"

"He came down the beach."

"Can I ask *why* he was there?"

"He said that he came to talk me into going back to a party in town, and that he saw the smoke."

She wanted to ask if Alex believed him, but she knew that would be crossing the invisible boundary he'd drawn. She thought of something else. "How did *you* know who he was?"

"What?"

"I assume Fletcher was burned. How did anyone know who had died that night?"

Alex shrugged, turning to watch the water in front of the boat. "They didn't identify him for a while, then someone noticed that Franks . . . Fletcher wasn't around. They found a lighter he carried on the man who died in the fire—and he was the right general size. They couldn't find any relatives. Then—" he didn't look at her, but she saw the way his jaw worked "—Dailey suggested that we advertise for family in different papers around the state. No one came forward, so the town put up the burial money."

"How sad to be that alone."

He looked right at Kristin. "Some people go through life without any attachments, without anyone caring. Just drifting."

She moved back a bit, needing to put a distance between herself and his words. "Everyone thought the man slipped and fell, just like Bob Lipton?"

"Just like Bob," he echoed.

His gaze turned to her, and she could see the deep sorrow there. One friend had almost been killed, and it could have been at the hand of another friend. She looked away. "The idea of murder makes me sick."

"Did Bob say anything else to you? Besides that he was pushed?"

She turned to Alex. "No."

"Are you sure?"

"He said something about the police, and that he was pushed."

Alex took a deep, hissing breath. "Do you really believe that Dailey could have done this?"

"I don't know. I don't know the man. I can only go on what's happened and on what people have said."

His hands flexed on the wheel of the boat. "Sometimes the most obvious isn't the truth."

She looked away, surprised to see that they were almost home, nearing the dock at the base of the bluffs between Alex's house and the Donaldsons'. From out on the water, a short distance from shore, she had her first glimpse of Alex's home. Its adobe-and-Spanish tile construction fit right into the surrounding land. Weak sunlight caught on multipaned windows that faced the water. Impressively strong looking, as if it could withstand anything nature could throw at it, the house seemed to contain the essence of the owner—strength, stability and belonging.

She pointed to it. "Your house?"

He nodded. "Has been for most of my life."

"Your parents?"

"My father is dead, and my mother is in Europe. My stepfather is an international banker and for the past six years has been in France."

Why had she thought he was completely alone? "You're an only child?"

"Does it show?" he smiled.

"No, I . . ."

He moved abruptly, stepping up onto the side of the cruiser toward the nose. He motioned back to Kristin. "Steer to the right side of the dock."

"What? I've never driven one of these things," she protested, and grabbed at the wheel as it jerked. The plastic still held the warmth from Alex's hands.

"It's like a car," he called over his shoulder. "I'll talk you in." He stooped to pick up a coil of rope and started to yell orders.

Concentrating on following his instructions, Kristin guided the cruiser toward the dock, cutting back on the engine. With the motor stilled, the boat touched the dock with only a gentle bump and stopped. Alex turned to Kristin from where he stood on the nose, the sun glinting off his hair. His very presence seemed a treacherous threat to her reason. "Good work. You didn't take off more than ten inches of paint at the water line."

Kristin scrambled along the side, grasping the low brass rail that ran to the bow. "Did I scrape it?" she asked, craning her neck to find evidence of scarring on the pristine whiteness of the side.

"Completely demolished it."

She looked up at Alex, finally seeing the teasing there in his dark eyes, something she'd never have expected right then. She moved back. "I thought you were serious."

"I'm always serious," he said, the humor beginning to fade.

Feeling heat rise in her face, she mumbled something about going back for her purse and turned. She didn't realize that her toe had hooked under the rail until she twisted. Her sneaker caught against the ungiving metal, her body pitched sideways, and she lost her balance. Reaching out to stop her momentum, her hands closed on nothing but air.

Seemingly in slow motion she watched the dark water rushing toward her, and when impact was made, the deep cold took her breath away and stopped her scream. Frigid water filled her mouth, blinded her eyes and blocked her nose. The rush of going under roared in her ears. When she broke the surface between the dock and the boat, she looked up to see Alex with an oar in his hands, his voice snatched away by the sounds of her struggle to stay above water.

Flailing wildly, she blinked against the streaming water on her face. The oar was being pushed out to her, and she grabbed for it, but it wasn't close enough. She grabbed again as it came closer, but it went right past her outstretched hand and jabbed her sharply in the shoulder. Her mind screamed in horror as she realized that Alex was deliberately shoving her back under into the icy depths. She wanted to scream that she didn't care if Dailey burned the whole world down, but she couldn't fight against the strength pushing her under.

Terror spiraled through her body as she spun downward out of control, then instinct took over as her feet hit the bottom. She turned, stroking away from the boat. She glided under the dock and shot to the surface on the far side. As she gulped in air her hands closed over the rough wood of the piling. The cold was everywhere. Her clothes had become an anchor, a millstone of sodden, heavy material.

She shook her head to clear clinging hair from her face, looked up and saw Alex over her, down on one knee. He held his hand out to her, and she struck at it but missed. Before she knew what was happening, Alex had her by her wrist, but instead of thrusting her back into the water, he was lifting her.

The next thing she knew, she was on the dock, rocking back and forth, off balance but alive. She swiped at her face and looked up at Alex.

When he reached out to her, she flinched. "I didn't think you heard me," he said, ignoring her actions and tugging at her jacket. "I couldn't think of anything else to do."

When the sodden weight slid from her shoulders and down around her ankles, the shaking began.

"The way the boat was swinging toward you, it could have crushed you against the pilings." He shook his head as he took off his own jacket and draped it around her. His dark eyes were on her, filled with what looked like genuine fear. "You scared me to death."

"Sc-scared you?" She gulped and her teeth started to chatter. "I thought . . ."

Before she could say anything else, Alex touched her face, wiping at the trickles of cold water that ran off her hair. He pulled her to him. "Let's get you inside and warm. This water can put you into shock."

He hadn't tried to kill her. He hadn't. And he was holding her as if she were a piece of fine crystal saved from shattering. But the horror didn't die easily, especially when she realized that the boat would have crushed her as it swung toward the dock. She couldn't think. She pressed her trembling lips together. Why had she thought Alex had tried to kill her? She swallowed hard and looked up at him, not caring what he could read in her eyes.

Alex moved back a bit and tugged the jacket around her, then began to button it so that her arms were imprisoned against her side. She felt helpless, totally helpless, yet the fear was leaving.

"Come on," Alex said softly, dropping an arm around her shoulders. "Let's get up to the top and inside." He urged her toward the stairs, never letting go of her. She didn't want him to. She knew intellectually that she should get as far from him as possible, but when he urged her forward with his arm around her, she went.

She willed her numbing feet to move, and with each step water squooshed noisily from the pressure. At the steps she worked one hand out the bottom of the jacket to grasp the rail. Slowly she made her way to the top, but she had to stop as she stepped out onto the grass. For a moment the world spun crazily, then Alex was there and her feet were leaving the ground as he lifted her into his arms.

"You made it this far," he said, holding her to him. "Let me take you the rest of the way."

Cradled to the warmth of his chest, Kristin closed her eyes, hating the way her whole being yearned toward him. She didn't open her eyes until Alex shifted her weight and a door clicked.

He carried her into a large room with massive ceiling beams crisscrossed overhead, leather furnishings, deep copper carpeting and an adobe fireplace. Streams of pale sunlight came through the windows, giving a deceptively gentle cast to the chilly day outside the curtainless expanse.

"You're half-frozen," Alex murmured when Kristin began to tremble again. He carried her across the room to double doors, which he nudged open with the toe of his shoe. He stepped into another large room, and all Kristin could clearly see was the huge brass bed covered with a pure-white spread and yellow, orange and brown pillows against the headboard.

Alex set her on her feet, her soaked shoes pressing into the thick carpeting. She looked up at him, needing to say something, but words wouldn't come. Instead her whole body shook harder, so she tensed, trying to stop the spasms. Alex eased her back until they were near the bed.

Gently he pushed her into a slatted rocking chair and stooped to take off her sodden shoes. He tossed them to one side, not watching where they went. Her trembling grew. Taking her by the hand, Alex pulled her to her feet, and before she could object he'd taken off the jacket, tossed it over the shoes on the carpet and begun to unbutton her shirt.

"J-just a minute," she stammered between chattering teeth.

"You have to get these clothes off," Alex said, his fingers continuing to undo the buttons. Before she could protest again he'd pulled her shirt off and tossed it on top of the jacket.

Her wet bra clung to the swelling of her breasts, the lacy material all but transparent, and as the warm air raised gooseflesh on her exposed skin, she gasped. "I—I c-can do th-that."

Alex appraised her from under thick lashes, his expression unreadable. "You can hardly talk, let alone get undressed."

"I can undress myself," she protested weakly.

"I doubt that you could do little more than fall down by yourself right now." He reached for the snap of her pants at her waist. "Stand still and let me help," he muttered, and she did.

She stood woodenly while Alex stripped the clinging pants from her legs, moving only to lift one foot and then the other as the pants came off. Left to stand in front of Alex in indecently skimpy bikini panties, she didn't fight when Alex took her to his bed. He tugged back the patchwork quilt and sheet then maneuvered her onto the fresh linen until she was lying against the softness of pillows. He pulled the blankets to her chin as if she were a small child he was tucking in for the night.

Alex stood over her for a moment, and his hand touched her cheek. "How about some hot tea?"

She felt foolish tears prickling her eyelids. She couldn't speak at all.

His hand stilled on her cheek, and his expression gave away nothing. "Why did you hit me when I tried to get you out of the water?"

Because I thought you were trying to kill me, she wanted to say. She gulped, trying to clear the hard lump in her throat. "I was scared," she finally said.

"Of me?" He looked shocked.

"Of drowning," she muttered. Her heart was hammering against her ribs, and she was beginning to look at Alex through the glint of ridiculous tears.

"Well, you didn't drown."

She watched him, and she had a flashing memory of that moment in Len's store when she had met his dark gaze. The cold water hadn't killed that memory, and she could almost hate herself for allowing that response. "No, I didn't."

"Tea for you, brandy for me," Alex said evenly, and turned to leave.

Kristin held tightly to the sheets. She needed to get home, to call David. He needed to know about Fletcher's visitor in San Francisco. A violent shudder racked her body. Fletcher and someone here. Dailey Cook? She found herself desperately hoping that he wasn't guilty.

She snuggled deeper into the warmth of the bed and looked around. This room—Alex's room—seemed so comfortable with its off-white walls, thick carpeting, long dresser and marvelous view of the ocean. A table by the bed held a telephone. She stared at the black instrument then pressed a hand over her eyes.

In her years of working for David, she had never faced personal physical danger. Suddenly she wondered if she would truly recognize it if it popped up in front of her, especially if it was packaged in the body of Dailey Cook—or Alex Jordan.

* * *

Alex stood in the kitchen off the living room, but he hadn't begun to make the tea. He opened a drawer to one side of the double sinks that sat under a bank of curtainless windows. He reached for a cigar then lit it absentmindedly while he stared out at the docking area. He nudged the drawer shut and exhaled on a harsh hiss.

His life had changed so much in the last few days, and he knew when the change had begun—in that moment when he first glimpsed Kristin's blue eyes across Len's store.

He fingered the cigar, rolling the slender cylinder between his thumb and forefinger. Only grim determination had gotten him through undressing her and tucking her into bed. The silky curves, the high swelling breasts tightened by the cold, the flare of her hips in that ridiculous excuse for underwear... He hit the sink with the flat of his hand, and his intake of air sounded unnaturally loud in his ears.

The more he found out about what was happening around here, the more he felt fear for those who were important to him. That included Kristin. Somehow he would protect her. Maybe Devereaux could contact Allcott and get her pulled from the case. A flashing image of her on the boat, her huge eyes, the glint of sunlight on her silvery hair, tightened his chest. The taste of her when he kissed her, the softness under his hands. She had even been sensuous standing cold and wet in front of him after her fall.

He moved abruptly, but his hand didn't reach for tea bags. It closed over the receiver of the wall phone. With sharp jabs, he punched Devereaux's number. After their brief conversation he punched another number.

When he returned to the bedroom, he stopped at the doorway with the tray in his hand. Kristin had fallen asleep. Alex crossed silently to the bed. He'd never seen anything so lovely in all his life. Delicate and beautiful. Silvery.

He watched her, the breath catching in his chest when she stirred and shifted then settled into a deeper sleep. In a very few days Kristin had become dangerously important to him, so important that he was having a hard time facing the fact she'd leave. She'd walk away and get on with a life that she chose.

He put the tray on the table by the phone then bent and touched Kristin. Only the tips of his fingers rested on her forehead, yet the connection he felt with her could just as easily have been steel bonds. With a shuddering sigh he turned from the sight of her in sleep and crossed to the door that connected his bedroom with the study.

With great determination he sat in front of the computer and booted it up. He'd gotten Jake and Emma away from Webb Tanner, a character he'd forgotten about until the moment he'd typed the name into the computer. Now Emma and Jake had made their break from Webb, got lost in the canyon and stopped.

"Are we going to make it?" Emma breathed as Jake helped her down off the back of the spent pinto.

Jake wished he could tell her everything would be wonderful, that they'd be back to Fort Roberts safe and sound in a day. But he couldn't. He looked down into her pale face, her lavender eyes wide with fear, and he became fully aware of the fact that his hands still spanned her ribs just under the fullness of her breasts. "Sure, we'll make it," he lied, and released her as if she were fire burning his hands.

"Jake?" she asked softly from behind him.

"Yes?" He didn't turn from scanning their surroundings.

"I'm really scared," she said on a sob.

He turned and didn't realize what he was doing until she was in his arms, cradled against his chest. He felt every inch of her along the lines of his own body, every curve, every angle. Softness, gentleness, yielding.

It had been a long time since Jake had felt anything that touched him in such a way. He closed his eyes and literally had to hold his breath.

In that moment, when he knew he was going to kiss Emma, he opened his eyes and saw the Indians right behind them.

The phone by the computer rang, and Alex lifted it quickly to keep it from disturbing Kristin's sleep.

Jake Warner stood in front of Kristin. She knew it was an impossibility, that the man only lived in books, yet she saw him coming toward her on the beach. Tall and dark, with intense black eyes, he faced her. His boots sank into the sand, water swirled around the black leather, and his hands rested on ivory-handled pistols in holsters on each hip.

"Well, just what do you think of me?" the man asked in a rough, seductive voice, the hat brim low on his forehead.

Kristin stood very still, the waves washing around her feet, yet she wasn't getting wet. "You?"

"Me. Mr. Jake Warner—hero, cowboy, lover."

"Lover?" she asked. "You don't love anyone in those books. Why would you think you're a lover?"

He looked confused. "You don't love me?"

"No, I don't." She frowned at him. "Am I supposed to?"

"I guess not." He looked at her intently, his eyes shadowed by the hat brim. "Who do you love, if you don't love me?"

She felt warmth surround her, and she didn't have to think at all about her answer. "Alex."

"Alex?" Jake laughed at her, coming closer, yet he seemed less and less substantial all the time. "Him? Why?"

"I don't know," she said. "I just do."

"That's not good enough. You have to know," he countered, and Kristin realized that she could almost see the distant beach through the man.

"But I don't."

"Then I'll be leaving you," he said softly. He touched his hat and dissolved before her eyes. Only then did Kristin realize what she'd said.

She wanted to take it back, to make it not so, and she called out for him. "Come back! Don't leave! I have to tell you..."

"Kristin?"

Her eyes opened slowly at the sound of her name whispered above her, and she knew she'd been dreaming. The warmth of the bed and the steady beating of a light rain that had begun falling had lulled her to sleep.

She had to blink repeatedly to focus on Alex bending over her. Curling hair, black eyes, soft eyes. What had she told Jake in the dream? Could it be the truth?

Part of her hoped not, and part of her knew that hope was futile. Just as futile as she knew it would be to expect to leave this man without experiencing pain and loss. "I... I must have dozed off," she managed, her voice sounding thick and vaguely hoarse.

Alex stood back and rested his hands on his hips. " know. You were asleep when I came in half an hour ago. Did you have a bad dream?"

Kristin moved awkwardly, trying to scoot up and keep the blankets over her breasts at the same time. "I don't remember," she lied, as much to herself as to Alex. She flinched as her back touched the cool metal of the headboard.

Alex turned and crossed the room to look out the rain-smeared windows. "More rain," he said softly, and looked back at her.

She stared at Alex. "More rain," she echoed. But she didn't look at the window. Something was wrong. Very wrong. Gooseflesh rose on her arms. "Alex. What is it? What's wrong?"

He stood very still for a long moment, then he slowly came back to her. In the low light she could see deep lines bracketing his mouth. And his eyes. Pain, heart-wrenching pain showed in them. A foot from her, he whispered unsteadily, "He's gone. Bob died."

Kristin had never really known Bob Lipton, but she felt overwhelming grief at the waste of life, at the violence that had taken it before its time. And she felt anger that anything could make Alex hurt this way. "Was someone there with him?"

"His daughter came down from Oregon this morning."

Kristin gasped as she experienced a suffocating pain and rage. She started to say something, anything to get rid of the agony, but nothing would come past her trembling lips. With her hands in fists, she hit her thighs and struggled breath. "Damn it," she finally choked out. "Damn... damn...damn...!"

Alex had her by the shoulders, drawing her off the bed to pull her to him, hugging her so hard that she could barely breathe. One pain overlapped with another, and she pushed her face into his chest. "He shouldn't have died," she whispered.

"No, he shouldn't have." As a tremor ran through Alex, he held to him, staying very still in his crushing grip.

"He...he was special to you," she said, a muffled statement, not a question.

"I loved him," Alex said unsteadily.

He shuddered, and Kristin felt tears choke her. "I'm sorry. So sorry." And she pulled him down onto the bed with her. Ever so gently, she stretched out beside him in the mussed sheets and blankets. She stroked his curls with a trembling hand and spoke in a soft whisper, "So sorry, so sorry."

She'd never seen a man hurt so much before. He was shaking with the pain, and she didn't know what to do except hold him and be there.

Dampness touched her cheeks, and she cradled Alex on her shoulder. And she didn't try to fight the truth any longer. Her dream had been based in reality. She could love this man with a singlemindedness that took her breath away. She could care for him and about him with an intensity that frightened her.

She could. She could, but she didn't want to. It seemed impossible yet inevitable. The lump in her throat almost choked her. "Alex, I know how you feel. I really do."

She felt him inhale. He shifted to support himself on one elbow beside her. His eyes were dry, but his face held sign of incredible strain. "But your friend didn't die, did he?"

"No, he didn't die. He might as well have. He...he' paralyzed...in a wheelchair. When Ray, my ex-husband heard about what happened, he called to tell me that I wa lucky it was Jerry and not me."

"Damn. Ray sounds like a fool." His breath came on shuddering sigh. "But then again, if he had been halfwa intelligent, he wouldn't have let you get away." He touche her, his hand at her throat, his thumb slowly rotating on th exposed skin. "No man in his right mind would ever let yo go."

Her hand lifted to cover his where it lay on her. "Yo don't even know me—not really."

"I know enough," he whispered. "I know that I need you. And that I want you here, with me, for as long as you want to stay."

She trembled at the smoldering fire deep in the darkness of his eyes. "Do you?" When had life ceased to be defined in blacks and whites? "Do you really? No promises? No tomorrows?"

"No tomorrows. Just now," he said simply, drawing her to him. For a long moment he simply held her. And Kristin let herself be held, her face buried in the hollow of his shoulder, her hand palm down on his chest so that she could feel each breath he took, each rapid beat of his heart. She had never wanted to be as close to a man in her life as she wanted to be with Alex.

"What do you want?" he whispered, as if he could read her mind. "Just tell me what you want from me."

"Right now I need you, too. I don't want you to leave me," she admitted at a huge cost. She didn't want to expose herself to him, to let him be important to her. Yet she was terrified he'd let go of her and that she'd drift off to some strange place without an Alex in it.

She lifted her face to look at him, praying that he couldn't read things in her eyes, that the gathering darkness in the room could keep some of her secrets safely hidden.

"It hurts, doesn't it?" he asked softly as he shifted his position. His voice sent deep vibrations across her breasts.

"What?"

"Losing someone, wanting someone." Gently Alex cupped the nape of her neck and bent to taste her lips.

A hunger in Kristin came with agonizing sureness, a need for the man and for his touch that knew no bounds. Rational thought fled, and she tasted him with her lips and her tongue. She explored him, relished him, drawing comfort and heat. Her whole body trembled, and her mouth opened farther to accept him, to give him an access that she should have guarded from him.

Slowly his mouth traced the lines of her face, the fluttering of her eyelids, the sweep of her throat. And with his touch Kristin felt a surge of desire that threatened to expose every bit of her vulnerability to Alex.

She wanted to rush headlong into his bed and into his life, taking no chance that reason would come to rob her of what she could have. He radiated heat and exuded a maleness that stirred her inner fires. He offered her a solution to a loneliness that she just now realized had been with her forever.

Temptation touched her lips with each caress of his mouth, her skin with each exploration of his hands. And she let herself go, let herself fall headlong into a swirling tempest.

"Love me," she whispered in a muffled voice as she twisted to press her face into the hollow of his shoulder. "Please."

"I've never been asked to do anything so easy in my whole life," he groaned against her hair.

The gentleness of his touch and voice almost made her cry. "Please," she whispered unsteadily. "Just love me."

Alex moved back from her, and she looked up to see him quickly strip away his clothes until he stood by the bed in his Jockey shorts, the cotton starkly white against his dark skin. In one swift motion he slipped into bed and reached for Kristin again. She felt her body fitting to the angles of his side, and she touched his chest, her hand spreading over the ripple of muscles. For a fleeting moment desire seemed to be mellowing into the pleasure of being held. Then Alex' mouth found hers, and the world shifted into an unexplored dimension.

Chapter 11

Her body had never belonged to another man the way it did to Alex. That knowledge came to Kristin in one swift brilliant second, and her whole being stiffened with shock. Dozens of fantasies raced through her mind, passions, dreams. A lifetime of looking and never finding until now.

Alex was over her, the shadows gentling the planes and angles of his face. With an unsteady hand, she touched him and felt his reality and what her touch could do to him. His eyes never left hers as he came to her. A kiss, a simple kiss, yet the sensations evoked by the caress brought a sob from Kristin.

Her bra was gone, her panties discarded along with his shorts, and she and Alex lay together, skin against skin, nothing between them, their mouths teasing and tasting. Needs built, twining together to create a wanting that soared toward a frenzy of desire.

His hands on her explored and discovered, turning her being to liquid fire. Their hearts pounded in unison, his beating against her aching breasts until his hands moved to capture the rosy peaks. Fire. Pure and simple. Consuming yet nurturing, feeding on itself to grow even stronger. Hotter. And Kristin arched toward it, inviting it, wanting it—scorched by it, yet replenished. And alive. So alive.

Alex knew now that there had never been another woman in his life. Blurred images had passed through his world and left, undefined and unmourned, only disguised as relationships. Never anyone like Kristin. Her softness under his hands all but drove him mad with desire. It made his blood heat and his body throb. All the world was right here, everything that ever mattered was in this bed, and he'd been a lifetime getting here.

He traced her textures, her heat, her flesh that quivered under his touch. The old Alex Jordan was being lost to him at that moment and renewed. He'd never be the same, never look at life the same way, never experience the world in the same way. His needs shattered and soared, and they all revolved around Kristin.

He buried his face in her neck, uncertain about opening his eyes. Would he be able to take in that much glory and still survive? Her scent, her taste, her feel were all around him, then her hands began their own exploration.

"This is insane," she whispered vibrantly through the haze of passion.

If this was insanity, it felt glorious. And he reveled in it. It made him more focused than he'd ever been in his life. Kristin trailed her lips to his ear, then across his cheek to his mouth, a path of fire. And he caught her tightly to him, his tongue finding delights while her hands gave them.

Kristin had never felt more wanton in her life, yet more proud of what she could give another person. She heard Alex moan when her hand spanned his stomach then followed the narrow line of soft hair downward. She felt his whole being tense as she found his heat and his strength. His life grew and pulsed in her hand.

His touch skimmed over her trembling stomach, drawing her body as taut as a bow string. Then his mouth left hers, and she almost cried out from her loss until she felt his lips on her breast. His tongue swirled and teased the nipple, and her cries echoed around them, followed by a low vibrant moan that drifted off into the stillness. Burying her fingers in the thickness of his hair, she arched back and breathed his name over and over again.

Hot pulses throbbed through her, then his lips dipped lower, tasting the hollow of her navel. Lower still, his tongue flicking her skin, sending chills and fire to every part of her. He tasted the inside of her thighs, then her fingers shifted, digging into his shoulders and her whole body lifted with sudden waves of pleasure.

He found the center of her being, gently tasting and teasing, and she cried out for more, much more. Alex shifted, and his hand took the place of his mouth. Kristin lifted her hips, pressing her moist heat against his hand, moving in slow circles, ready and willing to take him into her.

His fingers did magical things, seeking, reaching, finding, darting in and out, the magic surrounding her in an explosion of color. Then Alex was over her, his dark eyes glowing with the promise of even more delights to come. She opened herself to him, willing him to take her, but he hesitated, dipping his head once more to kiss her fiercely. Then he drew back and accepted her invitation.

His taste and hers lingered on her lips, and his heat filtered through her. "Please," she moaned. "Now."

"I'll never hurt you," he vowed. "Never." And he touched her, quivered for one hesitant moment, then entered her. And she rose to him, encompassing him inside her as deeply as was physically possible.

She wanted to remember everything that happened, to set it in her mind for later to be taken out and cherished. But suddenly sensations shot through her. Pleasures so secret and so special spiraled upward to explode into chill and heat, rippling across her skin, drawing out every inhibition she'd ever had.

The beat grew, the rhythm faster and faster until the two of them reached a peak of perfection. And from that height, Kristin saw love and oneness. Her body sang with happiness as it fused with Alex's. The shattering release threw them both beyond reason into a brilliant realm of love.

Love. As the word materialized through the haze of pleasure, another word came with it. *Home.* The word spun around Kristin, settling into her soul. And she clung to it as the blissful descent began. Sensations dispersed, shimmering and delighting her in new ways as they ebbed. And her last thought before she fell back sated and breathless, before her body tangled with Alex's, was what home had to do with this man. Love? She could consider that later, and she closed her eyes.

Kristin drifted for minutes, or maybe hours, in a gentle dreamlike state, small aftershocks making her sigh as she snuggled against Alex's side. When she began to rouse, she pressed her lips to his chest, tasting the subtle mingling of saltiness and maleness on his skin. Nothing made sense to her anymore, but she didn't care. All she cared about was the man by her, his heat mingling with hers, and that feeling of delicious satisfaction and belonging that permeated her being.

"Kristin?" Her name was a rumble against her cheek.

She spread her hand on the firm strength of his stomach and began to move it in slow circles. "Mmm?"

"You know we need to talk."

"Not now." She sighed, unwilling to let reason intrude on this moment.

"All right, love, later. But we'll talk."

"Of course," she breathed, and as her hand trailed higher, she felt his skin tighten. Then her fingers found his nipple.

"Of course," he echoed on a groan before he rolled over, pinning her beneath him.

Jake lay with Emma under the desert moon, both his body and mind satisfied in a way they'd never been before. All his life he'd been looking for people, for things—and he'd never known he'd been looking for Emma.

He felt her stir then cuddle against him. He stroked her silky hair and stared at the moon. Damn, life sure had changed for him.

It was too bad he couldn't stay like this forever. But he had to find Webb Tanner and be finished with him. Then he and Emma . . .

When Kristin roused from a sleep as deep and dreamless as she had ever experienced, she opened her eyes slowly. Lying very still in the deep shadows of the silent room, she realized where she was and reached out for Alex. Her hand touched nothing but the cool emptiness of the other side of the bed.

With the euphoria gone and Alex beyond her reach, Kristin felt a sudden thud of return to reality. Maybe she could love him in less than four days. But she knew she would have to leave him. The thought of him being her home was foolishness. Opposites might attract, but they had a hard time making a life together. She stopped the thought. There hadn't been any mention of a permanent life together. It had only been in her mind.

That thought hurt more than it should have, and she sat up abruptly to stop the thinking. "Alex?"

Nothing. Reaching into the shadows, she touched the small lamp on the bedside table and snapped it on. Its low light barely touched the darkness beyond its glow. Nothing moved, nothing made a sound. Cautiously she got out of bed, the warm air brushing her bare skin as she padded to the dresser. Opening drawer after drawer, she finally found what she was looking for.

She took a dark blue flannel shirt from the drawer, shook it out and slipped it on. The soft material fell to her thighs, the cuffs well past her hands. She rolled the sleeves up, buttoned the front and turned to listen. There wasn't a sound beyond the slight sigh of wind and the gentle patter of rain on the glass.

Kristin crossed to a side door and looked into a small room. She reached for the light switch, snapped it up and saw Alex's study, a room lined with books and dominated by a computer console on the wall shared by the bedroom. But Alex wasn't there.

She hesitantly stepped inside and inhaled, not at all surprised to find that the room held the essence of Alex. She looked around, then crossed to the nearest bookshelf filled with well-used volumes ranging from how-to books to thick biographies of famous people. One whole section was on Europe, another on South America, still another on Russia.

On shelves next to the computer sat a set of Jake Warner books. She scanned the titles and found *The Day of Reckoning* near the middle. If they were filed in order, she was reading a book that Alex had written about halfway into his career. She touched the nearest volume but didn't take it.

She looked at awards hung on the wall framing French doors—awards that ran the gamut, including Hearts of the West Award for his last three books. His first award had been for *The Day of Reckoning*. "Good going, Webb Tanner," Kristin murmured. She ran her fingers through her loose hair but stopped when she heard a door close.

Her heart beat faster as footsteps came through the house, getting closer. She moved quickly toward the doorway to the bedroom and got there at the same moment Alex emerged from the shadowy hallway.

He saw her, stopped and simply looked at her, his dark clothes blending eerily with the darkness behind him.

"Where were you?" she asked in a voice so unlike hers that she could have sworn someone else had spoken.

He shrugged and took off his jacket, tossing it onto a chair by the door. "At the town meeting."

The admission brought back all the difficult issues Kristin had denied while she and Alex made love. She hugged herself tightly, her fingers pressing into her upper arms. "How did it go?"

"It was ugly. Everyone's upset, angry, fed up and hurting."

And so are you, she thought as she filed away every detail of the man across the room. Her gaze swept over the strong legs in well-worn denim, the broad shoulders under a natural knit sweater, the clean lines of his face. And she found herself matching them with the memories of their lovemaking. His imprint was on her as surely as if he had branded her. "I should have gone with you," she said simply, and meant it.

Alex came closer, the low light intensifying lines etched between his eyes. Stopping at the foot of the bed, he touched the brass but looked right at Kristin. "Why?"

Kristin didn't want to say that he might have needed her with him, so she said the obvious. "To hear what was being said, to see if there was anything we could use to figure out how to stop what's happening up here."

"Your friend was there—Lewis. Needless to say, the townspeople weren't too happy having anyone associated with Restcorp there." He stroked the brass tubing of the bed, never taking his eyes off Kristin. "We need to look through the cottage, Kristin."

"All right. I can call him." She swallowed hard. "But *you* need to see Dailey."

When he would have protested, she cut him off. "Alex, you have to. You have to know . . . one way or the other, for your sake. For your sake."

His hand closed over the brass so tightly that his knuckles dotted with white. "I don't know if I want to."

She went to Alex, close enough to hear his breathing and see the fine network of lines at his eyes. "Yes, you do," she said softly.

He touched her with a single finger at the base of her throat, covering the pulse that beat there. "How do you know what I what?"

"If it was me—if he was my friend—I'd need to know."

His hand fell from her, and she felt as if a bond of iron had eroded and cracked, leaving her alone and unsupported.

"And you could put a friend in prison?" he asked tightly.

She shrugged, but nothing could pass the constriction in her throat. What could she say to Alex? His loss would be staggering if Dailey was the one doing the damage—if Dailey was the one who had killed Bob. "I—I don't know," she finally managed.

"Neither do I." Alex sighed and abruptly reached for Kristin.

She closed her eyes, sinking into the circle of protection in his arms. This was the place where she didn't have to think, reason or face reality. She could let go and experience that incredible sense of belonging that she only found here. Alex's touch could make the world stand still.

His voice, soft and low, surrounded her. "We'll get things settled in the morning. But until then..."

"What?" She looked up at Alex. "Until then, what?"

"Be with me," he said in a rough whisper.

"Yes," she whispered, and stood on tiptoe to find his lips with hers.

With a low groan Alex answered the caress, meeting fire with fire. She held more tightly to him, her breasts crushed against his chest, her heart racing against his.

This man could become an obsession, she realized, then admitted there was no "could become" about it. He already was an obsession. Already she couldn't imagine existing without him. His hands stroked her, exposing every inner desire she'd felt since the first time she'd looked at him.

Then suddenly they were on the bed, tumbled in the mussed covers, and Alex was over her, looking down at her, his eyes burning with desire. And Kristin felt her body tighten in anticipation, yearning toward him. His gaze dropped to her breasts straining against their blue flannel covering, tautening as if he'd actually touched them.

With merely a look from him, she felt her blood turn to liquid fire. A heaviness descended within her, then a throbbing emptiness that almost screamed to be filled by Alex.

She worked her hands under his sweater to the rippling muscles of his chest, then lower to the soft line of hair. "There are so many ways that I could have been kept from knowing you," she whispered unsteadily. "And I never would have realized that you were in this world."

He shuddered as her hands moved lower, following the line of hair to tuck into the waistband of the suddenly restrictive Levi's. She tugged until the fastener popped. Alex groaned, and Kristin felt a rush of delicious power that she could elicit this response from him. She loved him for it.

Love. It sounded so right in her head that she almost said it aloud as she watched Alex strip off his clothes and relished the sight of him.

But in what seemed the space of a heartbeat he was back with her and no words seemed necessary. He lay beside her, and it was his turn to watch as Kristin slowly undid the buttons of the shirt she was wearing—his shirt. One by one they slid through the buttonholes until, as she reached for the last one, Alex covered her hands with his and helped her undo this final barrier. Gently he pushed aside the soft fabric, and his eyes caressed her, sweeping over her obvious arousal as her nipples peaked.

But Kristin felt no embarrassment at her blatant need. Everything felt right with Alex. His hand found her breast, catching her nipple between his thumb and forefinger, and she gasped, the sound almost a sob. Capturing his hand with hers, she guided it lower, across her rib cage, and he continued farther on his own, spanning then stroking the tensing muscles of her abdomen.

"You're so beautiful," he murmured as his hand moved even lower and she cried out, capturing him between her thighs. "So beautiful," he repeated, and he was over her, covering her, filling her in one strong thrust.

For a heartbeat neither of them moved, then Kristin lifted her hips, willing Alex to go deeper, to fill her more completely. Their rhythm started slowly and built until Kristin cried for more, and in the next moment, the two of them became one, soaring in body, soul and spirit.

Later, when Alex's breathing became regular and deep, Kristin lay by his side wide awake. *I love you, Alex Jordan,* she whispered to herself. And she didn't know what to do about it. Sometime later, in the dimly lit room, she felt Alex stir. He draped his arm around her middle and pulled her back against him. Despite his height, the two of them fit together as neatly as if they'd been born for it.

"I've got to make this quick," Alex said in a low voice close to the telephone receiver.

"What's the rush?" Devereaux asked.

Alex stood in his study next to his computer. He glanced over his shoulder through the bedroom door, at the light of dawn just beginning to creep through the curtainless windows. There seemed no reason to tell Devereaux about sharing the night with Kristin. Even as the thought entered his head, Alex admitted he'd shared more than just the night. He'd shared himself in a way he never had before. And when he'd woken with her cuddled against him, it had given him a sense of happiness that he had thought he'd lost forever.

Quickly, Alex told Devereaux about what they'd found in San Francisco. "I don't know what the tie-in is with Fletcher and Vespar Bay beyond the obvious—a hideout," he said in conclusion. "But I'm going to find out today. What I need you to look into is a man named Ben Lewis. He used to work for the government—maybe CIA or FBI. I don't know. Find out as fast as you can why he's up here."

Devereaux was silent for a long moment. "Alex, what else is going on?" he asked finally.

Alex swallowed hard. "Bob Lipton died from the fall."

"Damn shame. I'm sorry."

"So am I."

"Do you need help?"

He exhaled and stared out the windows at the ocean in the distance. "I don't think so. Not yet."

"Just yell if you do."

"Sure. Don't forget about Ben Lewis."

"I'll get on it right away."

"Thanks," Alex said, and hung up. He rubbed his eyes with the tips of his fingers and leaned back against the computer table.

Kristin had come out of a deep sleep with a start. She bolted upright in the bed, her eyes wide and searching, scanning a room grayed by the pale morning light. In a rush she remembered last night, and she turned, her hand held out, but Alex's spot on the bed was empty. Cautiously Kristin reached to touch the imprint of his head in the pillow. It still felt vaguely warm.

She listened for a minute then pushed back the sheet and blanket and got out of bed. Barefoot, she padded over and retrieved the discarded shirt and slipped it back on. She walked to the study door and stopped when she saw Alex standing by the computer, his head down, his eyes closed. He wore only Levi's, zipped but unbuttoned at the waist. She realized as she looked at him that she would never see him in the same way now that she'd known him as a lover, after she'd been held and loved with such exquisite gentleness.

"Alex?"

He turned with a jerk. "You're awake."

"Yes. You weren't there, and I thought you might have left again." She suddenly felt awkward, uncertain whether to stand where she was or follow her instinct to walk right into his arms. She compromised by going to him but not touching him. "I'm glad you're here."

"And I'm glad you're here." He touched her cheek lightly. "Since we're both awake, we should get started on this investigation. And since you're the professional, what should we do first?"

She pushed her toes into the carpet nap. "See if we can get into the cottage." She took a breath as his fingers lingered at the corner of her mouth. "And you have to find out what you can about Dailey."

Surprisingly, he simply nodded. "Why don't you find Lewis and see if we can get into the cottage to look around? I'll get in touch with Dailey." He looked at the wall clock that showed six-thirty. "Dailey will still be at home. How about Lewis?"

"I don't know," she said. His hand fell to her shoulder and his fingers began to knead her muscles there. "I can call Restcorp."

Alex's hand on her stilled. "I was wondering about something. Do you suppose there was another robbery and fire around the third of July?"

She'd wondered the same thing. "All Fletcher's other trips to the city were linked with robberies," she said, nodding. "I can go back to the city to look into the newspaper files, I suppose. Or I could call my boss—"

He stopped her. "I know where we can find out: Len. He keeps all sorts of old newspapers for the school paper drives. If we're lucky, he'll have one."

"After three months?"

He smiled down at her. "We're a small town here, Kristin. We have two paper drives a year at the school, in November and in June. In between, Len keeps the old papers in a shed behind the store. Could you go and look? I'll call him and tell him you're coming."

"What are you going to be doing?"

"Finding Dailey. Then I'll meet you at the cottage." He checked the wall clock. "How about meeting at noon? I don't know how long it will take to track down Dailey." He looked back at Kristin. "If I need you, will you be at the Donaldsons' house?"

"After I see Len. I'm still hoping that Mrs. Dixon might call. I hope she didn't try last night." She felt heat stain her cheeks at the memory of how she'd spent her night. "I didn't think of her at all."

Alex adjusted the loose collar of the shirt around her throat, and his fingers lingered there. "Neither did I, love." He smiled down at her. "I never expected this shirt to look so good on anyone, either."

Kristin reached up, gave Alex a quick kiss and drew back. "If you wore it, it had to look good."

"Do you think you might be a bit prejudiced?" he asked, his smile faltering.

"Just honest," she said, and ran back into the bedroom.

"Alex said you'd be wanting to look at the old newspapers," Len said as he unlocked the door to a gray wooden shed that sat under huge pines out behind his store.

While Kristin watched him, the cold breeze off the water cut through her plaid flannel shirt and Levi's. Her loose hair drifted across her face, and she pushed it back behind her ears. "We... he wanted some information from a San Francisco paper that was out during the summer."

Len pulled the door back. "What month?"

Kristin looked inside at neat five-foot-high stacks of papers, five of them to one side of the building, two on the other. The ones on the left seemed to be dailies, all black-and-white. The other ones had colored comics on the sides. "July, but..."

He pointed to the second pile from the left. "Right there. Anything else you need?"

"No thanks." She stepped into the shed and reached for the top paper.

Alex stared at Dailey. He wished he knew if he could believe him. He'd never been able to when they were boys. Dailey had been so good at making up lies. But this time...

Alex sat at the table in the small breakfast room in Dailey and Gwen's house on the southern edge of town. The clear morning light showed the strain on the long-haired man's face. "You can't say anything, Alex. You have to promise me."

"God, why didn't you tell me before?" Alex swallowed bitterness at the back of his throat. If this was true, he should have known. He should have sensed something. "I thought..."

"I know what you thought. That I was starting those fires." He spread his hands flat on the checkered tablecloth. "I'm not above it, you understand, but I didn't do it. I couldn't take the chance of someone getting hurt."

"I was hoping you weren't behind it." Alex stared down into his coffee cup. "Gwen know any of this?"

"No, not yet. I'll tell her... later."

"You've got a good wife, Dailey. A damned good wife."

Dailey leaned forward, his shoulders hunching. "That's why I can't risk losing her," he said with vibrating intensity.

"You wouldn't."

"You don't understand." His eyes looked bleak. "If I lose Gwen, I'd lose everything."

Alex understood completely. If Kristin left... He blocked the thought. Later. "She'd stick with you, man. You know that she loves you."

"Does she love me enough to understand that I've had a drug problem, that I used to shoot up? That I put anything into my arm that would give me a high, that would make life bearable? That's part of my past now, my so called 'free' days. Would she understand that I've lied to her since we met?"

"You *could* explain things to her."

He laughed harshly, the sound echoing in the pine-paneled room. "She thinks I was in Atlanta for a vacation. I was there for rehabilitation—rehab." He sat back. "She's talking about children. She'd be scared to death that I'm not stable, that I might start again at any time. And I could. That's why I see the group in Santa Rosa when I need to. They help. They understand. They've all been there and know you're never cured. You're off the junk and recovering—but you're never cured."

Alex had never had an inkling that Dailey used drugs. He stopped that thought. He hadn't been around Dailey for a while. The man was thinner, more intense, but the same kind of man. "I'll help any way I can, you know that."

"Thanks." Dailey exhaled heavily. "Can I ask *you* something?"

"Sure."

"What's going on between you and the house sitter?"

Alex almost lied, almost said nothing at all, but thought better of it. "She's becoming important to me, Dailey. Damned important."

"I thought so."

Kristin took the three papers for the third, fourth and fifth of July with her and went back to the Donaldsons' house. With the door bolted behind her, she went into the bedroom and put the papers on the bed.

She reached for the telephone and rang the Restcorp number. "Is Mr. Lewis there?" she asked the man who answered.

"Sorry, he's not in yet."

"Could I leave a message?"

"Sure."

"Tell him his watch is ready. He knows the number to call."

She hung up, pulled her legs up Indian-style on the bed and started at page one of the first paper. Ten minutes later she hadn't found a thing for the third or fourth of July. She opened the last paper, turned the first page and stopped.

The historic Nob Hill home of Parker Warren Stuart was destroyed in a spectacular fire early on the morning of the Fourth of July. The blaze totally engulfed the home, a guest house and servants' quarters.

Mr. Stuart, seventy-three, the only surviving member of the historic Stuart shipping family, was killed in the fire. His body was found by rescuers in his bedroom suite on the ground floor. He had been confined to a wheelchair for the past five years because of heart problems.

Several priceless works of art were lost, and the Stuart jewel collection has not been accounted for. Valued at nearly one million dollars, the collection of diamonds has been in the family since before the Second World War.

Police are still investigating, but the fire is believed to be related to several burglaries over the past five months. The chief of police will be making an announcement...

Fletcher stole one million dollars in jewels? Kristin stared at the story. What happened to the jewels? What had happened to the jewels from *all* the robberies? None of the clippings said a thing about their recovery. Then she understood. The jewels. Vespar Bay. Fletcher had hidden the jewels up here for safekeeping. But how did the fires figure into it?

She read the story again. When the telephone rang, the shrill sound made Kristin jump. She leaned across the bed and reached for the receiver. "Hello?"

"Kristin?"

She didn't recognize the soft, unsteady voice. "Yes?"

"It's Gwen."

Kristin sat back against the headboard. "Yes, Gwen."

"I've been trying to find Alex. He was here this morning talking to Dailey. I need to talk to Alex."

"I don't know where he is right now. What's wrong?"

"Remember I told you how Dailey takes off and disappears sometimes?"

"Yes."

"He's gone. He just walked out. Said he had to think, and he didn't go to school. I don't know..."

"Did he mention anything about Alex?"

"No, but since Alex was here earlier, I thought—" She sighed. "I tried his place, and there's no one there. I thought maybe you would have seen him."

"I will later, if you want me to give him a message."

Gwen hesitated. "Just tell Alex to call," she said after a moment. "I need to talk to him."

"Sure."

Kristin hung up and stared at the phone. Had Dailey run when Alex confronted him, or... She sat bolt upright. What if Dailey hurt Alex? She looked at the clock. Ten-thirty. She had to wait until noon to go meet Alex.

She looked briefly at the paper again, then sat back and reached for the Jake Warner book.

Jake knew that if he got behind Webb, he could get the drop on him, but the hill was made of rough granite, and bits tumbled downward with each step he took.

Closer, closer he crept. Then Jake saw Webb's back. The man was crouched behind a huge boulder, looking down over the valley. Jake knew he could shoot him right then, but he didn't. He saw movement down the hill and off to the side. A flash of color. Jake knew that the Indians had found them.

The Indians...

Alex drove past the Donaldson house at eleven o'clock. He almost stopped to see if Kristin was there, but he kept driving. He'd felt spent after talking to Dailey, and he'd gone to a phone booth. He'd tried to call Devereaux, but there was no answer. After three tries, he'd sat in the truck for a long time thinking. Finally he'd decided to head for the cottage.

He'd be there early, but he needed peace and quiet—a little time to think before Kristin arrived. God knew, with Kristin around he had a hard time doing any rational thinking.

He drove past the driveway for the cottage and parked his truck out of sight down the road. He walked into the woods, weaving silently through the trees, then he crossed the driveway, and headed toward the logging-camp side of the clearing where the small house stood. After just a few minutes he could see the cottage. No one was there—not Kristin, not Lewis. So Alex waited in the trees, out of sight, absorbing the peace of his surroundings.

Just a second later, he tensed as the door clicked open, and Lewis, in his uniform, walked out into the sun. Alex watched as the man stopped and stood very still. Then, instead of going up the driveway toward the road, he stepped off the porch and headed right for the spot in the trees where Alex was hidden.

Barely daring to breath, Alex pressed as close to the huge redwood as he could and didn't move. Lewis came close before Alex realized that he was going to the path that led to the logging camp.

He passed within ten feet of Alex without seeing him and disappeared into the thick forest. Alex watched until the dapper man was out of sight, then he sank back against the tree. He didn't want Lewis to know he was out here, if only because it looked a bit suspicious for a man to be skulking in the forest.

Alex stood straight. Lewis was gone, and with a glance at his watch, Alex realized that Kristin would still be a while in arriving. The last time they'd come to the cottage, the door had been unlocked. Alex looked around, saw no one and made his decision. It wouldn't hurt to look around while he was here, while he had the place to himself.

Quickly he stepped into the clearing and headed for the house. He took the steps two at a time, reached for the doorknob and turned it. It opened with a click, and the wooden barrier swung back silently.

Cautiously Alex looked inside, into a living room that filled the entire front of the house. The room made Fletcher's apartment look neat. Not only had all the furniture in this room been ripped apart, but the walls had holes at what appeared to be eighteen-inch intervals. Carpeting had been rolled to one side, and flooring was dislodged in spots. Pictures were propped against the ruined walls, and a trapdoor in the ceiling was pushed aside.

Alex stared at the scene, stunned. Then he understood. This house had been Fletcher's. And someone had ripped it apart looking for something. He knew in that instant. They had been looking for the jewels from the robberies, the jewels that had never been mentioned as recovered in the newspaper articles.

He took one step inside but froze when he felt something hard jab at his back. "Set a trap and catch a rat," a man's voice said.

Alex recognized the voice at the same time that he realized the pressure on his spine came from a gun.

Jake Warner bided his time. He knew his attacker would slip sooner or later. Then he'd be ready to take over. At least Emma wasn't here. At least she was

safe—until the enemy went looking for her. He touched
the gun on his hip...

Alex closed his eyes for a fleeting moment, got his bearings, then slowly raised his hand. He didn't have a gun.

"Just missed you in San Francisco at Fletcher's place,"
the voice said. "You and Kristin just couldn't give up. I
thought you would, but you couldn't, could you?" The gun
jabbed his back. "I actually hate having to do this, but I've
got no choice. You left me none, you and the girl." He
sighed, maybe with real sorrow, Alex didn't know. "First
I'll take care of you. Then I'll go get Kristin."

Chapter 12

The Hunter nudged Jordan sharply in the ribs. He was going to make this work, one way or another. He wasn't going to let anyone—not even Jordan—stop him.

"Turn slowly. Go down the stairs, then go right and across the grass to the trail that heads to the old logging camp."

The Hunter moved when Jordan did, staying behind him, more than aware of the size difference if they were to face each other.

"Another accident?" Jordan asked as he walked down the steps and onto the grass.

"This town deals better with accidents than with murders. You should know that better than anyone," the Hunter responded.

They walked in silence across the damp grass and into the forest. The air was cold and still. No wind, no noise, not even birds. A strangely unearthly feeling hung in the air as

they followed the path. Then the camp came into sight—th
mill and the mess hall. The Hunter stopped Jordan at th
side of the mess hall and half pushed him in the direction c
the front door. "In there."

Alex knew he had to act now or forget it. He started fo
ward, stumbled deliberately, and when he heard the ma
behind him swear, he knew where he was by the sound of h
voice. He gauged it right as he spun around and struck th
hand that held the gun. Hitting the metal with the heel of h
hand, he saw the gun fly sideways. He turned to run, ir
tending to head for the cliffs and the beach.

His attacker moved quickly, coming up behind him. Rigl
when Alex could hear the labored breathing, he felt the ma
hit him from behind, sending him facedown into the groun
no more than a foot from the steps to the beach.

He rolled and swung with all his might, cracking the othe
man in the head, but it didn't stop him. Hands were at h
throat, thumbs pressing into his flesh. Alex brought both h
hands up between the man's arms and with a sharp ou
ward movement, broke the stranglehold.

Alex scrambled up and headed for the steps. But befo
he could reach them, he felt another powerful blow in th
middle of his back. It sent him reeling forward toward th
edge of the cliff. It was all he could do to keep himself fro
flying over the edge.

Rolling to the side, he twisted and caught a glimpse of
huge rock coming right for his head. Then time stood stil
The world exploded into a million red shooting stars, pa
filled his whole body, and in that moment, he truly regre
ted only one thing—not being able to love Kristin for a lif
time.

He hit the ground, and the pain intensified in his left arm. Then his mind held nothing but the certain knowledge he had probably just died.

Jake Warner swung up onto his horse, which he'd left hidden behind the scruffy cottonwoods. When the screams of the tortured man rang in the air, Jake didn't react. The Indians could have Webb Tanner and do what they wanted to him. Tanner deserved everything he got. Jake had seen justice done, and now he was moving on.

The sun was low, its purple and red colors smeared in the sky that canopied over the desert floor. Totally alone, Jake rode slowly away from his past. He narrowed his eyes, looked ahead and nudged his horse. For a moment he wondered about his future. Then he shrugged and continued forward, never looking back.

Kristin dropped the book in her lap and stared down at the cover slashed with red and gold. Justice and truth had prevailed in the book. She just wished that life was that simple. A sudden convulsive shiver shot through her, and she tossed the book onto the bed.

She'd been waiting for over an hour, and it was making her so nervous she felt sick. With a glance at the phone, she muttered, "Come on, Ben, call."

Something fell in the front of the house, and Kristin found herself holding her breath. Nothing else sounded, and she sank back, exhaling. Her nerves were worse than tense. She glanced at the clock. Almost noon. She reached for the phone, dialed Alex's number, and when it rang for the sixth time, she put the receiver back in place. He must be on his way to the cottage.

She refolded the newspaper to expose the story on the Stuart robbery and death, then she stood. That was when she heard a shuffling sound. The cat? No, he wasn't big enough to do that. Carefully she started for the door that led into the kitchen. But before she could get there, a man stepped into the doorway, blocking the route. Ben.

"Hello, kiddo," he said with a smile.

Kristin rolled her eyes toward the ceiling. "Damn it, Ben, you scared me to death!" She moved back and sank down on the side of the bed.

He leaned against the doorjamb with one shoulder. "What's going on, kiddo?"

She almost started to tell him, but the phone rang. "Just a minute," she said, reaching for it. "Then we'll talk."

Ben nodded and watched Kristin.

"Hello?"

"A collect call from Mrs. Dixon," a small female voice said. "Will you accept the charges?"

"Yes, yes I will."

"Go ahead, please."

"Hello? Mrs. Delaney?"

"Yes, that's me."

"I'm Mrs. Dixon. Mr. Fletcher's landlady. My niece Lillie, told me that you came by and wanted me to call you I tried last night, but . . ."

"Thanks for getting back to me."

"I can tell you right now that I don't know where you uncle is. He hasn't been here for quite a while."

"I know. What I was wondering about was his friend. thought you might know his name?"

"Hunter, Mr. Hunter. I don't have any idea where he i though. He's only been by a few times."

"You've talked to him before?"

"Oh, yes. Such a nice man. Very well spoken, and he's got a flirty way with him. He always called me kiddo."

Kristin stood very still. "Ex-excuse me?"

"Kiddo. Such an old-fashioned expression. A very nice man, that Mr. Hunter. Nice looking, too."

Ben? Oh, God. Kristin stared at the wall by the bed and wished that she could breathe. She had to swallow hard before she could speak. "Oh, is he?"

"Very distinguished, with gray hair and a mustache."

"Th-thank you very much."

"Do you need—"

"Nothing, thank you, nothing else," Kristin said abruptly, and she put the receiver back in place, hating the way her hand made the plastic on plastic clatter.

"Something wrong, kiddo?"

She touched her lips with her tongue. The whole world, she wanted to say. But as she took a breath that hurt as it entered her lungs, she knew what she had to do. She had to get out of here, get to Alex and tell him.

"Wrong?" she echoed. "No, nothing." *Get him out of here,* she commanded herself. *Any way you can.* "I'm just tired. This whole thing..." She ran a hand over her face and made herself look at Ben. He looked the same, but everything had changed. "Maybe we can talk later."

When the phone rang again, she almost jumped out of her skin. "Just a minute," she muttered, and grabbed the receiver before Ben could do anything. "Hello?"

"Kristin, David here."

"David..."

"Two big things. Dailey Cook is a recovering drug addict. He was in Atlanta at a rehab center, and now he's in a support group in Santa Rosa. The other thing. Ronald Fletcher was mixed up with the government about a year ago. He got off. They couldn't prove anything, but the agent who found him was Ben Lewis."

Kristin tried to stay calm, to not give anything away to Ben. But it was hard, so hard. "Are . . . are you sure?"

"It's right here in front of me. It was right after that incident that Lewis left the Agency. I still don't really know why, but . . ."

"I know why." Kristin took a deep breath. "David . . ." She tried to think, to get something across to him that Ben wouldn't pick up on. "I'm glad you called. It looks like Dailey Cook might be behind all of this. He's got to be crazy. He obviously needs therapy, and I'm going to try and talk Alex Jordan into getting him to turn himself in."

"What are you talking about?" David asked.

"Sure, he'll do time eventually, but until then he needs help. A lot of help."

"Kristin, listen to me. The man's a recovering addict. He's in therapy now."

"Yes, I know he wouldn't turn himself in. He's crazy, David, really crazy. But he needs to get help."

"What's wrong?"

"A lot of therapy. Someone to look out for him."

"Are you in trouble?"

"God, yes. He really could hurt someone."

"Someone's there with you right now?"

"Ben just dropped by to visit, so I have to be going."

David breathed a soft curse and asked, "It's Lewis who's behind this, isn't it?"

"Yes."

"Does he have a gun?"

"I don't know."

"Does he know that you suspect him?"

"I'm not sure."

"I'm hanging up and calling the sheriff. Stall Lewis for ten minutes, and be careful." With that, the line went to a dial tone.

"I really have to go. Sure, I'll tell him. See you later," she said into the dead line. She hung up.

Kristin took a breath. *Look at him,* she instructed herself. *Just look at him.* She turned and felt thankful that he was still standing in the doorway. "That was David."

"So I heard." He stared at her for a long moment then slowly shook his head. "You know, don't you?"

She stood. "What are you talking about?"

His hand went into his pocket, and she knew even before he pulled it out that he had a gun. "Never mind." He looked almost regretful. "I was hoping you wouldn't, kiddo. I was really hoping that. I never wanted to see you hurt."

"Ben, please don't do this." She clutched her hands tightly in front of her so they wouldn't tremble. "You don't have to."

"Oh, but I do." He stood straight. "I do have to."

Ten minutes. Just ten minutes. Kristin thought about the sheriff and knew she had to do something on her own. She took one step toward Ben, and she could see his face tense.

"Don't do anything crazy. Not here."

"Ben . . ."

"Come on, kiddo. Let's go."

Buy time. Buy time. Alex would come, or the sheriff. Just keep Ben talking. "Why are you doing this?"

"Money. Not the reward, the money from the take from the robberies. I know you figured that all out when you were at Fletcher's place in the city." He actually smiled, a smug expression under his mustache. "I deserve the money. I found Fletcher and set him up here."

"Why here?"

"I happened to hear one of the agents mention coming here a few years back. He painted such a lovely picture—peace, quiet, no hassles, a distance from the city but close enough to drive." He shrugged. "The perfect place."

"Yes, perfect," Kristin agreed, listening past his words for sirens. No, David would have told them no sirens. "It's wonderful here."

"Do you mean that?"

"What?"

Ben came a step toward Kristin. "I never figured you'd like a place like this."

Kristin stared at him. "I do," she said, and meant it. It only confused her more. The truth was she didn't want to leave here, not if it meant losing Alex. She had found a home—not a place but a person. And wherever Alex was, she wanted to be there. "It's . . . it's peaceful."

Ben laughed, a sharp, intrusive sound. "God, I can't believe we're standing here talking about this place." He glanced at the gun. "Under the circumstances, I figured you'd be begging."

"Did Fletcher beg?"

His head jerked up. "Fletcher? No, he just hid the whole damned take from the robberies then tried to double-cross me. I don't expect you to believe me, but it was an accident, him falling. Lipton wasn't. I'll admit that."

"Why did you have to push him?"

"He'd figured out too much, and he wasn't about to keep quiet."

She trembled and hugged her arms around herself to keep it from showing. "And he was on the cliffs?"

Ben looked confused for a minute. "Actually I was trying to get him away from the camp. He found me there looking through the buildings. Then he remembered seeing me with

Fletcher. I thought I'd stayed out of sight when I was up here, but he'd seen me from his boat. He realized there was some connection when he ran into me at the camp. He would have figured out everything sooner or later.''

"Poor man," she breathed.

"Poor fool. He couldn't stay out of it, not any more than you or Jordan could."

That drew up every nerve in her body. "I—I was doing it as a job. You know that."

Suddenly Ben seemed anxious to go. He motioned with the gun. "I want to get this over with."

Kristin hesitated. Buy time, any way you can. "Where are we going?"

"For a ride," he said cryptically. "Now, kiddo. *Now.*"

She looked him in the eye and knew he meant it. She would have to find another way to stall. She took a step toward Ben, and as he backed up toward the refrigerator, a howling scream echoed all around. A gray blur shot through the air, and Boy launched himself from his vantage point on top of the refrigerator right at Ben.

Cat and man tumbled backward into the kitchen, the fur ball obliterating Ben's face and head. Landing in a squalling pile on the hard tile, the cat and man completely blocked Kristin from escaping through the front door. Leaving curses and fur flying behind her, Kristin jumped to clear Ben's thrashing feet and ran through the service porch to jerk open the back door.

She stumbled out onto the deck and steadied herself. With one quick glance around she ran across the deck, jumped over the side and landed squarely on the soft grass. As soon as her feet were under her, she took off running toward the side of the house.

"I've got Jordan!" Ben shouted from somewhere behind Kristin. "Keep going, and you'll never see him again!"

She stumbled, lurched forward, almost to the trees, not believing him, not wanting to believe him. "He was going to meet you at the cottage, wasn't he?" Ben yelled.

His words stopped Kristin dead within four feet of the garage and the driveway. She gulped in air and turned. Ben was on the deck, his gun leveled at her. Clenching her hands into fists, she stared at him.

"Stay where you are, kiddo. I don't want to shoot you."

She didn't move. Not Alex. Please, not Alex. Her eyes never left Ben as he jumped off the deck and came toward her across the damp grass.

He came within ten feet of her. "Good girl." He took another stride closer. "So Jordan is important to you."

She bit her lip, wishing that her heart would quit bouncing against her ribs. Alex. She couldn't lose him now. Not now, not ever. "Where is he?"

"I'll show you." He motioned to the front of the house. "Where are your car keys?"

Kristin hadn't used the rental car since that first day in the town, and she had to think for a minute about the keys. "Under the front seat," she said as she walked slowly in front of Ben past the garage.

"Bad idea. Heaven knows who could steal it." Ben chuckled.

Could she hate anyone the way she thought she hated Ben at that moment? She didn't have to think twice about it. Yes.

When they got to the car, Ben went around to the passenger side and got in, never taking the gun off Kristin. "Get in, kiddo." When she hesitated, his voice hardened. "I mean it."

Kristin slipped in and with trembling hands searched under the seat for the key. When she felt the cold metal, she prayed that her hand wouldn't shake too badly when she tried to put it in the ignition. "Where's Alex?" she asked as she started the car.

"I told you, we're going to see him."

"Ben..."

"Let's go," he muttered, and motioned behind them with the gun.

Kristin stalled the car twice backing out, and by the time she was on the road heading north, she could barely breathe. "I don't understand why you're doing this, Ben."

"You know about me and Fletcher."

"Why set fires up here?"

They were nearing the Restcorp gates, and Ben motioned Kristin to keep going, but he slouched lower in his seat. The gun never moved from its aim at a spot just below Kristin's ribs. "The take from the robberies is hidden around here. It could be anywhere from the cottage to the logging camp."

"I still don't understand," she said, wondering if anyone at the Restcorp trailers would see her and remember when the sheriff asked. *If* he asked. She looked ahead, glancing surreptitiously in the rearview mirror, hoping to see someone behind her. The road was clear.

"I used the fires, the thefts, the explosions to stop Restcorp, to keep them busy with phase one so they wouldn't begin to bulldoze the camp. They plan to, and I had to know where Fletch hid the jewels before I could let them do that."

It all made perfect sense to Kristin now, horribly perfect sense. "And that's what you're after, what you've always been after."

"That's it, kiddo." He motioned to the side road that led to the camp. "Pull in there and drive until I tell you to stop."

"The car won't make it . . ."

"I know. Just go until it gets stuck in the soft ground."

Kristin walked into the central clearing of the camp after the car had finally gotten stuck in muddy clay soil back about two hundred yards. Ben had the gun at her back, and when she stopped, he said softly, "To the old mess hall."

"Where's Alex?" she asked for about the tenth time.

"You'll see, kiddo," he said, and pushed at her with the gun at the small of her back.

Then she had a horrible thought that almost stopped her heart. It *did* stop her from walking, and she turned, not caring that the gun was within inches of her middle. "Ben, did you . . . ?" She could hardly think the word, much less say it. "Is he dead?"

Ben stared at her as if he hadn't heard her, then shot his free hand out straight hitting her a stinging blow in the shoulder. "Move. Now."

She turned, foolish tears burning her eyes, and she tumbled down the overgrown path to the old building. She bit her lip hard, her whole being hurting in the most awful way when she thought of something happening to Alex. If he wasn't alive, if there wasn't an Alex Jordan in this world, she didn't want to be here, either. There was no home at all.

At the entrance to the building Ben kicked the door open, then nudged Kristin inside. Chilly and silent, the building echoed with emptiness. Ben came to her side, and she looked right at him.

"Kristin, you know that I like you. I always did. I've always wanted things to work out for you."

"Tell me where Alex is and let us go. Tell me where Alex is, and you can get your jewels and leave."

"I don't have them. I still don't know where they are, but I will. I need time. More time." Without warning, Ben caught Kristin by the upper arm. "I can't let you leave, kiddo, I can't," he said, his voice touched with a strange tinge of sorrow. "I wish I could. Damn, I wish I could."

He pulled her toward the kitchen, its door wide open.

"So you'll kill me for the jewels?"

He stopped, and his fingers dug into her arm. "Yes. And I truly regret it."

"Are the jewels worth killing people?"

"They're worth everything, kiddo, everything," he said softly and motioned her to the door of the pantry. "Unlock it and open it."

She fumbled with the simple latch, her fingers shaking so badly that they almost refused to do what was needed. Then she had it, and she opened the door. Daylight from the kitchen windows filtered into the interior of the six-by-eight-foot storage room, and Kristin gasped.

Alex lay sprawled on the bare wooden floor. Eyes closed, he didn't move. One arm lay twisted at an odd angle from his body.

"He's still alive," Ben muttered as she ran into the small room and dropped to her knees by Alex.

This close she could see the matting of sticky blood on the left side of his head just above his ear, an abrasion that cut across his left cheek.

"Alex," Kristin whispered. Gingerly she touched his throat, and her relief was enormous when she felt his pulse—a strong, sure beating. She slipped her hand down to his chest where his jacket parted, needing to feel that steady rising and falling under her palm. She looked back to the door. "What did you do to him, Ben?"

He shrugged. "He ran into a rock."

"He needs help. You can't just ..."

"Yes, I can. I have to," he said softly. "Don't you understand?"

"I don't understand killing," she said shakily, scrambling to her feet. "God, you know that better than just about anyone."

"Jerry Rule knows all about it, too, doesn't he?"

She felt giddy, light-headed, as if the whole world had begun to float. "You ... you ..."

"Too bad you won't be unconscious while you're in here."

"Damn you! You're ..."

"No recriminations, kiddo." He backed up as he spoke, one hand on the door. "Life's not always fair. Hell, it seldom is." Then he was out in the kitchen.

Kristin realized immediately what he was going to do, and she sprang toward the door as it began to swing shut. But she wasn't fast enough. It slammed, and she ran into it full force with the flats of her hands. All the light was shut out, and in the darkness she heard the bolt click into place. With her hands curled into fists, she beat on the solid wooden barrier. "Ben, please, don't," she screamed. "Let us out!"

"Sorry it has to be like this," Ben said, his voice muffled by the door. "It'll be over before you know it."

Over? She fell back, groping in the dark until she found Alex. She knelt there, reaching to touch him. "Alex? Alex?" She tugged at his shoulder. "Please, wake up."

His stillness terrified her. Awkwardly she touched his face, then the sticky dampness of matted hair and a puffiness in his scalp. "Alex?" she breathed. "Alex."

She sank back on the hard wooden floor, tugging until she had Alex cradled on her lap. Wait, just wait. Someone will find us. Someone will come. She stroked Alex's hair at h forehead. The sheriff, David, someone. It would just be a matter of time.

She remembered a childhood fact scale—three weeks without food, three days without water, three minutes without air. Food she could do without. Water wouldn't matter for a long time. She had plenty of air. The pantry wasn't anywhere near airtight.

She stiffened when she heard footsteps. Maybe Ben had changed his mind and come back to let them out. Kristin began to stand, to ease Alex off her lap, when she heard a strange sound outside the door. A sloshing, as if water was being splashed around. Water. Why? She inhaled and felt her throat constrict. Not water. Something peculiar; something pungent. Gasoline!

"Ben?" His name came out in an almost indistinguishable croak. She stood in the middle of the room, the weight of Alex against her foot. "Ben!"

A hiss, a whoosh, then smoke mingled with the gasoline odor. Fire!

Chapter 13

Kristin felt fragmented as raw fear exploded in her. Ben was going to take care of her and Alex—burn them to death by setting fire to the building. Blindly she groped for the door, felt it under her hands and pounded as hard as she could against it. "Ben! Ben!"

She moved back, lunged at the door and only felt it give slightly. Again and again she hit the barrier with her body but in the end it held. Frantically she felt for the hinges Outside. No chance of knocking them loose.

She groped to her right, her hands running over the shelves, then the back wall. Bare. The left wall. Nothing.

She looked to her right, and her stomach contracted when she realized she was back at the door. She could tell from very faint glow outlining the barrier top, bottom and sides an orange-yellow halo that shimmered. Flames.

She leaned against the wood, wood that was becoming ominously warm. This couldn't happen. Not now. Not t her and Alex. "Oh, Alex," she whispered, afraid to inhale very deeply of the pungent mixture of gasoline and smoke.

"Kristin?" The sound of her name from the darkness was more of a groan, but she spun around.

She couldn't see anything. "Alex?"

She heard shifting, a moan, then a muffled "Yes."

Dropping to her knees, she inched forward, waving her hands out into the darkness until she felt solid life under her hands. His arm, then his chest. He was sitting up, leaning against the side wall, and she literally fell forward to get to him.

He groaned, the action shuddering through his body at the same time his arm circled her. "Wh-what happened?"

She held him, needing that moment of connection before she could find any words. She had to force herself to move back, but she didn't break contact. She never let go of his arm. "Alex, are you all right?"

"I—I . . . think so. I don't understand. . . ."

She was close enough to feel his breath on her face, and she could almost make out the deeper shadows of the man. "Ben locked us in the pantry and set fire to the building. We have to get out now."

He struggled to sit straighter, and the groan that came from him was almost primeval. "Oh, God, my arm." He sucked in air when he moved, and she could tell he tested his arm. "Broken, maybe. And my head . . ." She felt his body shudder. "Damn him," he groaned. His arm moved free of her hold, and his hand touched her throat, then her face. She could feel the unsteadiness in his touch as his fingers rested on her cheek. "Did he hurt you?"

"No, I—I'm all right, but we have to get out. He's trying to kill us."

Alex drew her toward him, then his lips were on her chin, then on her mouth. The kiss was unsteady, but infinitely reassuring to Kristin. She drew back, framed his face with her hands and whispered, "I love you, Alexander Jordan."

"And you've got awful timing," he muttered roughly.

"The worst," she murmured unsteadily. "But if we...if we don't make it, I wanted you to know."

His good hand covered hers. "We'll make it, love. We have to. I didn't go through all of this to find you just to have someone like Lewis end it before it began. And we aren't dead yet." His fingers found her hair and tangled in the strands at her shoulder. "Help me to my feet, and I'll try the door."

"It's no use. It's solid, despite the condition of this place."

With a shuddering sigh, Alex whispered, "Any other ideas?"

"Can't A. V. Jordan write his way out of this?" she asked with a stab at humor.

"If it were Indians, maybe, but..." She heard him inhale, and his hand on her shoulder tightened to become almost painful. "There has to be some way..." He moved abruptly, sucked in a sharp breath. "Help me up."

Kristin braced herself with her hands flat on the floor to stand, but stopped when she felt something strange. A gap in the floor. Warped wood? It felt small, but she ran her finger along it to a corner, a straight line of two feet, then another corner. A door. A trap door!

"What is it?" Alex asked.

"A trap door. An opening in the floor."

He moved by her, almost hitting her in the shoulder. "Where?"

She found his hand and guided it to the gap. "Feel here."

"You're right."

Kristin crouched on her knees, found the edge again and tried to force her fingers into the gap to tug the wood back. "It's…it's too narrow. I can't get my fingers in it." She had a thought. "I've got a nail file…" She went through her pockets, found the file and pressed it into the slot. She wiggled it, but the frail metal snapped. "It broke."

Alex moved back, and she could hear his quick intake of air. "Here," he finally said, and almost struck her in the arm with something. She groped for it. "My keys."

She closed her hand over three or four keys tied together with a leather thong. Quickly, she found the largest and pressed it into the slot. She wiggled it back and forth, and it didn't do a thing at first. Then the wood shifted ever so slightly. "It's moving," she said, and Alex was right by her, feeling the wood with his hand.

Trying to work the key farther under the wood, she pressed her fingertips into the gap and could feel the underside with the tip of one finger. Pushing as hard as she could and ignoring the scrape of wood along the back of her knuckles, she pushed until her hand wedged under the heavy door. Suddenly it pulled straight upward, and Alex had it off her hands. The door fell backward against the wall.

Alex's breathing sounded sharp and uneven in her ear. "Are you all right?" she asked him.

"Fine. What's down there?"

She looked down into a black abyss, then reached into it, but felt nothing. Shifting until she was flat on her stomach facedown over the hole alongside Alex, she pushed her hand down into the unknown. Nothing but cold. Cold? "It's cold down there. Maybe it's a cellar or something like that."

She gasped when a rumbling roar sounded outside the pantry, and a whooshing sound skittered above them somewhere. Alex touched her, his hand on her back. "We'll make it," he breathed near her ear. "We will. I promise."

She nodded, knowing he couldn't see it. "We have to." She waved her hand around and her knuckles knocked on the side of the opening and what felt like a narrow step. "There, Alex. A step or ladder or something like that."

The smoke was getting stronger, and now she could hear the faint snapping hiss of burning wood. She turned, could make out his silhouette now, and she touched his face, unnerved to find it sleek with sweat, yet cool.

"You get down there. See what it is." He trembled under her touch. "I'll wait here."

"You can't..."

"I have to. I can't use my arm at all. Find out what's down there, then come back for me."

"I love you." She touched her lips to his, needing the support, then she turned from him and reached out for the hole.

Adjusting herself to the size, she threw her legs over the side and slid down into nothingness, supporting herself by her hands flat on the floor on either side of the opening. Suspended over a hole that seemed bottomless, she kicked sideways and struck her ankle on the step. Lurching to her left, she stepped on the support, letting her weight test its strength. Although it creaked, it held. She put both feet on it, held to the side and looked back to Alex, a dark shape near the side. "I'll be back."

"Go, Kristin, quickly."

She moved her right foot down, found another stair, tested it, then tried to find a third step. She felt nothing at first, then something solid was under the sole of her tennis shoes. She worked her foot over it in broader and broader circles until she knew that she had found the bottom—hard ground.

"I'm down," she called. "It's only three steps." She kept up a running commentary while she explored, as much for her benefit as for Alex's. She reached out in front of her with her hands, and jarred her shoulders when she hit a wall. "A wall made of dirt, really hard. It feels like I'm in a hole."

She went less than a foot to the right. "Shelves," she called out, and finally realized what she'd found. "A root cellar, Alex, a root cellar."

"Find the vents or an outside door of some sort," he called. "And hurry."

Quickly she moved through the darkness around all four walls. "There isn't a door. I can't find one." She inhaled smoke beginning to thicken in the air even down here. "There isn't a door!" She reached in front and found the stairs.

"I can see something," Alex called from the darkness. "Where are you?"

"At the stairs."

"Face them, then look left and up about four feet on the wall."

She did as he said, and at first didn't see a thing. Then she felt certain she was hallucinating. A glow. Fire? No, it looked pale and weak. "What is it?" she asked as she moved slowly toward it.

"A vent, I hope," Alex said above her.

Gradually she could make out a strange texture to the light, as if it came through clogged mesh. She moved closer, bumped her foot on something in front of her and stooped. A box—rough wood, hinges, a lock.

"Kristin, quickly. Did you get to it?"

She stepped over the box and reached out. She felt screening. A ventilation space. "It is a vent with screening over it." She ran her hands along it. More than two feet wide, but blocked somehow. If she could work the screening loose, the vent would be big enough for a person to push through. But it seemed so small for Alex to get through.

She turned, feeling blindly for the stairs, and struck her toe on the box again. They could use it to stand on, if they had to. She nudged it over below the vent then groped for the ladder and hurried up.

The small space was filling with smoke, and a dull roaring sounded beyond the door. An orange-tinged glow outlined the door. "Alex?"

"Here, love, I'm here." He touched her, his hand on her cheek then cupping her chin. "Get back down there, and I'll come down."

"You can't with your arm..."

"I will," he said, and she believed him.

She scrambled back into the cellar and reached above her to the ladder top. She felt Alex's shoe, guided it to the step then moved back. She could almost make him out as he came down the ladder, willing him to make it with each step he took.

She gulped in air thickening with smoke with each passing second, and the roaring overhead grew. "Alex, hurry. Hurry!" She wished she could hold him and love him. All she wanted to do was to live, to be with him, to be able to tell him how important he was to her. "Hurry," she whispered.

Alex eased himself forward, felt the edge of the opening and started into it. Kristin had hold of his left foot, easing it down, and he felt the ladder with the toe of his shoe. H turned, easing back and down, being careful to keep his left arm against his side. He knew that if he moved it again, he'd feel that piercing pain that would shoot from the crown of his head down into his shoulders and back.

He'd been hurt before, but never like this. The side of his head throbbed with a life of its own, and his back ached right between his shoulder blades. But his arm was the focus of all the misery. One step at a time. He went down slowly, jarred his arm and bit his lip hard to keep from gasping. He felt an incredibly painful clicking in his shoulder. Broken. Something out of place. Damn it, he hurt like hell.

Gritting his teeth, he made himself keep going down until he felt ground under his feet. With all the strength that he could gather, he straightened. "Kristin?"

She was there, right by him, her hand on his shoulder, and he reached out. She felt so soft and vulnerable. Love. He'd never considered the idea very much until lately. Now, when the world was being consumed by fire, he knew that he'd finally found it. A love unlike any other in his life.

"Where's the vent?" he asked.

He felt her tremble, then move from his touch. "Over here," she said, her voice coming from five feet to the right.

He headed toward the sound, moving carefully to minimize the pain, then he saw a glow. Reaching to it with his good hand, he felt screening between him and the dull light. "This is the way we go."

"It's so small." Her voice echoed softly all around him, filling him completely.

"We'll get out of here," he found himself saying. "I can get through it." At least she could. He reached for her, needing to kiss her, trying not to think in terms of never again. Her taste filled him as surely as the sound of her voice had.

Her fingertips were on his lips. "I found a box to stand on."

He wanted to hold her and never let her go, but he didn't. "Let's do it." He reached for the screening and tugged. The action shot pain into his other shoulder, but he did it again and again until wood splintered, thankfully rotten wood, and the screen tore away from the framing. Something still blocked the hole, and he had to stretch to clear brush and dead limbs that lay over it. Pain seemed red and hot, and Alex concentrated on blocking it.

Kristin saw the glow grow as Alex cleared the opening, and she could make out the sky, strangely overcast, dark and gray. Then she realized it was smoke. "That's it. We can get out there."

"Come here," Alex said, taking Kristin by one arm "How far up is it for you?"

She went in front of Alex, tugged the box to center it right under the hole and climbed onto it. "I can make it."

A crash overhead and a roar that sounded like a tornado wind made Kristin jump. "It's going to burn to th ground," she breathed.

"Preferably without us in it," Alex muttered. "Ge going!"

She leaned up and pressed the flat of her hands on th frame, then reached outside, pulling at grass and sma brush. Then Alex's hand was at her waist, lifting her as sh tugged, and she slipped through the hole and into air fille with smoke, ashes and heat. She turned on her knees an looked back into the deep shadows of the cellar. "Ale come on."

She glanced at the building, its roof a canopy of flames and smoke, the walls glowing from the inside out. "Hurry!" she yelled. "Hurry!"

His hand was there, and she grabbed it, pulling as hard as she could. Slowly his weight raised, her heels dug into the ground for leverage, and she could feel him coming out. Then his head was there, his shoulders, pushing through a hole that seemed too small, too inadequate for the man's size. She pulled, jerking as hard as she could, and he came out, sprawling onto the ground.

He looked up at Kristin, his skin filmed with dirt and sweat. One hand clutched at his hurt arm. "Thank God for that box," he gasped.

Kristin stared at him and felt as if someone had struck her. *The box.* "Alex, the box. It could be what Fletcher hid. All the jewels and whatever they got from the robberies." She was on her knees beside him.

He reached for her with his good hand and pulled himself up to his knees, his lips white and compressed from pain. Then he was dragging her with him along the ground, working his way back, getting farther and farther from the roar and heat of the fire. "Come on. We have to get as far away from this as we can!" he yelled.

"The jewels..."

"Damn the jewels!" Alex reached for her, tangling his fingers with hers and holding on so tightly she almost cried out. "You and me. That's what's important."

And she knew he was right, so very right. "Yes, us," she said, and scrambled to her feet.

It took all of her strength to help Alex to his feet, then they broke into a run, heading for the stairs in the cliff, trying to get to the beach below. Ashes fell like snow all around, and the roar of wood being consumed thundered in her ears, mixing with her labored breathing.

At the top of the stairs Alex motioned for Kristin to head down, and he stopped. Sirens sounded on the air over the roaring fire. Someone was coming to help, but it was too late. Ben was gone, the building all but consumed. All that needed to happen was the final collapse.

She moved to go down the stairs and felt Alex jerk back. Looking up, Kristin didn't understand. Alex stood back, straight and still, his head pulled to one side. Then she saw the glint of a gun under his ear and behind, Ben.

"You aren't going anywhere yet, kiddo," Ben said, his gun pressing into Alex's jaw. "I never thought you'd do it," he muttered, his face smeared with sweat from the furnace-like heat of the fire.

Kristin took a step forward.

"Don't move any closer," Ben warned, and Kristin froze. "You can't just walk away from this."

She squinted her eyes at the glow behind Ben. "You can't do this."

"I need more time. The jewels..."

She knew right then how she could buy time. "I know where they are." She took another step toward Ben and Alex.

Ben pushed the gun more sharply into Alex's jaw, jerking his head back to expose the vulnerability of the big man. "You're lying. I've been looking for months."

"No, I'm not lying. You helped me find them." She pointed to the building. "They were there all the time. In the root cellar—the way we escaped. I almost fell over the box in the darkness."

Ben darted a look toward the building, and in that moment Alex twisted sideways, ramming his right elbow into

Ben's middle. Kristin dove for the gun as it flew through the air. She touched the metal, warm from Ben's hold, and she turned to the two men rolling on the earth near the bluff's edge.

"Stop it!" she screamed, and fired once in the air. Both men froze. Ben rolled to the side and got to his feet while Alex shifted back, his injured arm hanging at a horrible angle at his side.

Ben looked at Kristin—at the gun in her hand—and smiled. "And what do you think you're going to do with that, kiddo?"

She held the gun straight out in front of her. "Stop you."

"You and who else?" As if she didn't exist, Ben shrugged and looked at the building. "I've got time to get in there and get the jewels."

"No, stay put."

Ben moved to the side. "I'm going, kiddo, and you're not going to stop me." He moved slowly, talking all the time, circling past Alex and Kristin. "Bye-bye, kiddo," Ben said, touching his forehead with the tips of his fingers.

"The building won't hold," Alex muttered, clutching at his left shoulder.

"It will for another minute or two," Ben said with a smile. "Long enough."

Alex shook his head. "You're a fool."

"We'll see," Ben said, moving backward and breaking into a run.

Sirens were close now, their high-pitched screams rending the air, and Ben ran toward the opening of the root cellar.

"Ben," Kristin screamed. "Stop!"

He didn't. He headed for the hole, and he was within ten feet of it. Kristin tightened her finger on the trigger, took aim, but stopped. It was as if she were watching an old movie, all yellows and browns—Ben spotting the hole, heading for it, and just as he got near the space, a rumbling sound vibrating through the air.

Slowly, ever so slowly, Kristin saw the wall of the gutted building begin to sway inward, then outward, the glowing wood framed by leaping flames. It undulated, then rippled as it began to collapse from the top to the bottom. "Ben!" she screamed. "Ben!"

He stopped and looked up as the wall slowly collapsed, hiding him in the swirl of dust and ashes.

"No!" she screamed, and the wall came tumbling down with an unearthly roar. Flaming wood piled over the ground, distorting everything in waves of heat and fire.

Alex stumbled to his feet and reached for Kristin. She let him take the gun from her lax fingers, let him toss it away from them and let him gently gather her to him. She sagged against him, grateful when one large hand pressed her head into his chest and the fire was shut out. All she could hear was his heart thundering against her cheek. All she could feel was his presence surrounding her.

Alex sat in the dark study alone around midnight. The last hours had been a blur, going to the hospital with Kristin, finding out his shoulder was dislocated and having it put in a support sling. They'd talked to the police, made out reports, and all the time Kristin had held onto his hand but seldom spoke unless asked a question. Shock and sorrow mingled in her expression.

The drive in the police car to his house had been in total silence. She'd looked at him when they stopped, then turned to the driver. "Could you go by where I was staying and make sure the cat has food and water?"

The deputy had agreed, then Kristin had gotten out of the squad car and helped Alex out. They were both spent, emotionally and physically, but there were things to be said, things to be settled.

When they'd lain in the shadows on the big bed, Alex had simply held her with his good arm until she fell into a heavy sleep. And he'd stayed with her, being there when she stirred, when she cried out. Finally, when her breathing had become regular, he'd come in here and sat in front of the still computer.

Kristin was his life. He knew that with a certainty that he had seldom known in his life. He wanted her with him here or wherever she would be with him. When she woke, they'd talk. He'd tell her how he felt then let her decide.

His shoulder throbbed, but he didn't want to take a pain pill, not until his life was straight. He ran a hand over his face and jumped when the telephone by the computer rang.

"Lots of excitement up there?" Devereaux asked.

"Enough."

"Are you all right?"

"Just a sore shoulder."

"What about Kristin Delaney?"

"She'll be fine."

"I guess it's too late to tell you that I found out that Fletcher and Lewis knew each other?"

"Way too late."

There was silence, then Devereaux said softly, "If you want to talk, I'm here." And he hung up.

Alex set the receiver back in its cradle and stared into the darkness.

The phone rang again after only a minute, and he caught it on the first ring. "Devereaux?"

"No, it's me, Jessie."

"Hi, Jess." He was pretty certain he knew why she was calling. "What's up?"

"That's what I'm calling for. I heard about what's been happening up there, about you being in some fire or something. Are you all right?"

"I'm fine, Jess."

"How about the book?"

"It didn't burn up, if that's what you mean."

"Is it done, or have you been too busy being a hero, yourself?"

Alex almost said that no, it wasn't done, but he stopped himself. In that moment he knew that the book was done. It just had to be put into the computer. "Yeah, one more day. I'll send it out Express Mail."

"Good boy, Alex. Are you going to tell me what happened to Jake Warner?"

"It's his last book, Jessie." Before she could argue, he said, "I'll be sending another book with it. I want it out under the name of Alexander Jordan."

"What's it about?"

"My past. I want it published so I can get on with my future."

He hung up without giving her a chance to say anything else, and he turned on the computer. With one hand he began to slowly hit the keys on the keyboard....

Jake didn't move when Webb Tanner fell backward. He didn't make a sound. It was over, once and for all. Tanner was gone. He wouldn't come back to haunt him again.

"Jake?"

He turned to Emma right behind him, her eyes wide and shining with tears. "He's dead," Jake said.

"I know. I know," she sobbed as she came to Jake.

He held her tightly, trying to absorb some of her pain. Her trembling all but unnerved him. Emma looked up, her lips softly parted. "What now, Jake?" she asked in a choked whisper. "This is over. You'll get your five-thousand-dollar reward. Is that it?"

He framed her face with his hands and smiled. "No, that's not it. This is." And he kissed her, slowly, surely and thoroughly.

In one easy motion, Jake spanned Emma's tiny waist with his hands and swung his flaxen-haired woman onto the back of his pinto. Then he got into the saddle, felt her arms go around him and her face press to his back.

"Let's go and find our home," he said, and turned the horse westward.

As the sun sank slowly over the dead body of Webb Tanner, Jake rode into the deepening orange-red light with Emma. He wondered if any man had ever been as lucky as he was at that moment.

"You lucky dog, Jake," Alex murmured, and sat back. "I saved your life and gave you a happy ending." He stood, knowing he'd ended one part of his life. But he looked forward to the future.

He went silently into the bedroom, expecting to find Kristin still asleep, but she wasn't. In the softness of the shadows, he could tell her eyes were open and she was looking at him.

Kristin took in the sight before her. In only Levi's, with his chest bare, Alex prodded at something so elemental in her that she could barely breathe. Had there been life before this man? She couldn't remember now. He stayed in the doorway. "You aren't asleep?" he asked softly.

"No, just thinking."

"What about?"

"Gwen, Dailey, Ben..."

"I called Gwen earlier. Dailey came back. They talked...finally, and she's going to Santa Rosa tomorrow with him. She wants to get involved in the support group there, and in Dailey's recovery."

One weight lifted from Kristin's shoulders. She sat up, tugging at the cotton shirt she wore with clean jeans. Her bare feet pushed into the softness of the bed linen. "What about Ben?"

"Gone. They'll look for the jewels when the ashes have cooled. They might be lost, too."

Sorrow filled Kristin for a moment, then something settled in her. Perhaps an acceptance of fate, she thought. The same fate that had brought Alex into her world. "And you? Does the arm hurt a lot?"

"It's bearable." He came toward her, stopping at the side of the bed to look down at her. "How about you?"

"I'm fine." Trite words, she knew, yet she couldn't think of what to say, how to put her feelings into words. Would Alex understand when she finally found those words?

He came closer, stooped and brushed the tips of his fingers along her cheek. She shivered at the contact. "We made it, love, we really did."

She simply nodded, and he drew back.

Before he spoke again, he sat down by her but didn't touch her again. She could feel the heat from his body near hers and see each breath he took. His gaze lingered on her face, then met hers. "When we were locked in the pantry you said that you loved me. I said that I loved you."

That was all that had kept her going since the fire. "Yes."

"I also know what you said before about needing to keep moving. I understand, believe me, I do."

She touched her lips with her tongue, almost surprised that she couldn't taste Alex there. She was certain he'd become a part of her in every way. "That's the way my life's been since I was small. But..."

He touched her lips with his finger to still her words. "Four days isn't very long to know someone. Hell, it's a blink of an eye." He shook his head sharply. "I'm no good at this," he muttered, and stood. "I'll be right back." He turned from her and went into his study.

Kristin almost held her breath while he was gone. When he reappeared at the doorway to the study, he strode into the room, came back to the bed and tossed a plain brown box he was carrying onto the bed.

"I'm sending it out to Jessie tomorrow with the last Jake Warner book. I want you to read it before it goes out."

She looked up at him, and she felt her whole world settle and focus into sharp relief. "Do you know me well enough to ask?" she whispered.

He looked right at her. "Yes."

"I love you, Alexander Jordan," she said, and reached for him, drawing him down with her onto the bed. "Four days, four weeks, four years. The time isn't anything. It's what I've found right here with you." She brought her mouth within inches of his and looked deeply into his eyes. "Life has become very simple for me suddenly. I love you."

"That's not enough, Kristin."

She didn't move. "What?"

"It's not enough to love me or for me to love you. I want life with you—not a month or a year. A *whole* lifetime."

"So do I. A lifetime," she echoed. "I knew that when I thought we were going to die. All I wanted was to be with you forever. I don't care where. Here or anywhere."

Alex stared at her intently for a long moment, then his mouth found hers. It was a gentle kiss, but one that moved her as deeply as any they'd shared in the past four days.

She felt his hand spread on her back, and she rested her head on his shoulder. Home. Had she ever thought it would be encompassed in a person instead of a place? She tasted the side of his neck, whispering his name over and over again.

Carefully Alex eased her back, lying by her side. The clothes were awkward to be rid of because of Alex's injured shoulder, but within minutes they lay naked, her head fitting neatly into his unhurt shoulder. Home, she thought and turned to kiss him.

Her breasts tingled against his chest, and she heard Alex whisper that he loved her more than anything in the world. Then he cursed the support sling for his shoulder. He couldn't touch her the way he wanted to, he murmured against her throat, then lower between her breasts. So she touched him, savored him and knew him in ways she had never thought possible.

Epilogue

Emma and Jake were married at Fort Roberts and again headed west. When they found the tiny settlement of Rio del Sol in California near the Mexican border, they stopped their journey.

They built their life together on rolling grasslands that spread as far as the eye could see. Jake became the first sheriff for Lane County, and along with his Emma, his five children and eventually his sixteen grandchildren, he lived a long, contented life.

Jake Warner was home.

THE END

Kristin stirred in Alex's arms, realized he was sound asleep, and she turned. The box with his novel in it had been pushed to the floor. Carefully, she reached for it and lifted it up into the bed. She pushed the pillows up against the headboard, tugged the sheet up to her waist and, after snapping on the small bedside lamp, she opened the box.

For three hours she read, and finally she laid the last typed sheet in the box. With her head back against the headboard, she closed her eyes. After reading this book she knew Alex even better. She knew the compassion, the caring, the anger at death, the killings, the revenge, the love for his friends and his fears. And she loved him more and more.

"What are you thinking about?"

You, her heart said. *Loving you. Needing you.* She turned to Alex, and the sight of him in the soft light made her spirits soar. He made her complete. He made her whole. "How long have you been awake?" she asked. Carefully avoiding the swelling from his fall, she smoothed back the clinging curls at his temple with an unsteady hand.

His dark gaze never left her face. "For a while."

The feel of him under her fingertips made it difficult for her to speak. "Why didn't you say something?"

"I wanted to watch you, to let you read without interruption."

Carefully she put the lid back on the box and placed it on the bedside table. Then she turned and, supporting herself on one elbow, gazed down at Alex. "I've finished."

"And what do you think about it?"

She touched him again, taking pleasure in the traces of new beard she felt under her fingertips, in his body heat and in the pulse at his jawline. "It's you, a part of you," she whispered as she bent to taste the spot her fingers had touched.

He tried to shift onto his side toward her but ended up sinking back into the pillows, muttering, "I can't even look right at you with this damn thing on my shoulder."

"Lie still," she whispered. "Let me take care of that." And carefully she moved until she was over Alex, straddling his hips and looking down at him through the so-light. She touched the heat of his chest just above the sling, then she began to trace lazy circles around his nipple. She could feel his breath catch as his nipple peaked. His desires and needs grew as rapidly as her own, and she smiled down at him.

His good hand covered hers abruptly, stopping its movements. "I have to know one thing," he said in an unsteady voice. "And I'll never get to ask, if you keep doing that."

She sat very still. "What?"

"You've seen every side of me, the good and the bad. Will you live here with me?"

His heart raced under her palm, and twice she had to try to speak before the words would come. "Only if it's for the rest of our lives."

"Yes," Alex said, and his hand lifted, reaching out to Kristin until its warmth gently covered her heart. "Welcome home, love. Welcome home."

* * * * *

Silhouette Intimate Moments

COMING
NEXT MONTH

#269 ONCE FORGOTTEN—Jan Milella

Claire's marriage to Jack had fallen apart several years ago. Now she was losing her daughter, too. Little Meghan needed a kidney transplant, and time was quickly running out. Jack was a doctor, perhaps the only one who could help Meghan. Soon Claire found herself hoping that together they could heal old wounds and remember a love once forgotten in this desperate race against time.

#270 STRANGER ON THE SHORE—Carol Duncan

Sarah Wilson possessed a "sixth sense," but she couldn't forsee any profitable outcome from a relationship with free-lance writer Jordan Matthias. The man had a reputation for exposing psychic frauds, and she wasn't about to reveal her own special abilities to him. But he did have an uncanny effect on her other five senses, and she wondered if he'd be interested in the secrets locked in her heart.

#271 REBEL'S RETURN—Sibylle Garrett

Afghani Prince Ahmed Khan was a rebel with a cause. In his fight for his country's freedom, he had sacrificed everything—family, title, wealth—and found imprisonment in his self-imposed isolation. But when he met Toni Prescott, he knew that only her love could set him free.

#272 KNIGHT SPARKS—Mary Lynn Baxter

As Carly's superior officer, Captain Rance Knight was off-limits, so she tried to ignore the sparks that flew whenever he was near. But then they were thrown together on a case, and even though their forbidden love could end their careers, Carly was willing to be seared by his fire.

AVAILABLE THIS MONTH

#265 LUCIA IN LOVE
Heather Graham Pozzessere

#266 FORBIDDEN JADE
Doreen Roberts

#267 HOME FIRES
Mary Anne Wilson

#268 ROOM AT THE INN
Marilyn Pappana

Silhouette Desire

1989
IS THE YEAR
OF THE MAN!

What makes a romance? A special man, of course, and Silhouette Desire celebrates that fact with *twelve* of them! From Mr. January to Mr. December, every month spotlights the Silhouette Desire hero—our **MAN OF THE MONTH.**

Sexy, macho, charming, irritating…irresistible! Nothing can stop these men from sweeping you away. Created by some of your favorite authors, each man is custom-made for pleasure—*reading* pleasure—so don't miss a single one.

Diana Palmer kicks off the new year, and you can look forward to magnificent men from **Joan Hohl, Jennifer Greene** and many, many more. So get out there and find your man!

Silhouette Desire's

MAN OF THE MONTH…

MAND-